JEN'S PRIDE & JOY

NEVA COYLE

THOMAS NELSON PUBLISHERS
Nashville • Atlanta • London • Vancouver

Also by Neva Coyle

Fiction
Cari's Secret, 1994

Non-Fiction
The All-New Free To Be Thin
The All-New Free To Be Thin Lifestyle Plan
Learning to Know God
Making Sense of Pain and Struggle
Meeting the Challenges of Change
A New Heart . . . A New Start

Copyright © 1995 by Neva Coyle.

Published in Nashville, Tennessee, by Jan Dennis Books, an imprint of Thomas Nelson, Inc., Publishers, and distributed in Canada by Word Communications, Ltd., Richmond, British Columbia.

Scripture quotations are from the KING JAMES VERSION of the Bible.

Library of Congress Cataloging-in-Publication Data

Coyle, Neva, 1943–
    Jen's pride and joy : a novel / by Neva Coyle.
       p. cm.
    ISBN 0-7852-8028-6
    1. Young women—United States—Fiction. I. Title.
PS3553.0957J46 1995
813'.54–dc20
                               94-27183
                                 CIP

Printed in the United States of America
1 2 3 4 5 6 — 99 98 97 96 95 94

About the Author

*N*eva Coyle is a full-time free lance writer who is very active in the ministry of her local church. She is also the co-author of the best-selling book, *Free To Be Thin. Jen's Pride and Joy* is the second in a series of Christian romance novels set in her hometown of Redlands, California. The first book in the series, *Cari's Secret,* was released in spring of 1994.

Neva is happily married and the mother of three grown children. Many of the story lines in this series grew out of family discussions in her own household.

Neva is also a proud grandmother.

CHAPTER ONE

*J*ennifer reached for her thick woolen muffler and wrapped it carefully around her neck. She purposely left it a little loose in front so she could pull it up over her mouth when she stepped into the freezing weather.

"President Kennedy announced at an early morning press conference from the oval office plans for representatives from the U.S., Great Britain, and the Soviet Union to meet later this summer in Moscow to discuss the control of nuclear weapons testing." Jen ignored the radio's newscast and stepped back into the kitchen to retrieve her sack lunch from the refrigerator.

"Spring stays stubbornly around the corner—the wind chill factor is five below," the broadcaster calmly announced.

"Windchill factor. Never heard of such a thing back home," she muttered. All the LA stations reported were the temperate readings expected at the beaches and in the upper and lower valleys. "Well, girl," she said into the mirror hanging in the lobby of her apartment building, "less than three months to go and it's back to sunny California." Bracing herself, she ducked her head into the wind and thrust her mitten-covered hands deeper into her coat pockets.

"Not goin' to be many customers today, I'd say." The

heavy black man always had an opinion about something or another as he let the employees in the side entrance at Halloran's. Jen had worked at the upper-class department store for the last two years.

"You're probably right, Willie," she responded, tugging at her frozen scarf. "Maybe we'll get some work done then."

Making her way up the stairs to the second floor, she crossed through the lingerie department and bounded up the silent escalator, which wasn't due to be turned on for another five minutes.

"My goo'ness, miss, you're going to get caught comin' up tha' down es'lator some of these days."

Jennifer snapped her scarf at the cheerful cleaning woman. "You'd save me, wouldn't you, Sally?"

"Yep, guess I would." Sally laughed.

Each morning her routine was the same. Her coat and boots were safely tucked inside an employee locker with her damp scarf. She scarcely had time to try to tame her unruly red hair before checking her purse with the security guard behind the counter. After punching the time clock, Jen headed back down the same escalator she had come up a few minutes earlier.

Reaching her department a few minutes early, she began straightening a clearance table while she waited for the department manager to give her an assignment to work on between customers—assuming they had any customers today.

"Good morning." Mr. Jeffers' tone was always matter-of-fact, and Jen wondered if he knew the difference between a good morning and any other kind of morning. He never listened for a response anyway; he was more interested in the paperwork he never seemed to be without.

"Morning," Jen replied.

"It'll be slow today," Jeffers commented without looking up.

"It's cold out there," Jen offered.

"I know," he said. "It'll be a good day to get some stock work done."

Jennifer winced; she knew she would be getting her wool plaid skirt and matching sweater dirty and hoped it wouldn't be snagged or otherwise ruined by the end of the day. *I should have worn my corduroy jumper,* she thought. It already had a stockroom scar from the last time she pulled duty in the "cavern."

"Hey, you!" Megan called from the other counter. "How's business?"

Megan's black hair gleamed under the spotlights that showed off the bright gold and silver costume jewelry in her department. Jen had welcomed Megan's bubbly personality—and her friendship—her first day at work. Megan had been a real comfort. Leaving Redlands and coming to Chicago had terrified Jen in the beginning, though she wouldn't dream of telling anyone back home.

"Well, it's early yet," Jen called back.

"With this weather, it's probably not going to get much better either." Megan straightened a display of necklaces. "Just think, you could be laying in the sun back home in California."

"Sure," Jen said, "getting a tan in March. Listen, Meggie, only tourists from Chicago lay out in California in March."

By eleven that morning, Jen had waited on only one customer, a woman who wasn't sure what to choose for a wedding gift and decided to browse some more. At 11:15 she had a second customer, a kindly woman in her late forties or early fifties who asked to pick up an item being held for Mrs. Johnson. A set of monogrammed hand towels, she informed Jen.

"I know right where it is," Jen smiled. "I saw it yesterday."

Plucking the box from a high stock room shelf, Jen thought she heard something rattle. *Hand towels don't rattle,* she mused. She opened the box to investigate.

Just as her eyes caught an expensive gold chain sticking out from between the towels, she spun around, aware that someone was right behind her. "I'll take that." Kindly Mrs. Johnson's face had changed as much as her tone. "And, my dear, I will need you to come with me."

Jen dropped the box. The gold chain, along with an expensive locket and a pair of diamond earrings, fell on the rough surface of the stockroom floor.

"What's this?" Jeffers' voice boomed from behind the woman.

"A security matter, Jeffers," said the woman. "I'm taking Miss Whipple upstairs for questioning. You'd better come along."

"But I can't," Mr. Jeffers said. "I don't have any other help today. The weather."

"I'll take over." Yvonne suddenly appeared in her mysterious way. She seemed to show up at the most opportune times. "I'm free right now. I can stay."

Jen could barely hear herself think, much less answer the questions being asked of her in rapid succession in the security office.

Jeffers paced back and forth as the demure Mrs. Johnson proved herself to be anything but demure.

"How did you know that package was there, Miss Whipple?"

"I saw it yesterday."

"Wasn't it kind of high for you to just 'see'?"

"I was looking for something."

"Oh? What?" Jennifer jumped as the older woman

leaned suddenly closer and looked directly in her eyes. "I said, what were you looking for?" the woman repeated.

"Signs. Clearance signs. Mr. Jeffers wanted to do a special clearance table and asked me to find the signs."

"Jeffers?" The interrogator peered at the nervous department manager.

"Yes, I did. But I didn't know about the stolen, uh, misplaced merchandise."

"How long had the package been up there?"

"I don't know." Jennifer fought to keep back her tears and at the same time struggled to keep her temper from flaring. "I only saw it yesterday. As you said, it was a little high to be seen."

"Yes, one would have to know it was there, right Jeffers?" the woman said, never taking her eyes off Jen. "Jeffers?"

"I guess one would have to know it was there." Jeffers looked apologetically at Jennifer. "You would hardly stumble across it accidentally, I guess."

"You guess?" The stern woman wouldn't let him off so easily.

"It seems reasonable to me that whoever..." Jeffers' voice trailed off.

"Get Miller on the phone," the woman ordered.

"Mr. Miller?" Jeffers asked.

"Of course Mr. Miller—Mrs. Miller wouldn't come even if you called her, now would she?"

"Yes, yes. Right away. I'll call Mr. Miller." Jeffers walked to a desk in the outer office and dialed an in-house number. Jen watched him through the glass window. As soon as his back was turned, the woman gave Jen a brief smile, and Jen thought she could even detect a slight softening of the expression in her eyes. However, as soon as Jeffers returned her expression hardened once again, and Jen assumed she had been mistaken.

"They're paging him," Jeffers said flatly.

Jen could hear two short beeping tones, a pause and one more. She glanced around.

The gray metal desk was devoid of any paperwork or personal items that might reveal who worked there. Only a small Courier and Ives calendar hung on the glossy light green wall at the side of the desk. Behind the desk was a matching metal credenza with employee schedules pinned on a bulletin board above. The shiny tan and black asbestos tiles were laid in their every-other-square pattern, and some of the squares showed wear. Fluorescent tubes hung from fixtures in the high ceiling and cast an unflattering pall over the room's sparse furniture and tense occupants.

"There's Mr. Miller, now." Jeffers sprang to his feet and closed the door behind him as he approached the man just coming in the outer office.

Jennifer started then turned her attention to the woman sitting near her. Mrs. Johnson, or whoever she was, patted her hand and smiled. "Don't you worry, this will all be cleared up very soon." Then Jen watched in amazement as the woman's demeanor turned sour again when the two men entered the room.

Dan Miller crossed the room toward her with his hand extended. "Miss Whipple? Jennifer, isn't it?" Jen nodded. "I'm Dan Miller."

"He's the assistant store manager, Jennifer," Jeffers offered.

"I'm sorry we have to meet under such, shall we say, unpleasant circumstances." Dan withdrew his hand and took a step back toward the older woman. "You've met Elizabeth Simms, I see," he said, nodding toward Jen's interrogator.

"But I thought . . ."

"I'm Beth to most folks." Jen could almost see her expression softening again.

"But you're not most folks, are you Jen." Her tone hardened. "You've been caught handling stolen merchandise."

Beth turned to Jeffers. "I think we can take it from here, Mr. Jeffers. I know your department is shorthanded today."

Dan Miller took Jeffers' elbow and ushered him to the door. Jen saw Mr. Jeffers' shoulders relax a bit as he was dismissed from the room. Only once did he cast a furtive glance in Jen's direction as he crossed the outer office and walked through the door.

"Miss Whipple—Jennifer. May I call you Jennifer?"

Dan Miller's voice was polite and gentle. Jen noticed his warm hazel eyes as he swept his hand across the front strands of his golden-brown hair. *It was a habit,* Jen thought; he didn't seem to realize that every strand of his hair was already perfectly in place.

"May I call you Jennifer?" Dan repeated.

"Jen."

"Jen?"

"Yes, I prefer just being called Jen."

"Okay, then—Jen."

Dan stood and walked slowly, pushing back his sport coat with his hand as he slid it into his pants pocket.

"We have a problem, Jen," he said.

Jen watched as he turned to face her. "What kind of problem?" she asked.

"You've been caught handling, shall we say, suspicious merchandise. What's more, you seemed to know exactly where it was when Beth, posing as Mrs. Johnson, asked you for it."

"She didn't ask me for it."

"Oh?" Dan looked quizzically at Elizabeth.

"She asked me for an item that was being held with her name on it. I didn't know about the jewelry."

"How do you know it was jewelry?"

"It fell out of the box when I dropped it."

"I see, when you dropped it."

"I saw the box up on the top shelf yesterday when I was looking for something else, and I pushed it to one side and saw the name on it. I was on my way to do a clearance display and didn't think any more about it until today when she came in and asked for it." Jen nodded toward Elizabeth Simms.

"She knows the rest. I took the box down and noticed that it rattled slightly. Towels don't rattle. I got down off the step stool and opened the box just as Mrs.—I mean, Mrs. Simms came in."

Dan looked at Beth.

"That's right, Dan."

"Then what?"

"Then nothing. I learned about the jewelry the same time Mrs. Simms did."

"Jen, would you excuse us for a moment?" Dan stood and without waiting for Jen's answer, signaled for Elizabeth to follow him, leaving Jen alone in the sparse room.

Closing the door behind him, Dan glanced over his shoulder at Jen. She looked alone and frightened—or angry, he wasn't sure which. Turning to Mrs. Simms, he started to speak.

"I know what you're going to tell me," Elizabeth said, "so don't waste your breath. We caught the wrong person."

Dan walked to the far wall of the outer office and leaned against it. "Yup," he said, "that's what I was going to say."

"Well don't. I figured that out the minute I saw her face when she dropped the box and the stuff fell out."

"Why didn't you just let her go then?" Dan asked with an

irritated edge to his voice. "Anyone can just look at that girl in there . . ."

"She's not a girl. She's twenty-two. I checked her file."

"Okay, that young woman then."

"Pretty young woman at that Dan," Elizabeth observed.

"Stop it, Beth. We have a problem here."

"I know. So, what shall we do with it—the problem, I mean?"

"I wish I knew. " Dan looked through the office window at the lovely young redhead. "I wish I knew, and I wish she wasn't involved."

CHAPTER TWO

$\mathcal{R}$eentering the security office where Jen was waiting, Dan Miller looked concerned. Elizabeth crossed the room and took a seat beside Jen.

"What we say to you, Jen, in these next few moments is critical," Mr. Miller began.

Jen looked at Beth; she wore her softened expression.

"I'm confused," Jen said.

"We know you are, dear." Beth reached for Jen's hand. "You have every right to be not only confused but somewhat angry."

"We need to bring you into our confidence, Miss Whipple."

"Jen," she corrected.

"What Dan means, Jen, is that we find ourselves needing to ask you to help us, and we hesitate to do so because you could walk right out of here, and we wouldn't blame you if you did. However, we are aware of your outstanding work record, your faithfulness, and your dependability. We need you, Jen."

"Need me? How?"

"Jennifer, what I am about to tell you, could help us, but it could endanger you. We need your help, but we cannot tell you with what until we are sure we can count on it.

However, how can you make a responsible decision unless we tell you first—"

"Which we can't," Beth said, finishing his sentence.

"Let me get this straight." Jen stood for the first time, and Dan noticed that she had to tilt her head to look up into his face. He wasn't aware how small she was until that moment. Taking a step toward Dan, she put her hands on her hips and shrugged her long red curls behind her shoulders.

"You need my help but can't tell me with what until I agree to give it to you, even though giving you my help could endanger me." Dan searched her mysterious eyes. "That's right," Dan said.

"But can you tell me I'm not in danger if I don't help you?" Jen asked.

"Boy, Dan, she's got a good head there." Elizabeth searched Dan's face but for the moment couldn't read him.

Dan looked at Beth, then back at Jen. He closed his eyes and brushed a hand unconsciously across his forehead. Finally, he said, "No, I can't honestly say that you are not already in danger." Dan breathed deeply, then let it out slowly. "Oh boy, oh boy," he muttered.

"Then what are my choices here?" Jen asked.

"Not good ones, I'm afraid, Jen," Dan said. Jen turned away from Dan, and he turned back to Beth. "This is a fine mess, Simms."

"Boy, don't I know it," she answered.

"Where do we go from here?" Dan asked.

"It depends on her."

"You know, Jen, you could go home," Dan offered.

"Home?" Jen turned to face them both.

"Home. Back to California."

"Is there anything you don't know about me?" Jen was surprised to find anger swelling within her.

"Oh, yes, I'm sure there is." Dan stopped himself. He felt sorry for this young girl, but it wouldn't go beyond that. He had purposely kept his emotions in check where women were concerned, and he wasn't going to let this pretty little redhead make a difference in that decision. "I mean, of course there is. We only know where you came from and . . ."

"Where you live," Mrs Simms added, "and of course, where you go after work and where you go on weekends, and . . ."

"What?"

"She's kidding you, Jen," Dan said, casting an annoyed look in Elizabeth's direction.

"Well, we soon will." Elizabeth smiled at Dan.

"As I see it, I can't go home. I've only got two and a half months before I graduate. I've worked too long and hard to let that dream go up in smoke now. Besides, my mother is overanxious about me being here as it is. This would scare her to death."

"You're a student?" Dan was surprised.

"Yes, Mr. Miller, I am." Jen stuck out her chin in an almost defiant pose. "I am a second-year art student at the Chicago Institute of Interior Design. My job here has helped me with living expenses. My scholarship didn't cover that."

"So you're not headed for a career in retail then." Dan laughed.

"Well, in a way I am. I want to have my own interior decorating business back home someday. But I have a lot of territory to cover and so-called giants to slay before I ever open the doors to my own store."

"Let's get back to the problem here, shall we?" Elizabeth's voice was serious.

Dan began. He explained to Jen that there was a shoplifting ring operating in the store. It appeared to be an inside job, however. Twice they had been close to making a break in the case, and both times the thieves seemed to know what was happening and managed to set someone else up.

"Like me?"

"Yes, just like you," Dan answered.

"What happened the first time?" Jen asked.

"She was from a small town in Nebraska, and we paid her way home. She was given several letters of recommendation, and we paid her full salary until she was settled in another position. However, we spread the word here that she was dismissed under suspicious circumstances."

"That's what you offered me, right?"

"Right. However," Dan hesitated, "she wasn't two months from graduation."

"Two and a half," Jen corrected.

"Now what?" Beth asked.

"Now we have to find another plan." Dan looked at Jen. "If we send you back to the floor, someone will probably want to know why we didn't dismiss you. You know, like we did the other girl. You could be asked lots of questions, by lots of different people, and we have no way of knowing what those questions will be and who will be asking them and why." Dan looked uncomfortable.

"What's the matter, Dan?" Beth asked.

"I don't like this. I just don't like it."

"It's too late, Mr. Miller." Jen's voice dropped almost to a whisper. "I already know too much to turn back now. What do you want me to do?"

"Nothing."

"Nothing?"

"Nothing until we get a cue from them. Can you do that, Jen? Do nothing, say nothing?"

"Maybe, maybe not." Jen's eyes began to sparkle.

"What do you mean maybe not?" Beth asked.

"Maybe I ought to say I am under suspicion still. Have you tried that approach?"

"No. And I don't want to try it now," Dan said firmly.

"Wait a minute, Dan, maybe she's got something here." Beth was definitely interested in Jen's idea.

"It's too dangerous," Dan protested.

"It's already too dangerous," Beth argued.

"I bet it's not dangerous at all," Jen said.

"Yeah, I bet." Dan knew that Jen was already in over her head. He also knew he had to keep his in order to assure her safety.

"Wait a minute. I think both ideas show promise," Beth said.

Dan didn't like the gleam he saw in Elizabeth Simms' eye. "What?"

Jen turned her entire attention to the older woman she had decided to trust completely—maybe even with her life.

"Jen says nothing."

"And?" Dan asked.

"But *we* let it be known in just a couple of important channels that we—that she's still under suspicion."

"I don't know . . ." Dan wasn't sure he liked the sound of her plan.

"Whoever's behind this," Beth continued, "will believe that our attention is drawn to her, that we're keeping our eye on her."

And they wouldn't be too wrong, Dan thought. He had to intentionally force his eyes and attention away from Jen and back to Elizabeth giving a rough outline of her plan. Jen stood near the corner of the small office. Suddenly they were all quiet. While Dan thought the plan over, Jen said a silent prayer. She had complete trust that God would protect her in the challenges of her everyday life, but this—this would be different.

Finally, Elizabeth broke the silence. "It could work, Dan."

Dan sat on the edge of the desk and looked at the young woman they were planning to involve, perhaps even endanger. Jen stood silent, her arms wrapped around her stomach, and looked at Dan.

"I don't like it," he said flatly. "I don't like it at all."

"What better plan do you have?" Elizabeth asked.

"How many more girls will you have to 'fire' and send home, Mr. Miller?" Jen had a point, he knew. This had to stop somewhere, sometime, and it needed to be soon. "I'm willing to help if I can," she added.

Dan looked from Jen to Elizabeth, then back to Jen again.

"Then I'm calling Rusty."

"Rusty?" Jen asked.

"You'll like Rusty, dear." Elizabeth was smiling at Jen.

"Come on, Beth." Dan was clearly irritated. "You're a professional, okay? Don't act this way."

"You just call Rusty, Dan." Elizabeth's plan was taking on a new dimension. Dan didn't like the original plan, but he liked the tone of the Elizabeth's voice even less.

CHAPTER THREE

*W*hat's going on?" Megan's voice was insistent on the phone. "Why'd you go home?"

"I've had a pretty rough day, Megan. Can't we talk about this tomorrow?"

"No. I'm on my way over."

"Megan," Jen tried to protest.

"I said I'm on my way over. I'll stop off and get some take out. Chow mein, okay?"

"Meg, you don't have to do that."

"Did I say I had to? I'm on my way."

Jen was glad to see Megan even though she knew she couldn't tell her the truth about what had happened at work. It would be comforting to see a familiar face and perhaps watch the little TV Megan had brought over when she first started staying at Jen's apartment on the nights she worked late.

Jen grudgingly admitted to herself that she was becoming a little nervous about agreeing to help Mr. Miller and Elizabeth break the case. A friendly face might just do the trick.

Megan was curious but not insistent about the details of Jen's encounter with store management. Many girls were hauled into the office for one thing or another. Megan was convinced that Jen would tell her—when the time was right.

Her job now was to be a friend, a job Megan took very seriously.

Curled up on the drab sofa that came with Jen's small furnished apartment the two friends decided to eat the Chinese food right from the boxes.

"No forks, Jen," Megan teased.

"No forks?"

Megan drew tissue wrapped chopsticks from the brown paper bag.

"Oh, no." Jen faked a collapse against the back of the couch.

"Oh, yes, my dear." She handed Jen a set of chopsticks. The girls awkwardly picked the food from the cartons, eating only what they managed to catch between the sticks.

Megan was the first to give in. "I'm getting a fork." On her way the kitchen the phone rang. "I'll get it, you rest. You've had a rough day, remember?" She picked up the receiver. "Hello? Yes, she's here. May I tell her who's calling?" Raising her eyebrows, Megan handed the phone to Jen. "A friend—for you," she said.

It was Dan Miller. "Please don't let anyone know who is calling," he began, "okay, Jen? We aren't sure who to trust at this point. Do you understand?"

"Yes, of course."

"How are you?"

"I'm fine." Jen shrugged off a curious Megan who was trying to get close enough to listen. "Would you hold on a minute?" Jen put her hand across the receiver. "Get away, Megan," Jen scolded her friend, "this is a personal call."

"Sorry," Megan left to sulk on the sofa.

"I'm back. That was my friend Megan. We work together. She came over with Chinese food. She'll probably stay the night, considering the weather." Jen paused, listening.

"Then you're not alone. Good. She works in fine jewelry, doesn't she?"

"Um-hmm."

"Has she ever said anything about missing merchandise?"

"Yes, once in a while."

"I'm calling because we need to talk, Jen. And I'm afraid it should be away from the store. Could that be arranged?"

"Of course."

"I want you to meet Rusty. Elizabeth should be in on it too."

"That's fine," Jen said, keeping a cheerful tone for Megan's sake.

"Do you think we could come to your apartment?"

"Here?" Jen looked around at her small furnished flat. She had wanted to do more to make it attractive, but living on her modest salary from the store, she had decided to make whatever came with the apartment do.

"Is that all right?"

"It's not—well, I guess it would work." Jen's heart pounded unexplainably.

"Good, would Saturday night be okay?"

"Saturday? I think I'm free. Yes, Saturday night then. The four of us. Sounds great."

"In the meantime, just go back to work tomorrow as normal and keep as low-key as possible," Dan's voice was reassuring. "You have classes between now and then?"

"Yeah, I skipped tonight, but I can't skip Wednesday or Friday and Thursday I work 'til closing."

"Okay, Saturday evening. What time do you get home from the store?"

"I don't work this Saturday. It's one of my few Saturdays free." Jen was suddenly grateful for the free day. She would have to do something with her apartment by Saturday night. After her speech about being an interior design student, her surroundings suddenly looked appalling.

"Okay, see you then," Jen said, hanging up the phone. She turned to look directly into Megan's determined curiosity.

"Who was that?" Megan asked.

"Just a guy I know." Jen tried to shrug off the question.

"Just a guy you know?" Megan would not be avoided. "A velvet voice like that, and you say he's just a guy you know?"

"Okay, a guy from school." Jen couldn't lie very well.

"Coming here, just the four of you?" Megan wasn't going to let the question go without an answer.

"Yeah, Beth, an older woman, her friend Rusty, and this other guy."

"Yeah, the other guy," Megan said, "I want to know about this other guy."

"He's just one of the students, I said."

"Go on," Megan persisted.

"We're working on an assignment together. A project."

"For school?"

"Megan, for crying out loud. What's the big deal?"

"Just this, my friend. How come I've never heard you talk about him before?"

"What's to talk about? I've never even noticed him before."

"You're noticing him now?"

"No, not really, we're just doing an assignment together." Jen looked disgusted. "Really, Megan Marie LaNosy, don't try to make it out to be something it's not."

"LaBianca," Megan said. "Megan Marie LaBianca, if you please. Okay, I'll not mention it again." Jen caught the sparkle in her friend's eye and the exaggerated Italian emphasis on her last name. "Until Sunday, anyway." Megan fished in the carton with her fork. "Does this guy have a name?"

"I'm sure he does. But that's for me to know . . ."

"And me to find out." Megan looked at Jen's stern expression. "I can wait, like I said, until Sunday."

CHAPTER FOUR

*W*hy the sudden interest in your apartment?" Megan teased Jen. "It never mattered before. All I've ever seen you do to spruce up the place is that jungle you grow in your kitchen."

"A few houseplants, Megan, not a jungle." Jen ignored her question.

"Could it be your company tonight has inspired you?"

Jen tried to make light of Megan's inquisitive teasing. "Maybe," she responded. "Maybe not. Maybe I just got tired of the same old brown carpet, same old brown sofa, same old brown everything. Everything around here is brown."

"Right," Megan observed. "You've been here almost two years and with less than three months to go, you are suddenly tired of the way the place looks."

Jen ignored her friend and Megan knew there wouldn't be any answers—not yet anyway. But there would be, she wouldn't give up until there were.

Jen had taken on quite a challenge on very short notice. Getting an inexpensive light-colored slipcover for the couch had set her back almost as much as a week's worth of groceries, but the difference it made in the room was worth it. She had found a pair of cheery throw pillows in a sale bin in the bargain basement, and with her employee's discount she had been able to pay for them with the small amount of cash she had left over from last month's careful budgeting. Then she had taken down the kitchen curtains; washed, starched, and ironed them; and arranged her houseplants near the window hoping they wouldn't freeze.

Carefully arranging pictures of her family and friends back in California on the bookcase shelves helped make up for the lack of interesting titles there. Schoolbooks, she decided, were not very impressive. On Friday she walked to the corner florist after work and bought some flowers to arrange on the small coffee table—she wanted to brighten up the front room of her small apartment as much as possible.

Classes had been uneventful and unchallenging all week, and she had, as usual, worked far in advance of the assignment schedule. She found herself nervous yet eager for Saturday to finally arrive.

She scrubbed her whole apartment before nine o'clock on Saturday and polished the woodwork until it sparkled. Filling a small wicker laundry basket with decorating magazines that had been stacked beside her bed made the room seem even more inviting, she decided.

Jen took a step back to examine her finishing touches. For a simple three-room apartment, she had made the best use of the furniture, pushing and shoving until it looked as warm as possible. She was thankful that the table lamps were turned on by a wall switch and that there was no overhead light to distort her limited decorating efforts with unflattering shadows.

About four o'clock Megan shrieked, "Jen, your hair! What will we do with your hair?"

"My hair?" Jennifer ran her fingers through the long curly tangles. "What do you mean *we*?"

"Get in the shower, wash your hair, and then I'll do it up for you."

"Up?"

"Yes, in a french roll or something." Megan pushed Jen toward the shower.

"I don't wear my hair up," Jen protested.

"Tonight you do. Where's your hair dryer?" Megan was already pulling out brush, rollers, combs, and hair setting lotion.

For the next two hours, Megan worked on Jen's hair while Jen waited for her to finish and leave so that Jen could put her hair back the way she always wore it. Once her hair was done, Jen picked a mint green sweater and wool slacks which seemed to pass Megan's inspection.

At six-fifteen, Jen bid her friend a very good evening, and Megan made her promise to call no matter how late it was when everyone left.

Once alone, Jen headed for the bathroom mirror, ready to restyle her hair. She looked at her reflection and instead simply pulled a few strands loose around her face and neck and reached for her makeup bag. She didn't wear much makeup lately; she was too busy, and she didn't want to send too many signals that she wanted attention. But tonight was different. Tonight she decided to wear a little makeup. *No special reason,* she told herself. *None whatsoever.*

At seven exactly she heard a light knock and crossed the room to the door. She paused for a moment, swept the room with a last-minute glance, and opened the door.

Dan Miller greeted her warmly. "Hi, Jen. This is Rusty, and you know Beth."

"Hi, yes I know Beth. Please, come in."

"I'm glad to meet you, Miss Whipple," Rusty began. "I'm sorry it has to be under such stressful circumstances."

"Please call me Jen." She waved toward the couch. "Sit down. May I get you something?"

"How about some coffee?" Beth asked. "Tell me where you keep it, and I'll make some."

Jen started for the kitchen and Beth followed. "It's in the little canister there." Jen was glad she had four cups that matched. "I made some brownies."

"I could smell them all the way down the hall." Dan's sudden presence in the tiny kitchen was overpowering. It was one thing for Megan and Jen to maneuver the small kitchen bumping into each other playfully as they heated a pizza or popped corn, but this felt different somehow.

"I'll bring some into the living room," Jen said.

"You've been dismissed, Dan. Better get out of the kitchen," Beth scolded in a lighthearted manner.

"No, I'm sorry," Jen began, "I didn't mean to . . ."

"It's okay. He's just in the way in here anyway." Beth quickly measured the water for the coffee and put the inexpensive percolator on the burner to perk.

"Hey." Dan's expression feigned insult. He wasn't going anywhere. He had liked the looks of Jennifer Whipple on Tuesday when they met in the security office—but he liked her looks better, much better, here in her small kitchen.

Her face was delicately framed with the little loose curls she had pulled down after Megan left. She looked perfectly at home in this friendly little apartment.

"I like your plants," Dan said.

"Thank you."

"Do they have names?" Dan asked.

"Sure, they do." Beth said gruffly. "Anybody knows this is an English ivy, that one's a philodendron, that's called a hen and chickens, and this hanging one is a piggyback."

"Hey, Simms, how'd you get so smart and domestic, even?"

Elizabeth snapped at Dan with a tea towel. "My mother was very good with plants. She taught me all their names. What she never could teach me was how to keep them alive."

Jen watched Dan and Elizabeth and began to understand that they were not just coworkers but friends.

"Is she right?" Dan asked.

"About what?"

"Their names. I want to know if she knows what she's talking about."

"Well . . ." Jen hesitated.

"Well, what?" Elizabeth turned to Jen in mock anger.

"That's not what I call them," Jen explained.

"And what do you call them?"

Jen felt young and immature, certainly not the hostess or the woman of the house.

"This one is Charlie," she began, pointing to a potted vine. She looked at Dan. His eyes said that he was delighted with her response.

"This is Matt," she said gesturing toward another. Pointing to a small African violet she said, "and this shy one here is Phyllis."

"Oh, brother." Elizabeth took the plate of brownies and headed for the living room. "You better help me here, Rusty. They're out to get me for sure."

Dan picked up the coffee pot from the burner, and Jen grabbed the cups and some napkins. Pausing unexpectedly in the doorway, Jen almost ran into him. Glancing back over the kitchen and then directly at Jen, he said, "Nice, very nice."

Jen felt her heart jump as he looked her straight in the eye. Much to her surprise, she didn't look away.

"Well," Rusty said, "we'd better get down to it. We've got a lot of work to do, and as much as I'd like to socialize, that's not why we're here."

CHAPTER FIVE

*I*t seems," Dan began, "that we have an organized effort or team that has found an effective way to pilfer merchandise. We don't know who, and we really don't know how it works. That's why we have called you, Rusty."

Rusty rubbed his temple as he listened. Why anyone would call this dark-haired man "Rusty" was something Jen didn't understand.

"I see," Rusty replied.

"All we know is that when inventory is taken, we find definite losses. But our security efforts seem to make little if any difference."

"You know all your agents well, of course." Rusty's statement actually asked a question.

"Of course," Beth answered. "But I haven't taken anything for granted. I haven't revealed to any of them the extent of the problem or that Dan and I suspect an inside job."

"Good." Rusty began to relax, leaning back into one of Jen's new pillows.

"That's why we decided to call you," Dan added.

"What's Jen got to do with all this?" Rusty asked, nodding in her direction.

"Well," began Beth, "we have taken a couple of hold audits." Then turning to Jen she explained, "Dan and I go in after hours and count the items in the hold areas of the stockrooms. Then we check the sales records to see if and when those items are sold. Later we go back in to see if holds are still there. Sometimes customers don't understand why we can't hold an item longer than just a few days. They don't understand that merchandise that is not on the floor not only can't be sold when it's back there on the stockroom shelf, but it can easily disappear. Almost into thin air."

"But we found something quite different in your stockroom, Jen," Dan continued. "We found the box with the monogrammed towels, hiding some jewelry."

"I wondered how she got involved in all this," Rusty said.

"Just like you, we were rummaging around, and by chance we pulled down the Johnson package and found the jewelry."

"Then we thought," Beth's eyes narrowed, "we had discovered a key."

"Maybe we have," Dan interrupted, "we just don't know to what."

"We thought," Beth said, "that the jewelry was going out of the store piggyback style."

"Piggyback?" Jen asked.

"Yeah, riding along with something else," Dan explained. "Our thought was that someone was planting targeted merchandise, like the jewelry, inside other merchandise, like the towels, and then it was riding out the door with a so-called customer."

Beth poured the last half cup of coffee from the pot.

"Hey, no fair," Rusty complained. "I need to have my wits about me, and you drain the pot."

"I'll make another," Jen said.

Getting up to go to the kitchen, she was surprised when all three of them followed her.

In the kitchen, Dan noticed there were only three chairs

around the little table pushed up to the wall. "Is there another chair, Jen?"

"It's in the bedroom, I'll get it."

"I'll get it. You finish making the coffee. We need Rusty alert, and this could be a late evening." Dan turned and walked through the living room into the bedroom.

"Rusty, I still think the merchandise is being piggy-backed," Beth said.

"Could be," Rusty responded.

"But I don't think it is necessarily going out the front door."

"What's that?" Dan returned with the fourth kitchen chair.

Rusty and Dan pulled the table out from the wall and Rusty slid the fourth chair behind it and sat down. Beth and Dan joined him at either side. Jen put the pot on to perk and put the rest of the brownies, still in the pan, on the table.

"Thanks." Rusty reached for the spatula and carved himself a double-sized serving.

"It is possible," Dan said, "that merchandise is being squirreled away for a later pick up, maybe even after hours."

"Ever run into anyone when you two have been slinking around in the store after hours?"

"Never," said Beth, "and that's made us wonder if someone knew we were coming."

"Ever tell anyone when you were going in at night?"

"No, we didn't."

"No one knew." Dan and Beth looked at each other and nodded. "We decided no one could know," Dan continued. "We didn't know who to trust."

"You two working on this alone?" Rusty asked.

"Well, yes." Beth looked at Dan.

"Until now," Dan said. "Now we need you, too."

"What about Jen?"

Jen had been silent all the while, listening to the conversation and keeping a safe distance.

Beth told Rusty how Jen had become involved.

At ten o'clock, Jen's phone rang. Picking it up, she was surprised to hear Mr. Jeffers' voice on the other end.

"Hello, Mr. Jeffers." Jen looked at Dan and raised her eyebrows. The three at the table remained silent.

"Yes, I'm fine, thank you." She paused.

"No, I don't think anything more will come of it." She listened, and Dan wished he could hear the other side of the conversation.

"Yes, I know I've probably seemed a little distracted this week. But, I'm fine, really. I've had a lot on my mind. I'm headed into finals at school, you know, and I'm working on a big project that I hope will be finished soon."

Jen poked at the rug with her toe as she listened to Jeffers.

"No, I don't think so. It really has nothing to do with me. I didn't put it there, did you? No. I didn't think so. Someone was up to some funny business, I guess. But they didn't get away with it, did they? As far as I know it's over. Yeah, me too."

Jeffers seemed to be satisfied, and with a few cordial words Jen said good night and hung up.

"He ever call you here before?" Dan was clearly irritated.

"No." Jen stared at the phone. "No, never. Even when he knew I had the flu."

"You think he's involved?" Rusty asked the three of them.

"Jen, you work with him every day, what do you think?" Beth asked.

"I don't know. He's under some kind of pressure, but I figured it was just trying to make his sales quota, scheduling sales people, displays, you know, the usual."

Dan watched Jen move away from the phone. He had

tried to picture her in this setting when he had called to set up this meeting, but he couldn't then. Now he would be able to—the next time he called.

"Who was here when I called?" he asked her.

"Megan. Megan LaBianca. She works in fine jewelry. She comes over a lot. We've been good friends for almost two years," Jen answered.

"I've already checked her out, Dan," Beth said. "She's clean. She's been at the store since she worked part-time in high school."

"Does she ever wear any of the jewelry from the department?" Rusty inquired.

"No. She has a difficult time even borrowing a dime for a phone call," Jen said. "In a merchandising seminar she heard you should dress very plainly and without any jewelry to show the merchandise properly. If someone wants to see a pair of earrings on a human ear, you shouldn't have to take off your own first."

"I've watched her." Beth said. "She doesn't just hold up her merchandise for the customer, she drapes it across her shoulder or puts it up to her own neck. Very effective, I must say."

"Her sales records prove she's an effective sales representative," Dan added.

"She ever buy anything?" Beth asked.

"Gifts mostly," Jen said. "She helps with family finances— her mother's a widow, and she has a younger sister. She mostly uses her discount at Christmas and birthdays and occasionally on sale merchandise."

"So, what plans do you have for Jen now?" Rusty returned his attention to the young woman seated opposite him with the unruly curls teasing at the neckline of her mint green sweater. Then he turned his eyes toward Dan.

Dan dropped his eyes toward the floor. "I don't know.

She has offered to help, but I don't want to . . . well, I don't want to put her in an awkward position."

"Are you in an awkward position, Jen?" Rusty was direct and Jen liked that.

"Yes," Jen said, "but Mr. Miller didn't put me there."

"How so?"

"Beth did," Jen smiled, "when she asked for that package."

"So blame me, then," Beth laughed. "I was trying to find out who knew about the package and what would happen if someone came to pick it up."

"Did Jeffers know about the package?" Rusty looked at Jen.

"I don't know. The attention was all on me. He was really nervous about the whole thing, but I thought it was just because of me," Jen answered.

Dan knew what it was like to be nervous around this young woman. He wondered if Jeffers' reasons were the same as his own.

"What now?" Dan asked Rusty.

"I don't know," he said. "I need some time to think this through and do a little detective work of my own. I'll probably be in the store from time to time." Rusty drained the last of his coffee. "If you see me, don't acknowledge that you know me, okay?" The instruction was directed at Jen.

"Okay," she answered.

"Well, we've got work to do. Could be some long hours, and tomorrow could be my last day off for quite a while. Guess I'll go out to the country and see the grandkids," Beth said.

"Grandkids?" Jen was shocked.

"Twins, just two months old." Getting her coat off Jen's bed, she bid the group good night and left. Rusty followed almost immediately, but not before asking Jen to keep a record of any questions Jeffers might ask her and to tell him if there were any more calls. He also commented that he would feel better if she would have her locks changed, just in case.

"In case of what?" Jen asked, then turned a questioning gaze to Dan.

"I'll get a new lock tomorrow. Can I come by and put it in later in the afternoon?" Dan asked.

"Do you really think that's necessary? I have a safety chain, and I do use it."

Rusty persisted. "I would feel better about it, Jen."

"Well, I guess so."

"Good," Rusty said. "Good night then. See you soon."

"Night," Dan said as he shut the door. He turned to Jen. "Jen, we still don't know how this will involve you or to what extent."

"I know," she said quietly.

"You all right? You still want to do this?"

"I'm okay. I do want to help if I can." Jen looked up into his eyes.

"I promise, I'll watch out for you as much as I can," Dan vowed.

"Thanks, that makes me feel better, I think." She smiled.

Jen picked up his coat and felt the warm softness of cashmere. His scarf was stuffed inside the arm and she pulled it out as she handed him the coat. He slowly put the coat on and carefully removed the scarf from her hand.

"There's just one more thing," he said softly.

"What's that?"

"Do you think you could call me Dan?"

"Not at the store."

Dan smiled. "Away from the store, then?"

"Away from the store." It was a simple agreement between them. They would be seeing each other away from the store. An agreement they both liked and both looked forward to.

CHAPTER SIX

*E*arly the next morning, Jen could hear the phone ringing just as she stepped from the shower.

"Oh, no!" she remembered. "I forgot to call Megan!"

After Dan left, it had taken Jen a while to get to sleep. Alone with her thoughts, she tried to identify the troubling feeling growing within her. Getting involved in a security matter at work was a little frightening, but that wasn't what was troubling her.

Scrambling for her robe, she reached for the phone. "Hello? Megan?"

"No, it's not Megan, it's Dan." His voice sounded wonderful.

"Oh, excuse me. Good morning."

"I was wondering what time you would be available for me to come and put on the new lock."

"You have one already?"

"I have a key to a department store, remember? I can get in anytime."

"Of course, how could I forget? I hope you didn't steal it," Jen teased.

"No, I wrote it down, they'll put it on my account. Do you have plans with Megan?" Dan asked, changing the subject.

"No," Jen said, "only a promised phone call."

"Then when would be a good time for me to come over?"

"After church I guess."

"Church? You go to church?"

"Um-hmm. Right down the street at First Community."

"I see. Well then, how about two o'clock? That give you enough time?"

"Plenty. Two will be fine," Jen agreed.

Hanging up, she looked at the clock radio by the bed. Eight-thirty. *I still have time to give Megan a call,* she thought, *and make it to the ten o'clock service.*

"Must have been a late night," Megan teased.

"Not really—I was just tired when everybody left," Jen explained.

They chatted for a few minutes, then Megan said, "Want to go for a movie later?"

"Oh, I don't think so. I have a few chores to do around the apartment and then . . ."

"You got a date?"

"No."

"Well then?"

"Well what?"

"How about a movie later," Megan suggested.

"No, not this time, Meg." Jen didn't want to take the chance that Megan could run into Dan.

"More project planning?"

"Maybe, and I still have studying to do for a couple of finals."

"Okay, I'll go with my mom over to my sister's then. My mom will be thrilled, even if my sister isn't."

"Oh, Meg, you love your family. Have a good time."

"Yeah, right. See you tomorrow."

Jen found a cake mix in the cupboard and decided it might be nice to have a little dessert on hand for this afternoon. Just in case.

She went to church, sang the hymns, and enjoyed the

choir's rendition of "Blessed Assurance," but she had trouble concentrating on the sermon.

Stopping by the market on the way home, she picked up some real cream remembering that Dan had asked for it the night before to put in his coffee. When she got home, she changed into some warmer clothes and wished that women could wear slacks to church. She picked a heather gray wool pair that her mother made before she left home. Even after two years, they were beautiful. She reached for an ivory silk shirtwaist blouse and her gray and ivory plaid wool jacket. A pair of gray anklets matched the slacks perfectly, and she slipped on her penny loafers. She let her curly hair fall loosely down her back but caught up the sides with matching combs. She had applied a light coat of mascara earlier, and now she touched her lips with a subtle shade of lipstick.

At exactly two, she heard a knock on her door.

"Dan?" she inquired before she opened the door.

"It's me," he said.

Standing on the other side of the door, he looked approvingly at her choice of casual clothes.

"That's nice," he said simply. "You have good taste."

"Thanks," she said. She felt a little embarrassed but was glad he approved.

"I even brought my own tools." Dan held up a small toolbox.

"Good. I didn't think of that." She moved to one side, and he crossed the room to take off his parka.

Without the three-piece suit he wore at the store, he looked like any other guy in the neighborhood on a weekend project. He wore a red V-necked sweater with a plaid shirt open at the collar. His Levi's looked just worn enough to be comfortable.

In just a few minutes, a new dead bolt was installed. Once

it was locked from the inside, it had to be opened from the inside.

"When you leave," he carefully explained, "you have to lock it with the key."

"There are two keys here."

"One's a spare. They always come with two," Dan explained.

Jen felt a little sorry that the project was finished and almost wished she had told Megan she would go to the movies. It would be a long day, now that the lock was installed.

"What's that I smell?" Dan headed for the kitchen.

"A cake."

"For anyone special?"

"No, just a cake," Jen felt embarrassed, hoping he might want to stay for a while.

"Make you a deal." Dan's whole face smiled as he good-naturedly turned toward Jen.

"A deal?"

"How about some Italian food? Spaghetti, ravioli, french bread, a little wine. Then dessert back here—that cake."

"I don't know . . . I wasn't . . . I mean I'm not dressed for . . ."

"Sure you are," he said. "I know a little place up on the shore, just off Wacker Drive. It will only take forty minutes or so to get there. How about it?"

Dan reached for his jacket. "Get your coat, I'm hungry."

Jen took her car coat from the hanger and grabbed a scarf and her gloves. It was not quite as cold as yesterday, but it was still cold enough to bundle up.

"Shall I wear my boots?" Jen asked.

"You probably won't need them. I do have a heater in my car," he laughed.

As they left, Dan insisted on a small ceremony to try out

the new lock with the key. Hearing the bolt snap into place he turned to Jen. "There. Am I an expert or what?"

Dangling the key in front of her, he said, "If you ever need an extra, just take this to Mike down in housewares, and he can make a duplicate."

"Sure will," she said as she dropped the key inside her small purse.

At the curb, Dan took Jen's arm and steered her toward his low Corvette. She couldn't even imagine such a car, much less imagine herself riding in one.

As they drove toward the edge of town, she began to relax. "Ever been out to the restaurants on the shore?" Dan asked.

"No, afraid not." Jen didn't dream of such extravagance on her small income.

"Good, I'll get to show you something new then."

Heading north on the expressway, Dan turned on the radio. With soft music in the background, the powerful motor purring contentedly under the hood of the sleek car, and Dan happily pointing out the sights, Jen thought she hadn't been so happy—maybe ever.

CHAPTER SEVEN

*W*here were you last night?" Megan was waiting at the bottom of the silent escalator that Jen always ran up.

"Last night?" Jen swept by her friend and headed up the escalator.

"Yes, last night. I thought you had a project." Megan looked inquisitive, almost hurt.

"I did. But I got finished."

"So why didn't you call?"

"I thought you went to your sister's."

"I did, but I got home early."

"Something came up," Jen said. "I'll tell you about it later."

Both girls stuffed their coats and boots in employee lockers and headed for the security counter to check in their purses.

"Later? Why not now?" Megan wanted to know.

"I don't have time now." Jen was already two steps ahead of her friend.

"Suppose we can get our breaks together?"

"How're we supposed to do that? Yvonne relieves us both, remember? She can't be in two places at the same time."

"After work then, let's go to your place after work. It's supposed to be snowing again. I'll call my mother."

"Sounds okay to me," Jen agreed.

"You don't think anything will come up again, do you?"

"I'll let you know." Jen playfully pinched her friend's arm as they parted and went to their respective departments.

From across the aisle, Jen heard Megan call out her name.

"Jen," she said in an alarmed loud whisper. "Jennifer, come look at this."

Jen glanced around. Mr. Jeffers hadn't appeared yet, and the store clock said it was ten minutes before they would open. Crossing the aisle, Jen saw at once what Megan was alarmed about.

"Look here, the display case is empty." Megan looked around to see if other merchandise was also missing.

"Isn't it supposed to be?"

"No, not this one. Only the fine jewelry is put in the vault, this was only costume jewelry. A little pricey maybe, but not the real stuff. Who would steal costume jewelry?"

"I don't know, Meg. Better call security. No wait, you stay here and keep an eye on things, don't let anyone disturb anything. I'll go call security back at my station."

Jen hurried across the aisle, found the store directory, then dialed.

"Mr. Miller, please. Miss Whipple calling."

"Jen?" Dan's voice was alarmed. "You all right?"

"Yes, but I thought you would want to know before we call security that there's costume jewelry missing from Megan's department. In fact, a whole case of it is missing. Megan just found it."

"Okay, go ahead and have her call security. It will be interesting to find out how long it takes them to get there and how long it takes them to notify me. Meantime, I'll call Rusty."

Jen started to put the phone down but heard his voice

again. "Jen, you stay away from there, okay? Have Megan call."

Jen did what she was told and returned to her department just as Mr. Jeffers appeared.

"Good morning." It was his usual flat greeting.

"Morning," Jen answered from behind a sale table as she began to straighten the merchandise.

Jen heard the beeps she recognized as Dan's page. He had been in his office just a moment ago, Jen thought, but now he must be somewhere out in the store.

Elizabeth Simms appeared on the opposite side of the floor and headed for the jewelry counter. She wore a heavy coat and carried a large purse. She looked like any other shopper, and Jen wouldn't have noticed her at all before last week.

"Can I help you?" Megan asked Mrs. Simms, trying to be calm and professional.

"Well, now miss, maybe you can." Beth was convincing in her disguise. "I'm looking for a gift for a friend's daughter. She will be graduating from high school soon, and I'd like to get her something nice. I bet you'd know what the young girls like these days."

"Well now, let me see." Megan began to browse her displays.

"Looks like you're a mite short on inventory. Not much choice here," Elizabeth observed.

"Well, we're rearranging the displays. We've got plenty to choose from."

Megan selected a few items and suggested them to Beth. The encounter would have looked to anyone else like a normal sales presentation. Beth watched carefully out of the corner of her eye and turned a little away as the security agents came to question Megan. Megan answered their questions as well as she could, explaining that she discovered the loss only a few minutes before.

Jen watched from behind the sale merchandise she was sorting. "What's going on?" Jeffers' voice startled her.

"I didn't know you were there, you scared me."

"Sorry. What's going on?" he repeated.

"Megan discovered some stock missing when she came to work this morning." Jen kept working.

"Great." Jeffers seemed disgusted. "I hope it doesn't turn up in my stockroom. Maybe I'd better have a look."

Later that evening Dan called.

"You alone?" he asked.

"No, Megan came home with me for the night. She's in the shower. She had a difficult day answering questions, rearranging what merchandise she had left into a display. She was pretty good at it, though."

"I know, I saw it." Dan sounded strange.

"You okay?" Jen asked.

"Just tired. Beth and Rusty are together now, trying to come up with some ideas. This whole thing is a real mess."

"I bet."

"No one knows anything, no one saw anything. No one has any ideas, and no one knows what to do next." Dan yawned. "I need a good night's sleep."

"Who's that on the phone?" Megan came out of the bathroom with a towel wrapped around her black hair.

"A friend," Jen said, putting her hand across the receiver. "I'm almost done."

"I can take a hint," Megan turned and went back into the bedroom.

"She's not in a very good mood," Jen told Dan. "She thinks I'm holding out on her."

"Oh?"

"We've become very close friends in the last two years. It's hard for me to keep all this from her."

"I'm sure that's true," Dan said. "But you understand why you can't tell her, don't you?"

Jen assured him that she did. Dan continued telling her about the missing merchandise.

"There were two beaded cashmere sweaters taken too," he said. "And a fur."

"A fur?"

"A mink." Dan heaved a deep sigh. "Who knows what else. An inventory will show what else is missing."

"Inventory?"

"Starts tomorrow. The department managers are not too happy about it, either."

"Oh, boy," Jen said, "I guess Mr. Jeffers has his work cut out for him."

"Not really, but his department isn't missing anything that we know of. We'll start with gifts and accessories, jewelry, and of course the coat department."

"Will Megan have to help?" Jen wondered.

"Probably."

"She'll love that."

"Won't we all." Dan fell silent for a moment then continued. "Jen?"

"Yes."

"Did you lock your door?"

"I sure did. All nice and tight."

"I'm glad Megan's there. I don't like to think of you living alone. I wish you were in a secured building."

"It is, well, sort of. The front entrance is locked after ten."

"Good. I don't want anything to happen . . . I mean, not that I think it will. After all you've lived there, how long, and nothing has happened?"

"Two years."

"What a shame," Dan said.

"Pardon me?" Jen didn't understand his comment.

"You've lived in Chicago two years and I only just now met you. And you'll be gone in two months. What a shame."

"Two and a half," Jen said.

"Oh, yeah, two and a half."

Jen hung up the phone and curled her knees up, hugging them to her chest. Megan peeked in from the bedroom and decided not to interrupt her friend's thoughts.

Two and a half months. She had looked forward to going home to California, but now she wasn't so sure. If she wasn't careful she could get sidetracked. She had her goals, and she would certainly need to remind herself of them often if she were not to be distracted. But right now, all she wanted to think about was Dan.

CHAPTER EIGHT

*I*t's Mrs. Halloran, Mr. Miller." Debbie sat behind her desk right outside Dan's office, dangling the phone from her hand. "It's the third time she's called this morning."

Dan glanced at his watch and felt his stomach tighten into a familiar knot. "This morning? It's only nine-fifteen."

Dan opened the door to his office. He had always liked this room before. But today it seemed cramped and confining despite it's size and large corner windows.

"Today of all days," he said under his breath, "I don't need any trouble from her."

He spun his chair toward the glass and surveyed the city view, then lifted his gaze to Lake Michigan in the distance. Even in the harshest weather, the lake was beautiful.

With a deep breath, he reached for the phone."Good morning," Dan said simply.

"Good morning? You call this a good morning?"

Well, it was, Dan thought, *until now.*

"What's up?" Dan wanted her to get right to the point so he could get back to the challenges facing him. He began to sort through his phone messages while Mrs. Halloran leveled her remarks at him. He held the phone away from his ear, and her voice carried out into the room.

"What do we pay you for, anyway?" She could be so

demanding. "Right under your nose they make off with our merchandise."

"Oh, that," he said flatly.

"Yes, that—and more."

"More?"

"Indeed, more." Dan heard her take a deep breath and let it out slowly; she was probably taking a deep drag on a cigarette.

"Go on." Dan was fingering a note that said Rusty had called. He wanted to get this conversation over as quickly as possible so that he could find out what Rusty had on his mind.

"You bet I will," the woman continued. "When did you think you would tell me about this burglary?" He could hear her fingernails tapping on a table.

"Soon."

"Well, did you know it hit the papers?" she demanded.

"I thought it might."

"And you let me read about my own store being robbed rather than tell me. I'm so embarrassed."

"Embarrassed?" Dan wrinkled his eyebrows, crunching them toward one another.

"Yes, embarrassed. I was playing bridge last night with the O'Connors. Ruth asked me about the robbery, and I hadn't even heard a word about it. Don't you think, young man, that if I am paying you to run the store, you should at least inform me there has been a break-in?"

"It wasn't a break-in."

"What?" Her shrill voice put Dan on edge.

"There wasn't a break-in," he repeated.

"But the paper . . ."

"The paper is wrong," Dan told her.

Mrs. Halloran took another drag on her cigarette. "Will you please explain this to me?" she whined.

"Somehow, someone, a group—who knows—managed

to get in, take a load of merchandise, and get out without breaking in." Dan tried to keep his voice even and matter-of-fact, not an easy feat considering how badly he wanted to yell back at the woman who bore the name of the store. "What's more," he continued, "it probably happened after hours. That means someone either had a key or figured out a way to get in and then out..." Dan turned his chair toward his desk. An idea began forming.

"As soon as you find out anything, anything at all, I insist you call me." Mrs. Halloran was very good at insisting.

"As soon as I know anything conclusive, I'll let you know." Dan carefully guarded his words.

"See that you do," Mrs. Halloran said. "You're paid—plenty, I might add—to watch the store, not sit idly by while some two-bit hood ransacks the place."

Dan rolled his eyes and hung up. Then he immediately dialed Rusty's number.

"Just got your message. What's up?"

"Interesting twist to this one, Dan. Rothschild's was hit in the same way last night."

"Really?"

"No break-in, no alarms set off. No nothing." Rusty's chair squeaked loudly enough for Dan to hear it over the phone. "I thought at first that someone at Halloran's had given somebody a key, or was in cahoots with someone. However, with Rothschild's last night, I am thinking something has to be different."

"What do the police say?"

"You know the cops. They ain't sayin' nothin'. Keepin' the lid tight on this one. Funny thing, though . . ." Rusty's voice trailed off.

"What's that?"

"They are saying how stumped they are in the rags."

Dan frowned. "The rags?"

"You know, the papers," Rusty said.

"You're starting that Dick Tracy stuff again, Russ."

"Well, we PI's gotta stick togetha," Rusty mimicking a mobster he saw in an old movie.

"Come on, Rusty. This is my store we're talking about here. Not some B-movie prop."

"Okay, okay. Just trying to bring a little fun into a day that promises to be total waste."

"Waste? How do you know this day will be waste?"

"These guys are moving at night. Guess I'll be pulling graveyard hours for a while until they move again."

"How do you know they'll move again?"

"Two hits, two runs, no errors. According to the papers they're hitting pretty good. Hey—" Rusty stopped, and Dan knew he had an idea.

"Yeah?" Dan encouraged. "I hear the wheels spinning over there."

"Listen, Dan. Could we meet somewhere and talk?"

"That's a good idea. Let me call you later and tell you where and when." Dan wanted to do a little more thinking on his own before he met Rusty.

"Okay, later then. I'll hear from you?"

"Call you later," Dan promised.

Dan turned from his large wooden desk and paced in front of the office windows. A cold wind blew across Lake Michigan, throwing frozen drizzle against the glass.

Dan walked to the opposite shelf-lined wall, and his eyes rested on the picture of a young dark-haired woman. His mind flooded momentarily with memories of her. *Marie.* Touching the picture briefly, he walked away then walked back and picked it up off the shelf.

Dan lowered himself onto the brown leather couch across the room. For a few minutes he looked at the picture of Marie. His mind didn't dwell on anything in particular;

then he suddenly realized that Jen and Marie would have made good friends. They were opposites, yet in many good ways, quite alike.

Marie's dark hair was almost black and hung smooth in a loose page boy, just touching her shoulders. But Jen's hair was almost unruly in a very charming way. Marie loved fine music and the quiet softness of rain beating against a window. *I wonder what kind of music Jen likes,* Dan mused. Marie had a way of brightening up every room she entered, just like Jen. Dan stood up, still holding Marie's picture. "Four years and I still miss you," he told the image. He propped Marie's picture on his desk and let his thoughts wander. Immediately, he saw Jen's face in his mind. He decided he liked the way a curl inevitably escaped and claimed it's independence from Jen's efforts to keep it under control. He pictured Jen's movements—always quick and determined. Though he had concluded that Jen's upbringing had probably not given her a lot of material comfort, he admired her confidence.

He glanced at Marie's picture. She had been quite content to let people wait on her; Jen, in contrast, was the perfect hostess, even in her modest little kitchen overgrown with houseplants.

He reached toward the picture, tracing the outline of Marie's face with his finger. Then he thought of Jen again. He would have to be careful where she was concerned. After all, she had her own plans and goals long before they met a little less than two weeks before. Plans that did not include him—or any man at the moment. He was fairly certain of that.

Nor could he make plans that included her—or anyone else. "I wish I could talk to you about this," he said under his breath to Marie's picture. "But then, it's my own fault that I can't." Dan's heart tightened with pain. "And then there's Joy. I can't forget about Joy."

Dan stood and took a few steps, stood again in front of the large windows. He thrust his hands deep in his pockets and fingered his keys. *There's no room for anyone, right now,* he told himself. "No room and no right," he said out loud. *No room.* That was his decision. *No right.* Mrs. O'Halloran would make sure he didn't forget that.

But if there ever was room, and if he had the right . . . Jen's face came to mind again.

He remembered the way she had settled back into the deep leather seat in his car the night he took her to eat Italian food. He thought about the way she marvelled at the sight of the city skyline and the way she was delighted with everything they were served at the restaurant. He could still see her as she kept scraping the little serving dish the spumoni ice cream came in, wanting to get every last delicious little bit.

He remembered her hair that night, pulled up behind her ears, and the night before when she had piled it on top of her head. He could see her dark eyes, which seemed to be deep blue one day and hazel the next time he saw her. He had approved of the light scent of the perfume she had worn, and he remembered with a smile the softness of her cheek when he had accidentally touched it helping her into her coat.

Yes, Jen, he thought, *if I had room in my life, or even if I didn't—if I just had the right I'd find the room.* "But I don't," Dan said aloud as he moved toward the desk again.

"I've got work to do," he said. "Better get to it." But his heart wasn't in it. His heart was down on the second floor, in the home furnishings department with the lively, vivacious young sales clerk who at that very moment was pushing an independent red curl away from her face. Dan reached once more for Marie's picture, then quietly and slowly put it face down in the bottom drawer of his desk.

CHAPTER NINE

*D*an walked nine blocks against the bit-ter March wind before he turned into a coffee shop. Rusty was supposed to be meeting him here, and he had asked for an extra hour or two to sort out his thoughts and try his theory.

"Just coffee," he said to the waitress. "I'm meeting some-one in a few minutes."

"Another just like it, miss." Rusty slid into the red and gray vinyl booth opposite Dan. "Been here long?"

"Nope. Just got here."

"Good. Jee . . . whiz, it's cold out there." Rusty usually modified his language in front of Dan, but he almost slipped. He had never heard Dan talk about being a relig-ious man, but he knew he hadn't heard a swear word come from him in the seven years they had known each other either. He admired this hard-working young executive and respected the way he made everyone feel important. Not the usual for someone of his stature and social standing—even if he had—what one could call a loose connection to the social set. Dan didn't talk about his past, although Rusty had read the papers and knew pretty much the whole story. But then, Dan didn't ask him about his past either, and Rusty liked it that way.

Rusty glanced over his shoulder toward the jukebox in

the corner. Bob Dylan's soulful voice filled the small restaurant. "If only the answers were that easy."

"Pardon me?" Dan said.

"Just blowin' in the wind. If that were true, we've got enough wind today to give us all the answers we need."

"You just want the easy way out, Rusty. The answers we're looking for are a bit too difficult, even for Dylan."

Stirring his coffee, Rusty ignored Dan's pensive mood. "I think I have a hunch on the heist," he began.

"That's an interesting word."

"Well, what do you call it?"

"*Heist* will do."

"I've been wondering if someone might have a key, or at the least a connection to somebody inside the store."

Dan laughed. "Yeah, I thought that at first, too."

"But then," Rusty continued, "I got to thinkin'. It doesn't seem too likely that someone would have the keys to both Halloran's and Rothschild's. And now, the Emporium."

"The Emporium?" Dan hadn't heard about that one.

"Yeah, last night. It's in the evening paper."

"Oh, great."

"I've been thinking, Dan. What do all these department stores have in common?"

"Well, let's see," Dan began. "I assume that you mean something more than the obvious, like merchandise, salespeople, wealthy owners, and so forth."

"Right, something more common," Rusty nodded.

"Common? Better not let the upper-crust owners hear you say that."

"Come on, Dan, think."

"Okay, let's see. We all use Brinks to haul away the money. We all use Sani-Fresh to haul away the trash—"

"What?" Dan's companion almost choked on his coffee.

"Brinks to haul away—"

"No." Rusty reached toward his coat hanging at the side of the booth on a chrome hook. "Who did you say hauls away your trash?"

"Sani-Fresh."

Rusty unrolled the morning's paper. "You say you *all* use Sani-Fresh?"

"I think so. They've had the downtown contracts for so long, they've gotten rich off the garbage of the rich."

"Look at this." Rusty held the paper out for Dan to examine a picture near the back page.

"What's this?"

"A picture of a meter maid giving a ticket?"

"No, not the cop. The truck in the background."

"A trash truck?"

"A trash truck, a Sani-*Free* truck." Rusty jumped up and went to a phone booth. Dan watched as he rifled through the yellow pages of the phone book. Rusty shrugged, made an *okay* sign through the phone booth door, and dialed a number.

"Come on," Rusty crossed the coffee shop with large steps. "We've got a break."

"Where are we going?" Dan slid in beside Rusty in his old Plymouth. "When are you going to get a new car?"

"When I get rich. We're going to police headquarters. They've got a lead."

Rusty brought his old car to a sudden stop in front of an expired parking meter. "Put some change in there, will you, Dan?"

The two men took the steps up the front of the police station two at a time. "Hey, Russ," the front desk officer called. "How ya' been?"

"Great, Mack, and you?"

"Can't complain," Mack laughed, "nobody'd listen."

"Tell Jake I'm here, will you, Mack?" Rusty called over his

shoulder as he and Dan headed down the hall. "Up here," he said to Dan. Rusty led the way upstairs to an unoccupied office. Soon Jacob Smith joined them.

"What have you got?"

"Look at this, Jake." Rusty pulled the newspaper from his pocket.

"So?"

"Tell him, Dan."

"Tell him what?"

"Who picks up the trash in the downtown area?"

"Sani-Fresh," Dan said.

"No kiddin'?" Jake made the connection immediately.

"No kiddin'," Rusty answered. "Know what else? There's no Sani-*Free* in the yellow pages."

"Pretty clever, I'd say." Jake looked at the picture again—this time more closely. "Almost identical to Sani-Fresh. Look at the markings on the truck, even the company logo. No one would even notice the difference. Wonder why Sani-Fresh hasn't complained?"

"Think the Sani-Fresh people are involved?" Rusty asked.

"They'd certainly have a lot to lose. They have most of the downtown business as it is. But who knows? Maybe they're just looking the other way." Jake turned to Dan. "How's the trash pickup system work?"

"We get several canvas trucks each morning. You know, the canvas sided carts that are, oh, I'd say four to five feet long, no more than thirty inches wide and just about as tall, I guess. After the cleaning crew gets done each evening after store hours they put the full ones back by the door and then next morning they bring empty ones and take the full ones away." Dan was beginning to see that Rusty's theory might be credible after all.

"Are they ever covered?"

"Sure." Dan laughed. "Upper-class establishments like

Halloran's, Rothschild's, and The Emporium can't have exposed trash now can they?"

"We're on to something here," Jake said.

"I've been thinking, you know, guys, an adult would be able to fit into one of those trucks. It'd be tight, but it could be done," Rusty said.

Jake reached for the phone. "Thanks, Rusty, we owe you one."

Rusty opened the door, and Dan followed him down the stairs and out into the cold March afternoon. "Getting dark, Dan. I'll give you a lift back to the store, okay?"

"Thanks."

Rusty started his old car, and as they pulled out into traffic Dan said, "Now what?"

"Now nothing. They'll take it from here. We're finished. They'll close in tonight or tomorrow. Those guys have been makin' quite a haul. But I bet it's not been to a dump."

"But what about . . ." Dan was confused.

"This is not the same case, Dan." Rusty stopped, then carefully turned right on a red light.

"It's not?"

"Nope. Not the same M.O."

"Oh." Dan had hoped it was over.

"Got anyone in the jewelry department you can trust?" Rusty asked.

Dan began to go over the staff in his mind. "I think so. Jen mentioned a girl named Megan. Remember? Said she had trouble even borrowing a dime for a phone call."

"I need to talk to her. That is, if you're sure she can be trusted," Rusty added.

"When?"

"As soon as possible." Rusty stopped in front of the canvas awning at the entrance to Halloran's. "How 'bout tonight?"

"I'll see what I can do. Where?"

"Someplace private. Maybe Jen's place again?" Rusty suggested.

"I'll let you know," Dan said.

"Better come along, Dan. I want you in on all of this, every step of the way."

"I'll set it up with Jen and call you." Jen. He would see Jen again. It was work, of course, but that was as good as an excuse as any.

"I'll go to the office and wait to hear from you. Tell the girls I'll bring pizza. And Dan?"

"Yeah?"

"Don't let anyone know you're talking to Jen. It's better if no one knows."

"Sure."

Back in his office, Dan decided to call the extension next to Jen's register. If anyone else answered, he would ask for Jeffers and make up a reason for calling.

"Home furnishings, Miss Whipple speaking, how can I help you?"

"Jen, it's Dan. Are you alone?"

"Yes, for a few minutes. It's slow here, and Mr. Jeffers is at a managers' meeting."

"Oh—I forgot about that meeting. But it doesn't matter. Listen, Jen, can we talk to Megan?"

"Megan?"

"I mean can she be trusted?"

"Megan?" Jen's voice carried a bit of surprise. "Megan can be trusted completely. Why?"

"Rusty needs to talk to someone in the jewelry department, and I thought of Megan," Dan explained.

"I see."

"Can you get her to go home with you tonight after work? Could we meet you two there?"

"Well, sure, I guess. I have a class, and I'll need to tell

Megan something." Jen fell silent briefly. "But don't worry, I'll manage to get her there. I usually go straight from here to class. It's going to be pretty hard to get home then back to class."

"If you went home, and after you got there explained to Megan what's going on, would there still be time to get you to class if I drove you?"

"Sure. That would work. You don't mind?"

"Not at all."

"Then leave it to me, okay?" Jen caught a glimpse of Mr. Jeffers out of the corner of her eye.

"Royal Dalton? Of course. And we have some pieces in stock. It would be better if you could come down and see them if you don't know what specific pieces you want."

"Mr. Jeffers, right?" Dan guessed.

"Right. Nine 'til nine on Thursday."

"Oh, Jen, Rusty said he'd bring pizza," Dan added.

"You're having a party that soon? Well, I'm sure we can help you out. Okay, we'll be looking for you then. Goodbye."

"You have a way with phone customers, Jennifer." Jeffers complimented her so seldom that it took Jen by surprise.

"Thank you, Mr. Jeffers."

"It's closing time, Jen. You go on. I'll count the drawer tonight."

"Thanks." Jen was glad she had straightened up the department earlier. "I have class tonight. I'd better hurry."

Catching up to Megan, Jen didn't have a hard time convincing her to come stay over. "Only on one condition." Megan's eyes sparkled with a mischievous look.

"What's that?"

"I can wear your gray and white sweater tomorrow."

"You can wear whatever you like." Jen laughed. "Half of what I have in my closet is yours anyway."

"Hey, what about class?" Megan asked.

"Don't you worry about my education. I'll do a make up if I have to."

On the bus, the two girls miraculously found a seat. "I'm hungry," Megan said, "what's for dinner?"

"Pizza."

"Pizza? You're kidding. Not one of those frozen things, I hope. They've got to do something about those. Come on, Jen, it's not a frozen pizza, is it?"

"No, it's not. It's being delivered."

"Yeah?" Megan paused. "How we gonna pay for that?"

"We don't have to. A friend is bringing it."

"You mean I'm finally going to meet your classmates?"

"Well, not exactly, classmates. More like my project partners," Jen hedged.

"What do you know? Our social life is improving, finally."

Jen laughed. If Megan only knew—but further explanation would have to wait until they were alone, safely secured behind the lock Dan had so carefully installed on her apartment door.

Dan. She could hardly wait, even though nothing could come of her seeing him, of course. She had firmly and clearly told herself so—many times.

CHAPTER TEN

*O*nce Jen explained the purpose of the evening's meeting to her friend, Megan seemed quiet and thoughtful.

"You okay with this, Meg? I should have told you about this some other way, I know. But Mr. Miller called and asked if they could see you as soon as possible. I thought . . . well, now I'm not so sure."

Megan's eyes were wide, and she sat motionless at Jen's kitchen table. She quietly began to pick the dead leaves off one of Jen's houseplants.

"These need attention," she said and got up to fill a teapot. "They could use a spot of warm tea."

"Meg, let me call and cancel the meeting. Dan . . . Mr. Miller will understand."

"*Dan?* You call him Dan?"

Jen picked up the phone and dialed. Megan jerked the receiver out of her hand and put it back in its place on the cradle.

"No, you don't. I've been wanting to talk to someone about some very strange things happening in my department, but I didn't know who. Now's my chance, and you're not going to take that away from me. I'm scared to death, Jen, but this has been bothering me for a long time." Megan poured the hot water into a cup over a tea bag.

Jen watched her friend dangle the soggy bag above the

cup, then put it in a teaspoon and tightly wind the string around it to squeeze out the rest of the water.

"Sugar?" Jen reached in the cupboard for the bowl.

"Violet doesn't like sugar."

"Sorry, I didn't know."

"Who's coming?" Megan put the warm liquid a few drops at a time around the base of Jen's African violet.

"Rusty. He's the one who wants to talk to you. Probably Elizabeth Simms. And of course, Mr. Miller."

"Dan." Megan said his first name looking directly at Jen, the unspoken question hung between the friends.

"Yes, Dan." Jen didn't want to say any more. There wasn't anything more to say.

"Who's Elizabeth Simms?" Megan let the subject of Dan Miller drop for a moment.

"She's the older woman who works as head of security at the store. You'll probably recognize her when you see her. She keeps a pretty low profile around the store. It works to her advantage when she needs to watch a clerk or customer who's under suspicion." Jen hoped her explanation was accurate.

"Can I trust them?"

Jen smiled. "That's what they asked me about you." Megan reached for the sugar.

"I thought Violet didn't like sugar."

"The rest is mine."

"Yes, Megan, you can trust them. I do. I really do. And maybe something you know will help them find who's taking this stuff from the store."

"I don't think I know anything really, it's just something I feel."

"Feel?"

Before Megan could answer the question, someone knocked on the door. "Pizza delivery!"

Opening the door, Jen was glad to see Rusty with a smiling Dan behind him.

Jen hesitated before shutting the door. "Where's Beth?"

"They're working on another case."

"They?" Megan's panicked expression made Rusty's heart soften toward her.

"The police have a solid lead on the burglaries. They'll be up all night watching the stores in town." He headed toward the kitchen.

"Hey, that'll get cold if we don't dig in." Dan led the way to the cupboard to get some plates. Jen reached for some napkins, and Megan cleared the table of the plants.

Discussing the situation over pizza, Rusty and Dan carefully explained to Megan all they knew about the mysteriously disappearing merchandise at the store. She listened intently and then took a deep breath.

"Wow. People really take things? Right out of the store?"

"Yes, Megan, they do. And what's worse, right from under your pretty little nose," Rusty added.

"That's where you're wrong." Megan pushed her plate away and wiped her mouth with her napkin.

"Excuse me?" Rusty said.

"I mean I know it." Megan looked at the three people crowded around Jen's small table staring at her in shock. "I mean I know it," Megan repeated.

"Just when it's getting good, I have to go," Jen said.

"Go?" Megan couldn't believe her ears.

"I have to go to class, Meggie, my friend, I have an exam tonight."

"I promised to take her, Russ." Dan grabbed his coat from off the back of the chair where he sat.

"I don't think this one will give me any trouble," Rusty joked as Jen started toward the door.

"I'll wait for her and we'll be back as soon as we can. Beth might be calling in," Dan said. "Find out what's going on."

In the car, Jen tried to concentrate on the exam just ahead. It consisted of presenting a proposal for an office decor. She had carefully planned and collected her color swatches according to the instructor's directions. She was to simulate a presentation to a corporate client. Her portfolio lay safely in the small back seat of Dan's car, and she mentally went over her approach and silently rehearsed her presentation.

Dan watched the young woman beside him grow quiet, seeming to change personalities as she thought.

"A penny for your thoughts." Dan broke the silence.

"I don't want a penny, I want an *A*." Jen said.

"Okay, an *A* then," Dan said with a smile.

"It's just that I have to make a presentation in front of the whole class tonight."

"A required assignment?"

"Yes, of the scariest kind." Jen's mind was racing with colors, textures, and shapes.

"I see."

Jen explained how difficult it was to make a simulated presentation to other students. "If I just had a real client," she said, "I'm sure I would do better."

"How about me?"

"Excuse me?"

"I've thought of doing my office over. Would you object to my sitting in on your class? You could consider me a prospective client." Dan's impulsive suggestion gave him an idea. "I mean it, Jen. Maybe you could even stay on after graduation and redecorate my office."

"You're kidding." Jen searched Dan's face looking for a clue that he was joking.

"Why not?" Dan watched Jen, but he had to divide his attention between her and the traffic.

"Because I'm just finishing school, that's why not. I have to work with someone for a while and get some experience first."

"How do you plan to do that? Do you have a lead on a job in California?" Dan asked.

Jen didn't. She had planned to take some time off, renew friendships, and go to the beach with Cari, her best friend.

"Would it bother you if I came into the classroom?"

"I don't know." Jen liked the idea, but she didn't know how the other students would react.

"Then it's settled. Where should I park?"

After class Dan was quiet as he turned the car toward Jen's apartment. Jen too sat silently. Dan must already regret that he had spoken to her about his office and didn't know how to get out of it, she concluded.

"Well, that's behind me." Jen said, breaking the awkward silence. "One more step toward home. That's what I've been telling myself all day."

"I'm impressed," Dan said.

"Really?"

"Yes, really." Dan was more than impressed. He wanted Jen to stay in Chicago. If she would redo his office, maybe he could find another reason to keep her here a little while beyond that, and then . . .

"Jennifer," he began slowly, occasionally glancing at her as he drove, "I'm interested. Very interested."

Jen's heart pounded at the sound of him saying her full name. This feeling was not in her plans. Dan Miller was not in her plans.

Dan grew silent and paid close attention to his rearview

mirror. Suddenly he turned down a street several blocks from Jen's apartment.

"Jen—" Dan reached over and grabbed her hand. "I don't want to scare you, but I think someone is following us."

Jen's pounding heart threatened to burst.

"I'm going to try to lose him. Okay? You okay?"

"Yes."

"Hang on, we're going for a ride."

Dan pressed the accelerator to the floorboard, and the Corvette leaped forward. He headed for the expressway and dodged between cars and onto the entrance ramp.

"If I don't get a ticket, no one can even begin to catch this car," he said, glancing toward the side mirror and then checking the rearview. "I'm not so sure a speeding ticket wouldn't be welcome tonight."

He drove a moment in the left lane and then darted between two cars to the far right. A dark luxury sedan sped up to try to make a similar maneuver. Several cars crowded in between, and the sedan was forced to remain in the left lane. Dan stomped the gas pedal once again and darted down an exit ramp as the sedan sped by in the far left lane.

"There's no way off until you almost reach Elgin. I think it's several miles at least until the next exit."

Dan slowed down at the bottom of the expressway exit. "You still okay?" He looked at Jen in the light from the street lamps.

"I think so."

"Sure?"

"Who would want to follow us, Dan?"

Dan smiled. "I don't know. But whoever it was I owe a favor to."

"You do? Why?" Jen was puzzled at his sudden good humor.

"Because they made you use my first name." Dan laughed out loud and turned once again toward Jen's place.

Rusty checked his watch as they let themselves in with Jen's key, "Hey, you two, I was getting worried."

"We took a detour. I'll tell you about it later." Dan smiled at Jen, then looked back toward Rusty and Megan still sitting at the kitchen table. "Any progress here?"

"A gold mine." Rusty stood and stretched. "Megan has been noticing some very interesting things in her department, Dan. She's very alert. What's more, she has agreed to help us."

"Oh?" Dan looked toward Megan.

"If I can," Megan said.

"Is it safe?" Dan asked.

"I will make every effort to make it as safe as possible." Rusty's reassurance comforted Megan, if not Dan.

"But for tonight, we've covered quite a bit, and now I need to think about what I've been told. A good night's sleep, and I'm sure I'll think of a few more questions to ask Miss Detective here." Rusty stretched and stood. "We've made quite a mess here, let me give you a hand."

The four reached for the pizza remains, and Dan laughed as they lifted the empty box together. "I could probably handle this myself," he told them.

At the door, Megan said good night to Rusty and promised to call him if she noticed anything further—though of course, not from any of the phones in the store. She stepped back a little and overheard Dan as he turned to Jen.

"You may think our conversation is over, but it's not. I'd like to call you tomorrow." He waited for Jen's response.

"I don't know . . ."

"We'll talk tomorrow. Think about it. That's all I'm asking." He touched her cheek with his finger. "That's all."

"I'll think about it."

Dan's whole face lit with his smile.

"Think, Dan—I said I'd *think* about it."

"That's good enough for me," Dan said, *For now anyway.*

Jen shut the door behind him, and Dan paused, waiting to hear the dead bolt slide, locking her securely inside.

"Jen?" Megan was standing in the middle of the room, both of her hands held palms up. "Jennifer?"

"Not now, Megan, I'm tired. It's been a long day and quite a night."

"Obviously," Megan said as her friend brushed by her and headed toward the bedroom.

Jen felt dazed. *Think? Think? How in the world does he expect me to think when my heart is pounding so hard I can't hear anything else?*

CHAPTER ELEVEN

*T*he next Thursday, Jen slept late. She was glad for her day off and didn't hurry to get up. She was scheduled to close on Friday evening and didn't have to be to work until ten o'clock that morning. She counted the hours from five-thirty on Wednesday until ten on Friday—thirty-nine and a half hours all to herself. Well, except for Megan staying with her.

Megan had arrived early on yesterday morning before work with a suitcase in hand. "I'm moving in," she had announced. "Mama thinks it's to take care of you until you finish with school. She's worried the pressure might be too much and that you need someone to make sure you eat right."

Jen was glad for Megan's company. She had asked Megan on several occasions to move in, but Megan's family ties were too strong to allow her that freedom just yet. "Mama says girls have no business living on their own and were never designed to be so independent," Megan declared. Jen and Megan had laughed. After all, it was 1963, and women made up over 40 percent of the work force. It was clear, the friends agreed, that if you wanted a career, you had to have it *before* you got married; you sure wouldn't get it after.

Retail sales wasn't the same as being a corporate vice president, that was for sure. But it was something more than either of their mothers had dreamed of doing.

"My mother can't even write a check," Megan had said.

"My mother handles all the family finances," Jen was quick to add, "but she's always grateful she isn't expected to earn them."

Not me, Jen mused. *I'm going to have my own business someday.* She reached for the clock ticking beside her bed. Ten. "I can't lie here any longer. I'll get so stiff I won't be able to carry my laundry." She stretched and with one swift movement she leaped out of bed, threw the top covers back with one hand and grabbed the top sheet with the other. She stripped the bed, threw the sheets in the corner, and headed for the bathroom to shower before tackling the rest of the apartment.

By eleven, she had sorted her clothes, sheets, and towels, gulped a cup of coffee, and began washing the few dishes left in the sink from Megan's second visit with Rusty the night before when the phone rang.

"Have you been thinking?" The sound of Dan's voice made Jen's heart jump.

"Sort of," Jen said.

"Sort of?" Dan said. "It's been a week already."

"I have to finish school, you know. Last minute details and projects are keeping me pretty busy."

"I know," Dan said, "but I was wondering—if you saw my office, would it help you decide?"

"Maybe so." Jen wasn't sure she could tackle a big job without more actual hands-on experience. "Maybe that would be a good idea."

"How about tomorrow morning?" Dan pressed.

"That would give me a little time before I'm scheduled to go on the floor."

"I know, I checked."

"Okay. Tomorrow at nine."

Jen woke early on Friday, unable to sleep. Megan was tossing, uneasy in the other bed, and the two friends finally got up and made coffee at five-thirty.

Megan sat at the table with one leg tucked under her and a blanket wrapped around her. She wore her fuzzy slippers and leaned with one elbow propped up on the table.

"Something bothering you?" Jen knew her friend's moods pretty well.

"Yeah, something is bothering me. I might have to talk to Rusty about it, though, before I tell you." Reaching out toward Jen she said, "Is that all right? I don't want to shut you out, but I think that this is something he needs to know first."

"Sure," Jen said. "I don't feel shut out."

Jen hadn't told Megan about Dan's offer and wouldn't until she knew one way or another whether she would take on the project. She hoped Megan wouldn't feel left out either.

The two young women decided to dress and leave for work early, treating themselves to fresh cinnamon rolls at Dolly's Coffee Shoppe and Bakery a few blocks down the street. Jen chose her gray wool blazer and coordinating pleated skirt. "They're wearing cotton in Redlands," she muttered as she pulled on the jacket.

"They're what, where?"

"I'm just thinking about the spring weather back home," Jen explained. "My mother is already working in her garden and the orange trees are blossoming. It's really beautiful there right now."

Jen's homesickness was overpowering at times. She had made the best of Chicago's city life, but she longed for the atmosphere of her hometown. She could almost smell the spring air, feel the magic of a Sunday morning when the whole family was scurrying around to get to church on time, and sense the excitement of a "family" picnic that was made up more of friends than actual relatives.

She missed Cari, who was the closest thing she had to a sister. And Grandma Nelson, who was actually Cari's grandmother but felt like her own. Jen had hated leaving Redlands so soon after Cari's grandfather had died, but life was for living. Grandma had told her: "You go on with your life, Jenny girl. You've got to make your own difference in the world, just like Grandpa did."

Jen wanted to go home. She knew this offer from Dan was the only thing that could possibly delay that decision.

Stepping out into the cool air, the girls looked at each other and in unison said, "Spring!"

"It really does feel like spring," Megan said, looking up between the city buildings to find the sky. "Look, the sky is blue, there's not a cloud anywhere."

Jen followed her gaze. "How can you tell? All you can see is that little spot between the rooftops."

"I know," Megan said, "I can feel the sky."

Megan and Jen went separate ways a few blocks from Halloran's. Megan was off to meet Rusty before work and to tell him what was bothering her, and Jen walked on to the store. As she approached the elevator to take her to the sixth floor office suite, she felt nervous. But when she reached the office door, she feigned confidence and swung it open.

"Good morning." The young woman, probably in her late twenties, Jen guessed, greeted her warmly. "I'm Debbie, Mr. Miller's secretary. You must be Jen."

"Good morning, yes, I am."

"He's been called away from the office, but he said to have you take a look and that he'd call you later. Come on in, I'll show you around."

Debbie led the way into Dan's office. Jen was amazed at

the view from the corner windows. "I didn't know you could see the lake from here."

"Oh, yes, and over there," she pointed off to the north just slightly, "you can see Wacker Drive."

"Megan was right," Jen said.

"Megan?"

"My roommate," Jen explained. "She said there wasn't a cloud in the sky."

Jen stood for a moment, taking in the beautiful view, and then pulled her attention to the office behind her. Nice furnishings, she noted, but a little on the stark side. The rich mahogany paneling lent a deep sober mood, and the blond furnishings were a bit outdated. Jen put her hand on a chair. "Popular ten years ago, but . . ."

"I know what you mean," Debbie agreed, "he inherited most of this furniture. It came with the job."

"How long has he been here?"

"About four years. It was the manager's office before. But then Mrs. Halloran had the penthouse offices built. Her office is up there."

"Is she the actual store manager then?" Jen was curious.

"In name only. She's hardly ever there. Just keeps it for appearances if you ask me."

"I see." Jen didn't really.

"Dan—Mr. Miller does the actual managing. All the work, none of the recognition. All the responsibility, none of the authority."

Jen looked at Debbie with interest.

Debbie shook her head. "I've said too much already. It's none of my business. Mr. Miller is great to work with. I hope you can do something with this office. It really needs his own personality."

"And what is that?"

"Warmth, life, and openness." Debbie pointed at the

heavy doors leading to the office. "Those have to go. They don't reflect his accessibility at all."

"Have you ever considered going into interior design?" Jen asked.

"Mercy no." Debbie took a step back. "I didn't mean to step into your area," she apologized.

"Oh, no," Jen reached toward the nice young woman. "I just meant that you're a keen observer. That's important to someone in my field."

"Well, you're the professional here."

"Not yet, I'm not. I will be graduating in a couple of months, then we'll see. If I take this project, it will be my first."

"Really?" Debbie was surprised.

"Really," Jen answered. "For the moment, I'm a clerk in the home furnishings department downstairs."

"See what I mean? Mr. Miller is quick to spot the potential in someone and encourage them toward higher goals, and what's more, it doesn't matter to him whether you're a woman or a man. If you show promise, he promotes you. You can't say that for every company."

Jen turned her eyes toward the picture of Marie on the shelf-lined wall.

"He even decided to change my job classification from secretary to administrative assistant. Gave me more responsibility and of course, requires more from me. But I don't mind, it really is a great job."

"Who's this?" Jen picked up the picture and examined it closely. *All my love, always, Marie* was scrawled across one lower corner.

"That's Marie Halloran Miller. Dan Miller's lucky wife."

Jen froze and her heart stopped. She forced herself to return the picture to its place. She stepped back and grabbed her stomach unconsciously.

"Jen, you all right?"

"I'm fine. I just had a long walk and haven't had anything but a cinnamon roll and cup of coffee. I really need to eat something before I go on the clock." Jen picked up her purse from the leather couch and her pad from Dan's desk. She walked toward the door on legs that suddenly felt like wood.

"When shall I tell Mr. Miller to call you?"

"Oh, I don't know. I'm working until six and have a class at seven. I work tomorrow, and I'll be busy on Sunday. Next week sometime would be fine."

Jen found her way to the employee's locker room and leaned her forehead against the cool metal of her locker. She was glad to be alone for a moment and wiped away the tears that found their way down her cheeks.

She heard someone come in and quickly regained her composure.

"Hi." It was Megan.

"Hi." Jen didn't want to face anyone, not even her friend.

"I saw Rusty, and we need to talk to you later. He'll be over about nine-thirty or ten, okay?"

"I don't . . . I guess so." Jen really just wanted to run away.

"What's the matter, Jen?"

"I have to be on the floor in a few minutes, Megan. We can't talk now." Jen went into the restroom and splashed her face with cold water. She caught a runaway curl and tucked it up into the strands of hair fastened with a comb.

"Talk to me, Jen." Megan followed her, and the two friends stood looking at each other in the mirror.

"Not now, Meg, please." Jen dried her hands with the cloth towel draping from the dispenser.

"Jen, I can't let you go to work like this. What is the matter with you?" Megan demanded.

"I won't be doing Mr. Miller's office." Jen turned and looked Megan straight in the face.

"What?"

"He had asked me to consider staying on for a while after graduation and redoing his office."

"Really?"

"Yes, really. But I won't be staying. I'm going home just as soon as I can." Jen turned and left the restroom with Megan in close pursuit.

"Why does this upset you so much?" Megan asked.

"I can't talk about it, Meg. I just can't. Please don't force it."

Megan watched helplessly as Jen turned and walked toward the escalator. Then she saw him, the same man she saw earlier. He was following Jen, she was sure of it, and she was glad she had told Rusty. Later they would tell Jen, but with her already so upset, Megan wished they didn't have to.

CHAPTER TWELVE

H *ow could I have been so stupid?* Jen chided herself all the way to her second floor department. Barely able to fight back her tears, she silently went to work, strangely grateful for the unending busywork of straightening stock and displays.

"Good morning," Jeffers seemed interested in a bit more than his usual paperwork. He stood in front of the counter Jen was straightening, awaiting her response.

"Hi," she said simply.

"Something the matter, Jennifer?"

"A personal matter. I'll be fine. Excuse me—a customer." She brushed by him, but another clerk approached the customer before she could cross the department. She glanced back to where she was working and saw Jeffers watching. She took a deep breath and walked toward her unfinished task. As she once again walked by him, he caught her arm with his hand. "Could I see you in my office, please?" Without waiting for an answer, he let go of her and walked toward his small desk in the corner of the stockroom.

Jen waited a moment, then followed. *Now what?* She hadn't had a good day so far, and it looked like it wasn't going to get any better. She pushed back the curtain covering the stockroom entrance and approached Mr. Jeffers' desk. As she approached, he stood and pulled out his chair and offered it.

"Won't you sit down, Jennifer?"

"No, thank you. I don't mind standing." Jen didn't want to be in here with her department manager any longer than absolutely necessary. He had never done anything to offend her or make her feel uncomfortable, but since that day in the upstairs security office, she had not trusted him either.

"I've noticed," he began, "that you seem preoccupied today. Perhaps you aren't feeling well?"

Jen looked down at her hands and began picking at her cuticles. "I'm fine, Mr. Jeffers."

"I don't think so." He looked at Jen with what she could almost interpret as sympathy.

"Really, I'm fine." Jen took a deep breath and decided to offer some kind of explanation. She couldn't very well tell him that after nearly two years of working toward her goal of finishing her education and returning to her beloved family and carefully—successfully—avoiding any relationship that threatened those plans, she had fallen for a man—a *married* man. Finally, she looked straight at Jeffers. "I've had some bad news."

"I'm sorry," Jeffers offered.

"It's not your fault. I can't go into it. As I said, it's personal. I just need a few hours, then I'll be fine."

"Look, Jen." Jeffers had rarely called her anything other than Jennifer. "You've worked for me for almost two years. You've hardly ever taken any time off, you've not had a decent vacation, and you have accumulated almost two weeks of sick leave."

Jen looked at Mr. Jeffers, wondering what his point was.

He continued. "What I am saying is this; it isn't a busy day, so far. I've got Charlotte until five and Doris is coming on at one. I'm sure if I call personnel, I can get an extra to cover if necessary. I'll be here all day. I was planning to be out on the floor anyway. Why don't you go home? Maybe you'll feel better tomorrow."

"I don't know . . ." Jen's voice trailed off. Her empty apartment didn't seem very inviting either.

Jeffers seemed insistent. "Look, I'm trying to help here."

"I know."

"Then let me make you a deal. Okay?"

"A deal?"

"You go for a walk. It's a nice morning. It's almost like spring out there. Some fresh air would do you good. You're a religious person—go pray or something."

Jen smiled. *Pray.* The first thing she should have done was the last thing she thought of doing.

"Then when you get back," Jeffers continued, "you can help me out back here."

"Back here?"

"I have to check in all this stock for the Spring Fling, and the paperwork is killing me. There'er returns to inventory, and I've been told there will be a hold audit over the weekend." He smiled and took her hands in his. His hands were soft; she didn't expect that. "Please?"

"Okay, if you're sure it will be all right."

"I'll call personnel now and tell them to send us an extra. Now you go on, take an hour or two. See you back here in a little while." Jeffers smiled at her. "Jen?"

She was already turning to go. "Yes?" She looked back over her shoulder and pushed a stray curl from her face.

"Nothing. Go on now, enjoy the spring weather."

Outside the store, Jen walked with no destination in mind. She barely noticed the traffic, and on impulse she caught a city bus toward the shore. She needed space and she needed air. Lake Michigan offered both.

As soon as he called personnel and offered an explanation for Jen's absence, Jeffers went back to his desk in the stockroom. Glancing around to make sure he was alone, he reached for the phone. "Outside line, please," he said to the store operator. After a pause, he began dialing.

"I want this stopped," he said firmly to whoever came on the line. "There is no reason to keep such a close watch on her at work." He was angry.

"No, she doesn't suspect." Jeffers wiped his high forehead with his handkerchief.

"I don't care what your reasons are. The other girls are beginning to notice. I can tell you her schedule. I'm here with her at work, and there's always Yvonne. We'll keep an eye on things here."

Jeffers listened nervously.

"I sent her out for a while. She seemed upset after coming down from Miller's office. I guess Debbie must have done a number on her."

He listened, then said, "No, she didn't say anything to me. I'm her boss, not her confidant."

"Mr. Jeffers?" A voice called him from the door.

"Hold a minute, will you?" he said into the phone, "I think my extra's here."

Putting the fill-in clerk to work with one of the other salespeople, Jeffers returned to the phone.

"You still there? Good. I know I can handle things here. Just do your dirty work away from my department. It makes me nervous. I have helped you up to this point. But this is too much. Take the rest of it and your watchdogs out of here." Even if it cost him his job, Jeffers wasn't about to have strangers stalking one of his clerks, especially Jennifer. Not here, anyway.

Jen got off the bus at the stop nearest the lakeshore. It

had been cool in the city, but here with the wind blowing off the lake unchecked by the tall buildings, it was cold. She hugged her coat closer to her and pulled a scarf up over her head. She buttoned her coat up as high as she could and then turned her collar up to cover her face. Her gloves were still in her employee locker, so she put her bare hands into her pockets.

Walking toward the lake, she noticed a man a little distance behind her. She quickened her step, and her heart began to pound. Afraid she was being followed, she decided she needed to stay near the bus line. She crossed the street to find a bus stop. Reaching the curb she turned and faced the man straight on. His collar was also turned up against the wind, and he pulled his hat lower on his head. Thrusting his hands deeper into his pockets, he turned and walked away.

She glanced around, and as soon as the approaching bus stopped, she boarded, hesitating at the coin box. She directly looked at the man standing on the curb a few feet from the bus.

"Well, mister," the driver said aloud, "if you're coming, come on."

"He's not coming," Jen said to the driver. At the command of the driver, the doors gave way with a sigh of the hydraulic system and the bus pulled away from the curb.

Jen walked slowly to a seat near the center of the bus and looked out the window into the face of the strange man. She thought she could detect a slight shrug as the bus left him standing there alone in the cold breeze coming off the lake.

Dan should be told about this, she thought. Then the pain of this morning returned and flooded her eyes with tears that could no longer be checked. Silently she cried, staring out the bus window until she reached downtown. She got off the bus, and with a transfer in her hand she boarded another. For several hours she rode, transferring from one route to another. Finally she went to a pay phone and called the store. Talking to one of the clerks in her department, she left a message for Mr. Jeffers that she wouldn't be in until tomorrow morning.

Toward evening she went home to her empty apartment. Megan was going directly home to be with her family for the weekend.

Opening the door to her apartment, Jen let the loneliness sweep over her. *I've been so foolish.* She wished she had never heard of Dan Miller. *I knew better than to get involved this close to graduation anyway—but with a married man?* Jen mechanically put her coat in the front closet and walked into her bedroom. Laying across her bed, she let a day's worth of stifled sobs escape uncontrollably.

Finally spent from crying, she went to the bathroom and took three aspirin for the pounding headache all the crying had brought on. Stripping, she stepped into the shower and let the hot water wash over her. She furiously scrubbed her body and shampooed her hair. Finding a warm robe, she wrapped herself up and went to the kitchen and heated some milk before she crawled into bed—hopefully to sleep.

Later, she woke to the sound of someone trying to get into the apartment. Momentarily disoriented in the total darkness, she sat up in bed.

"Jen!" Megan called from the front door. "Jen, are you in there?"

"Megan?" Jen stumbled to the door without turning on a light.

"Jen, the chain is on the door. I can't get in." Megan's voice was tinged with worry.

"Coming."

"What's going on?" Megan reached for her friend and the light switch at the same time.

The table lamps came on, and Megan was shocked at Jen's appearance.

"I tried to call you all afternoon." Megan held on to Jen with one hand while shedding her coat. "You okay?"

"Yeah, I'm okay. I've had a terrible headache all evening. I came home from work early."

"I know," Megan told her.

"I thought you were going to your mother's."

"And I thought you were going to class."

"Not tonight. Why aren't you going to your mother's?"

"A change in plans. Rusty is on his way over," Megan explained.

Jen rubbed her temples. Sighing, she said, "I'm tired of this whole thing, Megan. Docs he have to come tonight?"

"I'm afraid so, Jen. We need to talk to you." But while she talked, Megan started playing with the idea that it might have to wait. Jen was obviously upset, maybe even sick.

"I can't, Megan, not tonight." Jen turned toward the bedroom just as the phone rang. Megan answered it.

"It's Dan Miller, he's asking for you," she told her friend.

Jen continued toward the bedroom. "I can't talk to him tonight. Next week maybe, not tonight." She closed the door behind her and didn't listen to the explanation Megan gave Dan. She didn't care what Megan said to him. She wanted to go back to bed, back to sleep. Jen barely heard Rusty's voice when he came in just before she drifted off.

"What's the matter with her?" Rusty asked looking toward the closed bedroom door.

"I don't know. Mr. Jeffers told me she had some bad news. That's all I know. I came home right after work and she was sleeping. I had to wake her up to let me in."

"Something doesn't make sense here." Rusty glanced toward the kitchen. "Got some coffee?" he asked.

Megan nodded and started toward the kitchen. "Sure."

"I'm going to call Dan. Maybe he knows what's going on."

"I already talked to him. He's just a confused as we are."

"Yeah? I bet he is." Rusty smiled.

"He said he was coming over. I told him Jen didn't want to talk to him, but he said he was coming over anyway."

Rusty nodded toward the bedroom. "I think he's quite taken with our little sleeping beauty in there. Caught him off guard too."

"Oh?" Megan poured two cups of coffee.

"He's sort of sworn off women, ever since—well, that's his business, none of mine. Got any food in this place?" Rusty sipped the steaming black liquid.

"Not much. Let me look." Megan leaned into the small refrigerator. "Eggs. Catsup. Lettuce. That's about it."

"Got any bread?" Megan produced half a loaf. "Great, make way. You are about to experience the epicurean delight of your life. I make a mean fried egg sandwich. Got any mayo?"

"Look behind the milk," Megan said over her shoulder as she made her way to the front door to answer Dan's knock.

"Where is she?" Dan asked immediately.

"Sleeping." Megan nodded toward the bedroom door.

"I want to see her," Dan said.

"She's sleeping."

Dan crossed the room with large strides. "Megan, I promise I won't disturb her. I just want to see her—I have to know she's all right."

He carefully opened the door and went to her side. Squatting beside her bed, he could barely make out her profile in the dark. Megan silently crossed the room and turned on the bathroom light pulling the door almost shut.

"Thanks," Dan whispered. He could see that Jen's eyes were swollen from crying and that even in her sleep she gave an occasional small sob. Her soft face was almost covered with her long light auburn curls. He carefully pulled them back, one by one, away from her cheeks. He stood and then on impulse he bent and lightly touched her temple with his lips. Jen was unaware of his presence and his tender revelation of the deep feelings he had for her.

Megan turned from her observation post outside the bedroom door and brushed away a tear. Dan turned off the bathroom light and quietly shut the bedroom door behind him.

"What happened to her?" he whispered to Megan.

"I don't know. Jeffers said she went home sick." Megan had called the department looking for her.

"He told me she was out on an errand."

"Something has happened, Dan." Rusty approached with a sandwich in one hand and his coffee in the other. "I'm as baffled by this as you are."

"I thought you were going to keep an eye on her."

"I didn't think I had to, since she was supposed to be at work," Rusty defended.

"I'm glad you're both here," Megan said, motioning them into the kitchen. "And I'm glad she isn't. I don't want her to hear this until . . . well, you can decide if she needs to know about it at all."

"What's going on?" Dan was growing impatient and uneasy with Megan.

Rusty cracked open another egg and stirred it in the pan. "I hope that's for me, I'm really hungry," Megan said. She settled herself in one of the kitchen chairs, smoothed her black hair, and unconsciously tucked it behind one ear. "I think someone's been watching Jen," she announced.

Dan's eyes flew open in amazement and fear. "Watching her?"

"I can't be sure, but there's a man, the same man, every day, standing around the store. At first I thought he was one of the security guys. But this guy is so obvious. Trench coat, hat—the works. Even a little corny, if you ask me."

Rusty put the sandwich in front of Megan. "Notice anything else?" Rusty asked.

"Yeah. He's always on our bus when we go home from work. He's usually across the street when we go in each morning."

"Why didn't you say anything earlier."

"I wasn't sure. I thought I was imagining it. After all, Jen and I see Yvonne several times a day too, and she's not following us. I wanted to be sure first."

"Don't wait until you're sure." Dan's voice was edged with anger. "You tell us, you hear? Let us make sure. You tell us anything suspicious—anything!"

Megan cringed and Rusty put his hand on Dan's arm. "Hold on, Dan. She didn't want to holler wolf. That's all." Rusty turned toward her with a soft tone to his voice. "Meg, how did you become convinced that she was being followed?"

"In the store. Earlier, when she had finished in your office. She came down and I saw her just before we went on the floor. She was upset and didn't want to talk about it." Megan washed down a bite of her sandwich with lukewarm coffee. "She said she would see me later and then I saw him. What's more, he saw me see him."

"Wait, I'm confused." Dan rubbed his temples with his middle fingers. "He saw you see him?"

"You mean as if he wanted you to know he was following her?" Rusty turned a chair around and straddled it, resting his elbows on its back.

"Yes, like he wanted me to see him." Megan swallowed the rest of her coffee. "You can ask Yvonne. She saw him too."

"Yvonne?" Dan didn't recognize the name.

"She's the floater. She was just going into the personnel office. I thought she might know him. She smiled at him, but she didn't stop and talk to him or anything."

"Did he know her?" Rusty asked.

"I don't think so, he didn't act like it."

Rusty sat quietly trying to make sense of what Megan had just told them.

"Why would anyone be following Jen in the first place, and in the second place, why would he want someone to know he was following her?" Dan's forehead was furrowed with worry.

"Rusty," Megan said, "you're the detective. You tell us."

Before Rusty could answer, they all heard the bedroom door close. Dan closed his eyes as he realized that Jen might have been listening to their conversation.

"Oh, no," he said. "I don't want her upset any more than she is already."

He was starting to care about Jen as much as he worried about her. Now she was being threatened, by whom or for what reason he didn't know. But it had to be because of him. He knew that much. It had been four years since Marie. Maybe he didn't have the right, but he certainly had the desire. He knew he was—well, starting to care for Jen. Already she was being hurt because of him. He stood, then turned and walked toward the door grabbing his coat on the way.

"Rusty, I'm leaving this in your capable hands," he said. "You know how to reach me."

Hearing the door close, Megan stared at Rusty with a questioning look. "You've got me, babe. I have no idea what the he—heck's going on. But I'm being paid to find out, so that's what I'll do."

CHAPTER THIRTEEN

Calling in sick on Saturday, Jen waited until Monday to return to work. Megan stayed close to her friend and tried to interest her in going out, but Jen preferred to stay in and work on her studies. After all, she had only a few weeks left. Graduation was only her first goal, she had reminded herself several times; going home, the second objective; and getting a job came next. There was no room for anything or *anyone* else. She had come this far, and she wasn't about to let any distractions keep her from her dreams.

When Jen got to work on Monday, Mr. Jeffers had his head stuck in paperwork as usual. "Good morning," he said, giving his everyday greeting. Looking up, he asked, "Feeling better, Jennifer?"

"Yes, thank you. Much better." Jen kept busy with the never-ending task of straightening stock and displays, a task which often fell to her. No one paid as much attention to the appearance of the department as Jen did. She had an eye for attractive displays, and the other sales personnel were happy to let her do more than her fair share. "How'd the hold audit go?" she asked Jeffers as she worked.

"Hold audit?" Jeffers feigned ignorance. "I don't know what you're talking about."

"But you said . . ."

"Phone for you, Jen," one of her coworkers called from behind the counter.

"Miss Whipple," the voice on the phone began, "this is Debbie, Mr. Miller's secretary."

"Yes, Debbie, hello," Jen answered cheerfully. She wanted to forget her experience in Dan's office, and Debbie was not to blame for her mistake of going there in the first place.

"Mrs. Halloran has asked that you meet with her this afternoon. She will see you at two. Please tell Mr. Jeffers we will be sending Yvonne to fill in for you."

Mr. Jeffers was quite nervous when Jen told him about her summons to the penthouse offices.

"Don't be silly," Jen tried to calm him. "I've only had two sick days, there can't be anything wrong in my going." Jen went back to her routine work. But at one-forty-five, when Yvonne came on the floor, Jen had to admit that she was a little nervous. Megan had not been very calm either, and she warned Jen that Mrs. Halloran could be very intimidating. Many of the girls had said so. Some never returned to the floor after a meeting with her.

Jen took the elevator to the penthouse and stepped onto the most luxurious carpet she had ever seen. None of the swatches she worked with at school had even come close. Jen was sure this carpet wasn't even available through the store's decorating studio on the fourth floor.

"Miss Whipple, how good of you to come," Mrs. Halloran greeted her warmly. The penthouse office was more like an elegant home. Large comfortable furniture was grouped in the center of the spacious room that was obviously the reception area. "Come on in," Mrs. Halloran said as she led the way to her private office.

Inside, rich cherry wood furniture blended perfectly with walls covered in imported silk. Jen couldn't help but take in all the lovely accoutrements and decor. There was just the right amount of lighting suspended from the ceiling with small spotlights on original paintings and priceless statues. The room was quite striking—and quite clear of the paperwork one might imagine would be involved in running a department store the size of Halloran's. The top of the large executive desk was clean except for a gold pen, a silk paisley trimmed blotter, and a matching personal phone directory.

Giving Jen a moment to admire the room, Mrs. Halloran broke the silence. "May I offer you a cup of coffee, or tea perhaps?"

"No, thank you," Jen was not about to risk spilling something on the expensive ivory-colored upholstery or honeygold carpet.

"Very well, let me get right down to business then."

Mrs. Halloran sat behind the large desk and tapped her long painted fingernails on the glass-covered top. "It has come to my attention that you may be leaving us soon."

"Yes, in a couple of months," Jen offered.

"I'm sorry to hear that. Our home furnishings department will miss your artistic touch." She paused, looked Jen carefully in the eye, and then continued, "I also hear that you are quite a talented young designer."

"Not yet. I am barely finishing up my course work. I plan then to take an apprenticeship somewhere on the west coast, California, and hopefully, someday, open my own shop."

"You're quite an ambitious young lady." Jen could almost sense Mrs. Halloran relaxing, though she hadn't really observed any actual movement. "I admire that in a woman."

"Thank you," Jen said, not sure whether or not it was a compliment.

"Will you be going to San Francisco then?" Mrs. Halloran asked.

Jen shook her head. "No, I have family in southern California."

"Perhaps Hollywood then."

"No," Jen laughed, "not anything quite as glamorous as that. I am more interested in traditional California decor. Spanish, Mediterranean in flavor."

"I see."

"I will probably get a job in one of the smaller cities closer to my home. Maybe San Bernardino or Riverside."

"Oh, I've heard of those places. I've driven from LA to Palm Springs; they're somewhere in between aren't they?" Mrs. Halloran said, reaching into her desk drawer. "I have something for you, Jennifer. I know it's quite a surprise, but I think you have proven your loyalty to our store. You certainly have given us more than the average sales clerk does in the way of your display talent and your head for business. Mr. Jeffers tells me you have been his favorite staff member for these past two years. That's quite an accomplishment. Jeffers is difficult to please."

Jen moved uncomfortably in her chair. Praise was not something she received with ease. "I have enjoyed my time here. I just wish your decorating studio was in California. Then I'd be asking for a transfer instead of just a letter of recommendation."

"Please accept this little—well, you might call it a bonus—to help with the expenses of getting home." Jen had been saving as much money as she could to buy a train ticket. "Perhaps there is enough here to help with any last minute school expenses, and so forth." The woman cleared her throat. "I'm not criticizing you, you understand, but it might be wise to build your wardrobe before you go looking for a job. Clothes for school are one thing, but starting a career . . . well, it takes the right look. Don't you agree?"

Jennifer looked down at her straight skirt and matching sweater set. She had bought them with baby-sitting money when she was in high school. While they were still in good condition, they were quite dated. Hemlines had crept up above the knee and while Jen had not liked them very much, she had taken up most of the hems in her clothes to stay in style.

"Something quite dashing, even one of the new plastic mini-skirts with boots, and you'd look like a new woman."

Mrs. Halloran's comment made Jen feel like a project, not a person. "Thank you, Mrs. Halloran, I don't know what to say. This is certainly unexpected."

"Yes, I thought it might be." She handed Jen a sealed envelope. As Jen took it from her hand, Mrs. Halloran said, "Just when did you say you'd be leaving us?"

"School is out the third week in May, just a week before Memorial Day. I promised my friend Megan that I'd spend the holiday weekend with her and her family before I go."

"I see. Well, my dear. Thank you for coming, and again, thank you for choosing Halloran's while you were here."

As soon as Mrs. Halloran started to stand, Jen jumped to her feet. The two women shook hands, and Jen turned toward the door of the office. It seemed so empty and strangely quiet, this beautiful office suite—not even a secretary to keep this wealthy woman company while she "ran" the store.

Megan met Jen at the elevator door. "I've been waiting here almost ten minutes. I only have ten left on my break. What did she want?"

"To say good-bye." Jen looked at her curious friend and then remembered the envelope in her hand. "And to give me this."

"What on earth is that?"

The two girls went into the restroom to open the envelope and found Mrs. Halloran's personal check for fifteen hundred dollars stuck inside a small embossed note card. They looked at each other with disbelief.

It was more money than a year's worth of tuition and more than Jen earned in several months.

"What's she up to?" Megan wondered aloud.

"Who knows?" Jen continued staring at the check.

"What's it for?"

"She called it a bonus for—well—" Embarrassed by Mrs. Halloran's praises of her talent and work, she was even more embarrassed to repeat them. "A bonus, that's all. She suggested I use it for my trip home."

"Well, you certainly won't have to take the train, Dahling," Megan teased. "Why not fly first class?"

"Oh, Megan," Jen poked at her friend, "stop it."

Megan was just happy to see Jen smile once again. Maybe whatever was troubling her was over and done with. Megan could only hope.

Later that evening Dan called. "She's right here," Megan said and handed the phone to Jen. "It's Mr. Miller—and it *is* next week. Talk to him."

Jen shrugged and took the phone. "Hello—yes, I have given it some thought. I think I'd better just go on home after graduation as I originally planned." Jen paused, and Megan listened from the kitchen doorway.

"Yes, I'm sorry too. But I have my plans. I want to take some time off this summer. I've worked straight through with no vacation, and I plan to spend some time with my friend Cari and her new baby." Jen suddenly seemed sad to Megan. Homesick. She must be homesick.

"Yes, I think your office could do with a face-lift, but your own decorating studio could do the job. There are some talented people working for you right there at Halloran's." Megan watched Jen wait while Dan said something she couldn't hear.

"No, I don't think so. I've got last minute projects to finish, a final on period furniture and designers coming up in a couple of weeks. It's pretty hectic."

Megan watched the shoulders of her friend sag a little. "I'm sorry too, Dan. Really sorry." As Megan heard the sad note in Jen's voice, she thought there was something that her friend was not saying.

Jen quietly hung up the phone and sat for a moment staring at it.

"Are you crazy?" Megan wailed. "One of the most gorgeous men in all of Chicago is interested in you, and you give him the cold shoulder? Jennifer Olivia Whipple, what has gotten into you?" Megan wailed.

"Leave it alone, Megan. You don't understand."

"Oh, yes I do. I've heard you talk about God as if He's a personal friend, but when He tries to bless you with a wonderful attentive man you say, 'No thank you, God. I have other plans.' What on earth is wrong with you, Jen? This guy is wild about you."

"Megan, don't!"

"Oh, but I will. Listen to me Jen, I saw the way he worried about you the other night. I saw him come over here even though he knew you were asleep just to look at you to make sure you were safe. I watched him, and my heart almost stopped when he leaned over and kissed you, even though you didn't or wouldn't know anything about his being here unless I blabbed."

"He came here?"

"Ask Rusty. He was worried sick about you. I thought he would cry when he saw your puffy face. Where do you ever think you'll get another chance like this? Do you know what you are passing up? He makes himself available to you, and you just keep packing your stuff to go back to California without so much as a look back."

"Megan, wait! Don't. I can't." Jen started to cry, but Megan didn't let up.

"What is going on, Jen?" Megan stood squarely in front of her friend with both hands firmly planted on her hips. "I want the truth, and I want it now."

"Okay, Megan, get ready for the shock of your life. You asked for it, here it comes." Jen was furious. Pent up anger surged from the pit of her stomach, and she felt her head pound. "I was interested in Dan Miller all right, and I thought he was interested in me. I even fantasized about delaying my trip home—well, indefinitely for Dan Miller."

"I know he's interested in you," Megan shot back.

"Don't interrupt. Interested or not, he's not *available*, as you say . . ."

"He's not what?"

"It's not what he's *not*, Megan, it's what he *is*!" Jen was almost yelling.

"Okay, so what is he?"

"*Married,*" Jen screamed. "Dan Miller is married!"

The two friends stood stiff and angry as they faced each other. Megan choked back the tears as Jen gave way to hers. Megan reached forward as Jen collapsed in her arms. Sobs racked Jen's body, and all Megan could do was hold her. Eventually she smoothed Jen's hair away from her face and led her to the bedroom where the two friends sat in silence on the side of the bed.

Megan got up without a word and headed for the phone just as Rusty called.

"I was just about to call you," Megan said. "I want out. You can do all the detective work you want, but I'm out. I'm quitting Halloran's tomorrow, and Jen is too. Find yourself another partner. And tell Dan Miller to stay home, where he belongs." She hung up the phone and just stared at it when it rang again almost immediately.

Pacing the floor, Megan decided to take Jen to her mother's.

"But what about our jobs?"

"Hang the jobs," Megan said, "You've got your fifteen hundred bucks, and I've got my mama. Let's get out of here and try to get you through school. California's waiting. Is it big enough for both of us?"

"Megan, I love you," Jen said. "But let this decision wait until morning, okay?"

Megan agreed to wait until morning. When the phone rang again, she marched over to it, picked up the receiver, and dropped it alongside the table on the floor.

It can wait until morning, she thought, *everybody can just wait until morning.*

CHAPTER FOURTEEN

*A*fter a good night's sleep, Jen and Megan decided to keep their jobs and contribute what they could to the investigation. Megan still avoided Rusty's calls, but whatever was going on at work seemed more confusing than ever. Two days later, Megan was forced to take action.

Megan stood staring at one of the glass cases. "I know I put that rhinestone brooch in this case," she said. "I worked for half an hour getting this display right." Jen watched her friend from across the store aisle. "I was the last one here last night—I counted the drawer. And I was the first one here this morning."

Jen looked around. Seeing no one, she left her department for a moment and approached Megan.

"Who are you talking to?"

"Myself. I am sure I put something in a certain place last night, just like Rusty told me to, and this morning it's not only moved, it's gone."

"Are you sure?"

"I'm sure." Jen knew what Megan was going to say next before she could say it. "I'm sorry, but I have to call Rusty."

"I know," Jen admitted. "We made a commitment to help. We can't back out now."

"Hi, miss, can you help me?" Elizabeth Simms was posing

as a customer. "I want to select a gift for my niece. She's about your age, it's her birthday."

Megan smiled. "Yes, ma'am. Let me show you something I think she will just love." Megan led her 'customer' to the other side of the counter and convincingly displayed a number of bracelets. Beth selected a charm bracelet and asked that it be wrapped while she waited.

"Would you like to put a note in it?" Megan asked.

"That would be nice, thank you." Elizabeth waited while Megan rang up the purchase and then handed her the little bag. "You've been so kind, miss."

"Thank you for shopping at Halloran's, ma'am. Come in again, won't you?"

In her car, Elizabeth opened the package and read Megan's note. *Need to talk to Rusty, ASAP.* That's all Elizabeth needed to hear. Megan was going to help them after all.

That night after the girls arrived home from work, Rusty called. Megan was glad to hear his voice, and even though she'd been angry with Dan, she was also glad she had rethought her decision to leave Halloran's. Besides, she liked helping solve this case almost better than she liked her job behind the counter. And she liked being around Rusty.

"I thought you should know. I set a display, just like you told me to. Then I made a drawing of where I put things. This morning when I went in, the display had been rearranged and a fairly expensive piece was missing." Megan kicked off her shoes and sat sideways in the chair, putting her feet nearer the large heat register in the corner.

"You sure?"

"I'm sure. If I had not set the display on purpose, I would have not been as sure. But I memorized where I put things and checked them last thing before leaving."

"How did you check them?" Rusty wanted to make sure Megan knew what she was talking about.

"I cleaned the glass last thing before leaving and made a mental inventory. And, like I said, as soon as I got home, I wrote everything down and drew a sketch of what I put where."

"And?"

"And this morning it was different. Only slightly, but different. After I checked my written inventory, which I hid in a special place, I made sure which piece was missing." Megan could hear Jen stirring inside the kitchen.

"So someone came in during the night and moved things around, didn't just take things?"

"That's right." Megan marvelled at the discovery. "Someone who must have a key to the case, who is good at displaying merchandise, who knows the right pieces to take—there you have it."

"Good girl, Megan. You'd make a fine PI—ever think of changing jobs?" She laughed, but she kind of liked the idea.

"Let's start at the beginning," Rusty said. "Who has keys to the case?"

"Nobody really *has* the keys. They're kept with our cash bags."

"How does that work?"

"Each night the last person to leave the department counts the drawer. Then they put the money, all except for the change, in the cash bag. Then as they leave the department, they also put the keys to the case in the bag—so they take the keys with them."

"Could I come over, Meg?" Megan glanced at Jen munching a piece of toast in the kitchen. She was glad to see her eating something. She had observed that Jen was losing a little weight, and she really didn't have any to spare in the first place. *Mama would have a fit if she saw her,* Megan thought.

"Is that really necessary? We've been working really hard,

and Jen has some reading to do before she goes to bed. I'm not sure—"

"It's all right, Megan, I can read in the bedroom. I'm tired, maybe I'll just set my alarm and get up extra early tomorrow." Jen was standing in the kitchen doorway. She had pulled the combs from the sides of her long hair and let it tumble free. Megan could tell how tired she was.

Putting her hand over the mouthpiece of the receiver, Megan said, "You sure, Jen? I can put him off."

"Let's get this over with. If you're up to it, let him come."

"I don't work until ten tomorrow," Megan said, "what time are you going in?"

"Ten. I work 'til six."

Megan spoke into the receiver again.

"Okay, Rusty, come on over. I'll meet you at the front door of the building—it might be locked."

"See you in fifteen minutes," he said, and without saying good-bye, he hung up the phone.

Rusty wasted no time getting to the apartment. "Let's see the drawing," he said as he and Megan began their discussion over chocolate chip cookies and milk. Megan produced her sketch and the inventory she had written from memory. Rusty studied them; then he said, "Now, can you show me how the display changed this morning?"

Rusty watched as Megan drew another sketch. He compared the two drawings.

"You say the second display was arranged as well as the first?"

"Well, I don't know if I'd go that far. I arranged the first, and I'm really good at it." Megan laughed and Rusty decided whatever had angered her the night before was over.

"Okay, okay. But you said that the display was good."

"Yes, it was done so well that had I not made the sketch and inventory list, I would have only *felt* something was different, but I probably wouldn't have been able to figure out what it was."

"I see, so it's someone who not only has access to the keys to the case but also knows what they are doing with display."

"I think I already said that."

"I know." Rusty smiled at Megan and continued. "Who fits this picture?"

"Well, the department manager, I guess. But she's pretty involved outside the store. She's only working because she has to. She's divorced with two kids, and she lives with her parents, who help her out. She seems really busy outside work."

"Do you think she'd risk losing her job, or her kids?" Rusty asked.

"No, I really don't. She's a hard worker and gets very upset about shortages."

"Mrs. Halloran ever call her in for anything?"

"Once," Megan recalled. "Halloran was upset that there were fingerprints on the display case. She specifically insisted that the cases be cleaned the first thing every morning—before the store opens."

"Oh?" Rusty thought that was interesting. "What if they're cleaned the last thing before the store closes instead?" he asked.

Megan shook her head. "Doesn't matter. She insists on them being cleaned every morning."

Rusty made a mental note and moved on. "Okay, so the department manager is out—for now at least. Who else?"

"It has to be someone who has access to the cash bags."

"Or another set of keys," Rusty added.

Megan nodded. "Yeah, I didn't think of that."

Rusty reached for another cookie, but he lost half of it when he dunked it in his milk. "Rats." Megan handed him a spoon and continued.

"Another set of keys." She stopped and stared at Rusty.

"I know someone who has access to almost everything in every department—Yvonne." Megan's dark brown eyes grew wide. Rusty forced his thoughts back toward the case and away from Megan's beautiful face.

"Who's that?"

"She's an extra—a floater. She fills in wherever there's a need. She can work in every department and even works in the cash office at closing time when they're shorthanded."

"What's she like?"

"She's okay, I guess. Not really close to anyone, though. She comes and goes at break times. Seems friendly enough but not really close, you know?"

"Okay, say Yvonne has access to the whole store. Does she have any authority?"

"Sure, she's sort of a manager-at-large. She's got a real cushy job, according to some of the girls. Never has to do stock work, doesn't have to work in display, and only has to be in any department for a short period of time."

"Anything else?"

"Some of the department managers don't trust her. They think she is what they call a pipeline—a snitch, I guess."

"A pipeline to who?"

"Who knows?" Megan thought a moment. "Not to Dan, I don't think. Maybe Halloran herself?"

Rusty pushed back in his chair. "Anyone else have that kind of access?"

"I can't really think of anyone." Megan pushed the plate of cookies away. "I don't need any more of these," she added.

Rusty took another cookie. "Let's see what we've got. Your department manager seems safe, Yvonne questionable. What about other departments? Anybody else ever talk about missing merchandise?" he asked.

"Um-hmm." Megan had given into the temptation and stuck another cookie in her mouth. "Accessories. You know, gloves, scarves, handbags, belts, lace collars, handkerchiefs. You know I saw a hankie for eight dollars? Can you believe it, you can blow you nose on an eight dollar piece of cloth?"

Rusty blew a slow whistle. "Seems a little extravagant, don't you think?"

"More than just a little." Megan grew thoughtful. "Frances said they have also missed merchandise. They turned in a report to security but nothing ever happened."

"You mean Mrs. Simms knew about it?"

"I guess so. Although we never give a report directly to her. It goes to the department manager then to the security office."

"So Mrs. Simms wouldn't necessarily know. I mean, it's possible for the report to stop somewhere before it reaches her, right?"

"That I don't know," Megan said. "I don't know how the security office works."

"I'll talk to her about it." Rusty wrote on a pad he carried in his pocket. "Can Frances be trusted?"

"She went to high school with my brother. That's not the greatest claim to fame, I guess, but she comes from a good family. To be honest, I really don't know her all that well."

"Okay, I'll check that out too."

"You know, a girl was fired in that department last week," Megan remembered. "She wore a belt home."

"Oh? How often does that happen?"

"It can happen. Sometimes a clerk will wear something from the department for a while and then put it back. Sometimes a customer wants to see it on you, and before you can take it back, you have to wait on someone else."

"You mean it could have been unintentional?"

"Could be. Probably not, though. Otherwise, why would they fire her? They didn't even know until the next day when she brought it back. They caught her putting it back into stock."

"You know who that is?"

"Her name is Rochelle Lewis. She lives on the west side somewhere."

"Married?"

"I'm not sure, I don't think so."

"Meg," Rusty said, reaching for her hand, "you've been a really big help tonight. Thanks for letting me come over."

"It's okay," she said, and she did not pull her hand away. She felt safe confiding in Rusty. "I'm glad to be able to finally tell someone about all this. I've never been able to figure out why nothing has been done. Stuff leaves the store, and no one seems to care."

"Well, someone does care." Rusty glanced toward the closed bedroom door where Jen was. "What's going on with her?"

"She's been upset by some bad news, that's all."

"Anything to do with the store?"

"Only indirectly." Megan felt uncomfortable telling Rusty about Jen's problems. "I'm not sure I can talk about it, Rusty. I try to be a good friend and not tell tales, if you know what I mean."

"Sure. I respect that. It's just that Dan seems confused by her. He's really taken an interest in her, and it's been so long . . ."

"He's interested in her?" Megan jerked her hand from Rusty's and sat straight up in her chair. Her face hardened with anger. "What gives him the right? Just because he is an executive where she works doesn't give him the right to . . ."

"Whoa, Megan, slow down." Rusty caught her hand again. "What's this all about?"

"Dan Miller, that's what."

"Come on, you have to tell me now."

"I can't."

"Megan, Dan's not just someone who has hired me to do

a job, he's my friend. I've known him for seven years, and I have a feeling he's getting a raw deal here."

"Getting or giving?" Megan's eyes were filling with tears. She loved Jen almost like a sister. It had been difficult to watch her suffer these past few days. Knowing what she now knew about Dan Miller made it even worse.

"You know him so well, why didn't you tell me? I could have told Jen and she wouldn't have gotten so hurt and embarrassed."

"Hurt how? Embarrassed?"

"She began to feel Dan was interested in her, and even though she has always planned to go right home after graduation she was almost persuaded to delay it a while."

"Because of Dan?"

"Because of Dan. Then she found out that his interest was, shall we say, inappropriate? Or maybe it wasn't, maybe Jen just read into it something that wasn't there."

"It's genuine. I've watched him with Jen. He has come to care for her, and in such a short time, too. Surprised the heck out of me."

"Surprised you? It shocked me. And when I heard that he's married, I can't tell you—"

"Wait a minute, Megan. Dan's not married."

"But Jen said . . ." Megan's expression softened, and her voice dropped to just above a whisper. "She said she saw a picture of his wife, in his office the day she went to look at it. His secretary said it was his wife. Marie, her name is Marie."

"*Was,*" Rusty said, "was. Debbie told her this?"

Megan nodded, "You mean he's divorced?"

"No, I mean her name *was* Marie." Rusty looked closely at Megan. "She's dead, Meg. She died in a car accident four years ago." Megan's mouth dropped wide open.

"But I am sure Jen was told—or at least got the strong

impression that Dan is . . . that Marie is . . ." Megan slumped in her chair but held on to Rusty's hand. "Oh my gosh. I'd better tell her."

"Oh no you don't. Dan should tell her himself. Did Debbie also tell her about Joy?"

"Joy? Who's Joy?"

Rusty looked at his watch. "It's after midnight, Meg, I'd better go."

"Who's Joy?" Megan insisted.

"That's for Dan to tell Jen. Then she can tell you, if she chooses."

He stood and Megan was sorry when he took his hand from hers. "Don't you dare tell her," he said. "Promise? Let me talk to Dan. He needs to clear this up, not you, not me. Do you understand?"

"I just feel so bad that . . ."

"Don't try to fix this, Meg. Let them work it out themselves."

"I guess you're right."

"I am." He put on his coat and walked slowly to the door. "Come on, now. Lock this behind me."

Megan followed him, but he didn't open the door. Instead, he stood looking at her, then reached out toward her. She put her hand out, and he took it, pulling her closer. When she was just a few inches from him, he leaned over and put his cheek against hers. "I want you to know," he whispered, "I'm not married. Never have been." Megan caught the faint hint of his after-shave.

She smiled, and after he gently kissed her cheek, she pulled away. "I'm glad to know that," she said.

"See you soon?" he asked.

"I hope so," she answered.

CHAPTER FIFTEEN

*J*en had been happy to let Megan meet with Rusty alone. Trying to concentrate on the final few weeks of her education was difficult enough. She was grateful she had taken her studies seriously, working ahead of schedule on most of her projects.

The faint voices of Megan and Rusty drifting in from the kitchen provided her with the security of not being alone. She climbed into bed with a book on period furniture and designers, propped herself up, and began to study. She had memorized the names and characteristics of most of the important styles and was reviewing the early American furniture makers when she suddenly grew restless.

"If I don't know it by now, I'm not going to know it." She put the textbook down beside the bed. As she reached to turn off the bedside lamp, her eyes fell on her Bible.

Grandma Ginny had given it to her when she finished her first two years at San Bernardino College. Grandma Ginny was as close to her as if she were her own grandmother. She had spent so much time at Grandma's house with her friend Cari during the summer months each year it was hard to tell Jen didn't live there.

As Jen lifted the Bible from the table, a small bookmark fell out. *Trust in the Lord with all thine heart,* was written on it in calligraphy and small butterflies were scattered among the letters.

Jen sat up and began to leaf through the precious pages. "I've been too caught up lately to even remember my devotions," she whispered.

She often underlined favorite verses with a red pencil. Just browsing through them and reviewing them began to make her feel better. *Casting all your care upon Him, for he careth for you.* Cari and Jen had memorized that verse in Vacation Bible School when they were just little girls. She continued to sample the marked verses. Turning back to the book of Ephesians, she saw that she had underlined a verse in chapter three:

> *Now unto him who is able to do exceeding abundantly above all that we ask or think, according to the power that worketh in us.*

Fanning the pages back to the Old Testament, she read,

> *I sought the Lord and he heard me, and delivered me from all my fears. They looked unto him, and were lightened; and their faces were not ashamed. This poor man cried, and the Lord heard him, and saved him out of all his troubles. The angel of the Lord encampeth round about them that fear him, and he delivereth them. O taste and see that the Lord is good; blessed is the man that trusteth in him.*

Flipping forward a few pages she read,

> *For since the beginning of the world, men have not heard, nor perceived by the ear, neither hath the eye seen, O God, beside thee, what he hath prepared for him that waiteth for him.*

Oh, God, Jen sobbed into her pillow, *I did not wait for you. I ran ahead and let my feelings get in the way of your will for me.*

*I am so sorry, my Father. Please Lord, help me. Please forgive me.
I didn't know Dan was married. I let my heart stray. Please, Lord
Jesus, help me. Keep me in your will. You know that I need to finish
school and get on with my plans. Just help me finish school, and
help me at work—that's where it's the hardest. And Lord, help me
be a good witness to Megan. Let me show her the way to you. Amen.*

Dan Miller was a bad experience, Jen decided, but she
was the wiser for going through it. She was hurt, but she
wasn't ruined. God still loved her, and she knew it. He
would be her strength. He would give her wisdom should
she ever have to face Dan Miller again.

The bonus check from Mrs. Halloran had taken Jen
completely by surprise. It was not what she expected from
the owner of the large department store. Certainly the
woman was not given to generosity; surely God had something to do with it. It was the sign she needed to make her
plans to go on home. If she thought so before, she knew it
now.

Across town, Dan sat on the other side of a large formal
dining table, facing Dorthea O'Halloran. Halloran's had
dropped the O' from the business name two generations
before.

"I don't care," Dorthea said. "She's my only granddaughter and I will treat her any way I please." The older woman
was almost pouting.

"But she's my daughter," Dan said, "and I don't want her
growing up with every whim and wish granted as if life holds
no restrictions."

"But it doesn't—not for her." Dorthea smiled sweetly at
five-year-old Joy. "Does it, darling?"

"Stop it, Joy," Dan reprimanded his little girl. "Take your
fork out of your water glass."

"No," Joy said simply and without emotion, "I don't have to do what you say. Grammy said."

Dan's eyes flew back to Dorthea's face. Carefully placing his napkin on the table, he felt the familiar rage rise within him. Slowly, he stood to his feet. "Someday, I don't know how and I don't know when . . ."

"Are you threatening me, Dan?" Mrs. O'Halloran said in a mocking tone.

"No, I'm not threatening, I'm stating a fact. You have your way with her now, but she will someday turn on you. Just like—"

"Enough! I won't take this from you." Dorthea also stood facing Dan across the table. "Not now, not ever. I won't have you telling me how to raise the child."

"My child," Dan reminded her.

"Not necessarily," she said.

"Oh? What are you up to now?"

"By the way, I understand you've been seeing one of our salesgirls." Dorthea walked around to where Joy was and started picking up the vegetables Joy had been squashing into the imported linen tablecloth.

"Josie!" she screamed, "Come here and clean this mess!" Dorthea looked at Dan. "Well?"

"Well what?"

"Is it true or not?"

"I see them every day, you know that. I work with them," Dan said flatly.

"Not as much as you've been seeing one disgusting little redhead."

"Redhead? Does this redhead have a name?"

"How could you be interested in a common working girl, Dan? Think of the embarrassment it could cause Joy later. You're not planning ahead."

Dan was outraged by Dorthea's interference. "Embarrassment? You're the embarrassment, not Jen."

"Josie!" She swept her hand across the air in disgust. "Where is that lazy little—Oh, there you are, thank goodness you finally decided to come." Dorthea's voice always held a tone of contempt toward her household help. "Get Joy to bed and get Katrina in here to clean up this mess."

"I don't want to go to bed," Joy pouted.

"Now, my good little angel, let Josie take you to your room. You can get on your pretty pajamas and play with your lovely dollies, and then when you are ever so sleepy, you can climb into your bed."

"No. I don't want to."

"Joy, darling, don't be naughty now. Go with Josie, like I said," her grandmother pleaded.

"No, I won't." Joy stomped a foot.

"Joy," Dan said, "how about if I take you up to read you a story?" Dan reached for Joy's hand.

Joy shook her head.

"I don't want a story. I want to stay up and watch TV."

"Honey," Dan began, "it's past TV time for little girls. It's story time and then night-night time."

"No. I want to watch TV." Joy stuck out her lower lip and crossed her arms in protest.

"Okay, my little love," Dorthea said with a voice coated with syrup, "do whatever you want. Daddy and I want you to be happy. Turn on the big TV in Grammy's room. I'll come put you in your own bed later. Daddy and I agree that you can watch TV, don't we, Dan?"

Dan felt reduced to nothing. He didn't want to argue with Dorthea in front of Joy. As awful as it was, Dorthea was the only mother figure in her life. His own mother loved Joy, but she didn't get to see the child very often because she lived so far away. The fact that Dan felt responsible for

Marie's death didn't help him deal with Dorthea very well. That and the store. As long as he worked at the store, he would be under the thumb of Dorthea O'Halloran—no question about it. And he would stay at the store, for Joy's sake.

When Joy left the room, Dorthea turned on Dan. "How can you treat your own daughter like that?" she demanded. "You never know how long we will have her. She's only a child for a very short time."

Dan recognized the barb intended to stab at the tender wound in his heart. "Stop it, will you?"

"I was about to say the same thing to you."

"To me?"

"I won't have my granddaughter being exposed to common—well, to our employees on a social level or any other level." She turned to light a cigarette.

"Or other children? Or public school? Or Sunday school? I want Joy involved with normal kids, and I want her to go to Sunday school." It was an argument they had frequently.

"Sunday school? Where they teach you that God gives you everything you need? You only get what you need if you're born to it or if you're willing to work hard for it. You and I both know that's true. Doesn't that little child need her mother? Where was God then?"

Dan felt his heart constrict. "Sunday school," Dorthea began, continuing her well-rehearsed lecture, "where they teach you to trust in something you can't even see. I have learned you can't even trust the things you can see."

"I want her in Sunday school," Dan said again.

"To hear fairy stories and myths? I won't have it. The only god I know is work. The only miracles I've seen are the ones I've made for myself. That's what Joy needs to know. And that's what I intend to teach her."

"I'm taking Joy out for the weekend, Dorthea. Have her ready on Saturday morning." Dan turned to leave, but before he could reach the entry way he heard his mother-in-law's steps behind him.

"Listen you, don't you try to convince your little Jen to stay in Chicago by tempting her with a child—a wealthy child. It won't work. She's leaving in a few weeks, sooner if I had my way about it. But nevertheless, she's leaving."

"How can you be so sure?" Dan was determined to talk to Jen again and try to find out why she was so set against redecorating his office.

"Because I made sure," Dorthea snapped.

Dan spun around to face her. "What are you talking about?"

"Ask her about her little bonus check." Dorthea took a long drag on her cigarette and blew the smoke toward the ceiling "She wasn't too hard to convince. She's ambitious, I'll say that for her. I almost like her. Too bad she comes from the wrong side of town. I bet she had never seen that much money all in one place before."

Dan felt his temples throb with the anger, threatening to explode in his head. "You dirty—" Dan stopped his remark short. "You'll stop at nothing to keep control, will you?"

"I'm almost sorry she took it." Dorthea picked at her long fingernails then studied the cigarette burning between her index and middle finger. "I thought I might have been wrong about the little thing. Oh well, you'll find another one to drag home, eventually." She followed him to the door. "You don't get it, do you, Dan? You will never marry again, I'll see to that. You don't have the right after what you did to my Marie. You have too many responsibilities for a serious romantic involvement."

Dan turned and left, slamming the large door behind

him. He would never forgive Dorthea for this. *Jen, what has she told you? Why did you take the money?*

He could imagine Dorthea meeting with innocent Jennifer Whipple. His mother-in-law had a vicious and cunning tongue; she could be very convincing—and intimidating.

Dan's heart broke with discouragement. The merchandise shortages at the store were happening with more frequency. Sales were up, but if the hemorrhaging of stolen goods couldn't be stopped, profits would be measurably affected. And then there was Jen. A complication, to be sure. *I don't have room in my life between running the store, dealing with Dorthea, and worrying about Joy. I don't have the right because of what I did to Marie.* Dan let his thoughts drift to memories of Marie. *Or do I?* he wondered. Dan pondered his life now and what his life would be in the future without Jen. *Is this how it's going to be from now on? Filled with work and regret? Is that what Marie would want? Would the person who brought so much happiness into my life want me to continue without it? Would someone who needed so desperately to escape her mother's control want her own daughter held prisoner by it?*

Dan turned his sleek sports car toward the city. Maybe Jen would still be up. It wouldn't hurt to go by and see. He needed to talk to her, to tell her he wanted her in his life. And then Dan knew—he loved her. What's more, he wanted desperately to tell her so.

CHAPTER SIXTEEN

*J*ust as Rusty was about to pull his faith-
ful old Plymouth away from the curb,
he saw Dan's car round the corner. Waiting for his friend
to get closer, Rusty watched as Dan slowed and found a
parking place. He waited a moment expecting Dan to get
out. When Dan hesitated, Rusty opened the door of his car
and Dan looked in his direction.

"Hey, Dan," Rusty called. He looked for oncoming traffic, then crossed the street toward Dan's car.

"What are you doing here so late?" Dan asked.

"Leaving," said Rusty, "how about you?"

"Just coming." Dan glanced up toward Jen's apartment
window.

"I'm glad to see you. There're some things I need to talk
over with you. But it can't be here, the girls are in bed by
now. Jen went to bed around eight-thirty. But Meg and I
had a very interesting talk."

"Oh?"

"Yeah." Rusty went around to the passenger side of Dan's
car and slid in the front seat with Dan. "Let's go to Mickey's
Diner—they're open all night. We've got some serious stuff
to go over."

"Look, Dan, it's time we put our heads together and
compared what we've got here," Rusty said as they slid into
a booth at the diner.

The waitress interrupted their conversation, and they ordered hamburgers and fries.

"What've we got?" Dan asked.

"I had a very interesting talk with Meg," Rusty repeated.

"So you said."

"She has proof that someone has been in the jewelry cases in her department just last night."

"Proof?"

"She arranged a special display, noted every piece in it, and then made a drawing of the display from memory after she got home. This morning the display was changed just a little, and one of the pieces was missing."

"Couldn't another salesgirl have sold the piece and rearranged the display?"

"Ordinarily, yes. However, Meg was the last one to leave the department last night and the first one to arrive this morning." Rusty examined his hamburger and slathered it with catsup before stuffing a quarter of it in his mouth.

Dan picked up his, took a bite, and chewed it slowly. After he swallowed it, he washed it down with a long swig of Coke.

"She's sure that someone from the display department or the department manager didn't move it for some reason?"

"She's sure. No one checked it out for display, and the department manager called in late, sick kid or something."

"What do you make of all this?" Dan asked.

"Well, just this: We know someone has to have the display case keys—or at least access to them. We know it has to be someone who is in the store later or earlier than the clerks and who can walk around the store without being questioned or detected."

"Hmmm." Dan dabbed at a pool of catsup with a french fry. "There aren't too many people who fit that description, but there are a few."

"Maybe we could narrow it down a bit." Rusty wiped his face with a napkin.

"Okay, narrow it down."

"Who can walk around the store any hour, day or night, and no one would question it—that's number one. And number two, who has access to keys to the jewelry cases?"

"Me, Beth—no Beth doesn't have access to the keys without a signature. There is one person who could get access if she really tried, but . . ."

"Who's that?"

"Yvonne. She's what we call a manager-at-large. She works in any department where she's needed. She's all over and knows every department. She fills in for department managers on their days off, gives the salespeople breaks, and sometimes works in the cash office when the drawers are turned in."

"Does she have access to the keys after hours?" Rusty asked.

"No, I don't think so. She's not authorized to have them anyway."

"What else does she do?"

"She helps organize and supervise inventory."

"What does that mean?"

"That is when we count everything—and I do mean *everything* in the store."

"How often do yo do that?"

"We do it in departments on a limited basis several times a year. But we do it storewide only once a year."

"I see. So she knows about inventory, she knows about the paperwork involved in that sort of thing, I guess."

Dan pushed his plate a few inches back and rested both arms on the edge of the table. "You know, there is one other person we have both overlooked."

"Yeah, who?"

Dan shook his head. "No, it's a crazy idea. Forget it."

"Look, Dan, this is a crazy case. Come on, give."

"Dorthea O'Halloran."

Rusty's eyes opened wide, and he held the last bite of his hamburger suspended between his teeth for a moment, then put it on his plate again. "Mrs. O'Halloran herself?"

"The very one."

"You're right, that's a crazy idea." But Rusty was interested and intended to press the idea further. He'd have to move slowly, but it was certainly worth pursuing.

"She has keys to everything. She has keys even I don't have."

"Dan, I can't believe you'd even say her name in connection to this ca—this conversation."

"I'm not saying there is a connection. It's just an answer to your question. She has keys to everything, she has access to the entire store anytime without question, and she pokes around sometimes."

"What do you mean, pokes around?"

"Department managers are very nervous about her poking her nose into their departments. She has been known to reprimand a department manager for having his bagging materials out of order."

"You mean she noses around even in the paper bags?"

"Yeah, she comes in and finds little things in departments and then writes up the managers or clerks on the pettiest things. Some of our best employees have left because of her."

"Do you have access to those files?"

Dan nodded. "They're kept in personnel. I could get to them if I needed to. However, I don't know that I could just go in asking for them without raising questions."

"How about after hours?"

"I could do that I suppose."

"Is there a problem with that?"

"No, but there are hundreds of files. We have over a hundred and fifty people on the payroll right now."

"What if Megan and I came with you?"

"That would help, I guess. What exactly would we look for?"

"Dates, comments, anything suspicious. I won't know until we actually get our hands on one or two files that look curious. We could start with people Jen and Megan know who've been written up. You know people talk about things like that."

"Let's talk to them," Dan said. "I hope they're up for a little after hours detective work."

Rusty shifted back in his seat and looked at his friend. "There's something you need to talk to Jen about, Dan."

"Like what?"

Rusty hesitated. Remembering the speech he gave Megan, he decided to approach the subject indirectly. "Have you and Jen ever really gotten acquainted? You know, shared your hopes, dreams—all that stuff girls like to talk about?"

"Well, not exactly. We've mostly been talking about the store, the case—that's how we met. You've been with us most of the time."

"Are you interested?"

"Interested?" Dan was sure his friend knew that he was interested.

"Look, Dan." Rusty leaned forward on the table between them. "There's something you need to know. Jen's been very upset ever since she visited your office. I don't know if it was something Debbie said or what. Megan has been upset with you too."

"What did I do?" Dan asked.

"It's not what you did, Dan. It's what you didn't do."

"Didn't do?" Dan was confused.

"Think about it, Dan." Rusty had thought this would be easier. "What do you actually know about Jen? What does she know about you?"

"I know enough about her to want her to stay on in Chicago so I can get to know more about her."

"Does she know anything about you?"

"What's to know?"

Rusty let out a low whistle. "How about a little piece of your past, Dan Miller. Like you have been married—and have a daughter?"

"Oh, that."

"Yeah, that."

Dan was suddenly alarmed. "Has someone told her about Marie and Joy?" Dan wanted to tell her about them himself.

"I can't say that for sure. One thing I do know is that you need to make sure she hears it from you, don't you think so?"

"I haven't been able to get her to talk to me, Rusty." Dan's face clouded with discouragement. "After four years, I'm finally ready to reach out to someone; not just someone— Jen. There hasn't been anyone I've met since Marie that I have been interested in. But when I met Jen, that all changed. Every day I have felt Marie's death as a fresh wound. Now it isn't there every day anymore. Marie will always be a part of me, but her death seems in the past, finally in the past."

"You need to tell Jen, Dan. Not me."

"I was on my way there tonight to do just that when I met you."

"Sorry, pal, it's too late tonight. It'll have to wait."

"I don't have much time. She's planning to leave Chicago in a few weeks."

"Well, then, better make it first thing tomorrow. That's what I'd do."

Dan changed the subject. "How about the guy Megan saw following Jen, any more on that score?"

"Oh, yeah, I almost forgot about that," Rusty said.

"Who do you think it is?"

"I don't know, but I do know he is following her."

"Then it wasn't just Megan's overactive imagination?" Dan asked.

"Afraid not. I saw him myself."

"He see you?"

"Not really. He has no idea I was looking at him. Middle forties, I'd guess. Looks like an out-of-shape cop. Beer belly, swollen eyes, the works."

Dan looked worried. "Is he dangerous?"

"That I can't say for sure. But I thought it might be wise to get somebody to watch him."

"You mean watch over Jen, don't you?"

"No, I mean watch *him*. Where does he come from? Where does he go? Who does he report to and why? We need answers to all these questions."

"Is just one guy following her?"

"Yup. I think that's all there is. Thought he might be a two-bit private eye. Trying to get something on her or . . ."

"Like what?"

"I don't know what, that's why I think we should hire someone to find out." Rusty seemed a bit impatient with Dan.

"I don't want her hurt. I don't want her even frightened. You hear me?"

"I hear you."

"Who'd you have in mind?"

"Bobby Moore. He's light on his feet, quick as lightening. He's strong and he's discreet. Jen would never know he's around, I promise you that. He'll report to me, and I'll give him his orders. Okay with you?"

"Fine."

"It'll be expensive, Dan. Before you get through with all of this, it could cost you a bundle."

"As long as I'm working at Halloran's, I have no problem with money. You know that, Russ."

"Ever think about leavin'?"

"Sometimes. But what about Joy? Halloran's is her inheritance. If I'm not there to watch out for her interests, who knows what the old lady will do."

"I don't understand."

"Marie's father inherited Halloran's from his father and grandfather. When he married Dorthea, it didn't take him long to figure out why she married him. He was heartbroken. He really loved her." Dan ordered a cup of coffee and piece of pie, and Rusty followed suit.

"No kidding?" Rusty had never heard this about Marie's family before.

"When the old man had his first heart attack, he put the business in Marie's name and stipulated that in the event of his death Dorthea would be the manager, but only until Marie turned twenty-five. She would receive a handsome salary, but only if the store turned a profit each year."

"A nice job, still in control . . ." Rusty mused aloud.

"But with one big catch. If the store lost money, she would be out of a job and her salary would disappear. She only lived on Marie's money. This was made even more difficult by the fact that Dorthea hasn't a clue about business. The only thing she knew about retail stores was how to spend Mr. O'Halloran's money in them."

"But now that Marie is gone . . . ?"

"The afternoon of the funeral, Mr. O'Halloran went

from the cemetery to his lawyer's office and put everything in Joy's name."

"With Mrs. O'Halloran still the manager."

"Not really. He named me Associate Manager and essentially put Mrs. O'Halloran in only as a figurehead. She really doesn't have any say, except what I give her. But she has the title, and little Joy has all the power—and I have all the work."

"Brother, this is complicated." Rusty ran his fingers through his dark curly hair and rubbed his chin across the whiskers that were beginning to show.

"It gets worse." Dan slurped his hot coffee. "Mrs. O'Halloran still goes on most of the buying trips, but she has to run every order past me for approval. It kills her, and it infuriates me. She really does have an eye for appealing merchandise. She knows instinctively what will sell. I wouldn't have done that to her, but then she didn't marry me for my money either. After Marie was born, the O'Hallorans lived separate lives, if you know what I mean. She had her room—her apartment really—and he had his. She had her friends, and he had his. Sadly, most of his were women."

"And Joy? Why do you leave her there, Dan? Living in that woman's house must be a real strain."

"I'm not there that much. She does love Joy. She spoils her too much, but if I take her, who will they have? At least they have each other. Most of the time it's not too bad. She did a good job with Marie, I have to give her that."

"And Mr. O'Halloran died, right?"

"Within three months of Marie's death. I remember feeling very little when Dad O'Halloran died. I was totally shocked to find out that he had named me administrator of the trust he left for Joy. The whole O'Halloran estate is in trust for her. Dorthea is actually living in Joy's house, not the other way around.

"The household staff looks out for Joy, and they call me if there's a real problem. I try to go up two to three evenings a week, and be with Joy on weekends as much as possible. I guess it's not the best, but then I haven't been in much shape to try to be a full-time daddy either. At least Dorthea has provided Joy some stability. If I threw her out, then all Joy would have is servants. Besides, where would she go?"

"What about your parents, didn't they ever—I mean, couldn't they . . . ?"

"My mother wasn't that well right after Marie died, and my Dad had his hands full with the farm and taking care of Mom. A child as headstrong as Joy—well, she would have been too much for them I'm afraid. I thought of my sister, and she even offered, but she has four of her own. That's quite a handful." Dan picked at the remains of his pie with his fork. "I really need to wake up and get my life back on track."

"Is that where Jen comes in?" Rusty asked.

"I don't know, Rusty. She's really a nice girl. I'm very attracted to her. But she has this career thing."

Rusty leaned back in his seat and laughed. "Hey, they get over it. Once they meet a good man, feel secure and loved, they really don't want anything more than that. What's there to want besides good catches like us?"

"You'd better watch yourself," Dan said seriously. "Times are changing, you know. Women want more out of life these days that just housework and babies."

"Yeah, right. Maybe O'Halloran had the right idea. Give her all the prestige she could possibly want but none of the power. Keep her out front and under control at the same time."

Dan didn't think Jennifer Whipple was a woman anyone

could control; nor was her roommate. "Better not let Jen and Megan hear you talk that way." Dan laughed and reached for his wallet. "You'll get in touch with Bobby?"

"First thing in the morning. You gonna talk to Jen?"

"As soon as I can." The sooner he could get Jen and Joy together, the better—but somehow he dreaded it, too.

CHAPTER SEVENTEEN

*E*arly the next day Rusty called Bobby Moore and then Megan before she left for work. He wanted her to know about Bobby, and she agreed that Jen would only be upset if she knew about any of this. After talking to Megan, Rusty went to look up first Frances and then Rochelle Lewis.

At Halloran's Dan went to his office wondering how he would tell Jen about Marie and Joy.

"Well, good morning, Mr. Miller," Debbie said, quickly hanging up the phone as he came in.

"Good morning, Debbie, how's my morning look?"

"Rainbow Accessories will be here at eleven-thirty, the Ship 'n Shore rep is coming by at twelve-forty-five and wants to buy you lunch."

"Have Mrs. Halloran take both of those appointments. She has a much better eye for women's accessories and blouses than I do."

"Both vendors insist on seeing you, Mr. Miller."

"Nonsense. Call Dorthea," Dan said.

"I already tried. They won't see her."

"Why not?"

"Won't say. They both say they must see you."

"That means they both want up-front exposure. Okay, I guess it's part of the job. What else?"

"James from interior design is asking for an appointment, the department manager in ladies shoes is quitting, and Mr. Halloran's lawyer wants you to call him, something about an audit."

"Oh?" Dan took the message slip from Debbie's hand.

"Oh, yes, one more thing—Joy has chicken pox. She broke out this morning. Mrs. Halloran called and said she wouldn't be in, she's staying home with her."

"Chicken pox?" Dan couldn't believe it. Joy actually had something that other children had. "Amazing, absolutely amazing." Dan smiled.

Debbie reached for Dan's ringing phone. "It's Elizabeth Simms."

"Thank you." He took the receiver. "Hi, Beth. What's up?"

Debbie walked slowly toward the office door. Dan turned away from her; he didn't realize that she hadn't left the room. Beth was telling him about more missing merchandise. "What? Again? That's twice this week," he said incredulously.

Beth went on. "It's in women's accessories this time, Dan. Leather gloves, a few imported lace collars, a couple of silk scarves."

Debbie quietly closed Dan's office door and dialed a three-digit number. As soon as it was answered she whispered, "Are you crazy? This is too soon. Somebody is going to get caught."

"I agree with you, but it's not my decision. I'm only following orders," the woman's voice on the other end said. "Following orders and cashing my checks. Gotta go." And the line went dead.

"Yes, Mr. Johnson, he'll see you at twelve-forty-five sharp. Lunch will be fine." Debbie was talking into a dead phone when Dan came out of his office.

"I'll be back later," he told her.

"Remember, Rainbow at eleven," Debbie called after him.

"Eleven." Dan rushed by her desk and out the office suite door.

Crossing the second floor, Dan scanned the home furnishing department for Jen. Seeing she was busy with a customer, he went on over to where Megan was straightening a display of earrings.

"Another hit last night," he said quietly.

"Where?"

"Women's accessories."

"That's a new manager, too."

"Do you know her?" Dan left personnel up to Dorthea and Yvonne.

"Not her, *him*."

"Him?"

"Mr. McHenry. Nice enough, but a little different. He has strange taste and dresses his mannequins a little on the wild side."

"How long's he been there?"

"Since Mrs. Halloran got rid of Rochelle—a month now, I'd guess." Megan looked around to make sure no one was listening. "Anybody talk to her yet?"

"Rusty's doing that today. See what you can hear today, okay Megan? Listen to what the other girls say about this."

"Sure. I wonder how McHenry's handling this?"

"I'm on my way there now." Dan turned and walked away, not noticing that Jen had finished with her customer and had seen him talking with Megan. Jen knew she'd have to wait until their break to find out what their conversation was all about.

"McHenry's department was hit last night."

Jen jumped and turned to see her department manager. "You startled me."

"I'm sorry, Jen. I didn't mean to sneak up on you like that. You were deep in thought, I guess. I apologize."

"No, no. Don't worry about it. What did you say?"

"McHenry's department was hit. He's livid." Jeffers stood to one side with his never ending stack of paperwork in his hand. "Quite a haul, too."

"How'd you find out?"

"We came in together this morning for a manager's meeting. He went to his department to get a questionable packing slip or something that he wanted to bring to the meeting, and he noticed it right away. Seems he did a display late in the day and it was disturbed this morning. When he looked closer, he found it was more than just *disturbed*—if you know what I mean."

Jen turned and faced Mr. Jeffers with interest.

"Then what?"

"McHenry is not a quiet man, as you well know." Jen did know; she had heard him berating one of his clerks when she was browsing on one of her breaks. "He came back to the managers' meeting quite upset, and he let everyone know about it. You'd think one of us did it just to upset him, the way he carried on."

That evening Jen knew Rusty and Dan would probably want to talk to Megan. Jen had a class, and she was grateful she had an excuse to avoid talking to Dan Miller. She was curious, though; she wondered what new information they would each bring to the meeting.

Jen was gone by the time Dan and Rusty arrived. "Any luck finding Rochelle or Frances?" Dan had settled in the kitchen chair next to the window of Jen's apartment.

"Yeah," Rusty was glad to be in this little cozy place again. "I can't talk to Frances until tomorrow, but Rochelle is plenty bitter about what happened to her."

"It's not like she stole the belt," Megan began to defend Rochelle.

"She didn't even take it out of the store, Megan," Rusty said.

"But I heard she—"

"I know what you heard. But Rochelle said she found the belt in the hallway going back to the downstairs shipping room. The stock boy had missed a bunch of packages that were supposed to be sent out, and she took them down to shipping herself. She had her hands full, so she set down her packages, picked up the belt, and put it on simply as a way to carry it. Then she picked up her packages and went on into the shipping room. When she got back to the department, she took off the belt and tried to find out if it was a special order, but she couldn't see where anyone had ordered it. She was putting it back into stock when Dorthea Halloran came along and 'caught' her. She fired her on the spot."

Dan looked at Megan and started to speak when Mrs. Simms knocked at the door. She came in, shed her rain 'n shine coat and accepted Megan's offer of coffee. "I shouldn't drink so much of this awful stuff, but since you kids keep me up to all hours, I need it—it keeps me awake."

Dan and Rusty filled Beth in on the latest details. Megan stayed back a little, thinking.

Noticing how quiet she was, Rusty asked, "What's goin' on in there, Megan?" He reached over and touched her forehead with his finger.

"The shipping room. Nobody knows what goes on down there. We fill out the paperwork and put the merchandise in the proper bin; a stockboy comes by and gets it out; and we never see it again."

"Well, it's no mystery," Dan said. "It's a plain room with scales for weighing packages, postage machines, stock bins, tables, a back door to the alley where the delivery trucks come for pick-ups." Dan had been there a few times, but he did not make it a regular practice to check up on it. "Murphy runs the delivery department, has for years. He'll retire someday, but as long as he can do the work, no need to rush him out of there."

"He work alone?" Rusty asked.

"No, there are a few stock boys, part-timers, and we hire temps to help with the special sales and furniture deliveries. Yvonne keeps her eye on the place too." Dan turned to Megan. "How about you? You hear anything from the girls today?"

"Plenty. I guess McHenry fussed and fumed all day. He's insulted that anyone would steal from his department. Like his department should be exempt from such underhandedness." Megan shook her head, and Rusty noticed how her hair shook in response.

"Like a thief would tiptoe around his area because he might get mad." The group laughed at Megan's indignation.

"What else?" Dan asked.

"He's angry because he's asked for his cases to be locked and no one seems to care about it."

"Oh?" Dan raised his eyebrows.

"I don't mean that you didn't do anything about it, Dan, it's just that he says he's asked and asked and no one responds."

"Who did he ask?" Beth addressed her question to Megan.

"Everybody." Megan looked at the group around the little table and pointed at Beth. "He says he asked the security office first, then when he didn't get a response, he asked Mr. Miller's secretary, and she said she'd check with you." Megan gestured in Dan's direction. "Then he said he asked Mrs. Halloran herself. Well, he didn't ask Mrs. Halloran directly. Yvonne said she'd do it for him."

"Wait a minute, did you ever get a note on this, Beth?"

"No, Dan. Not that I know of," Beth answered.

"I didn't either," he said.

Megan spoke up again. "He says he wrote it up. Three times. If he did, he'd have a carbon copy in his filing cabinet."

"Better check that out when we search the personnel files," Rusty said.

The four of them sat for a moment, thinking. Dan broke the silence. "When's Jen due home?"

"By ten or ten-thirty. She takes the bus, and sometimes she misses the good connection."

Dan checked his watch; it was eight-forty-five. "She get's out at nine-thirty, doesn't she?"

"Unless the class runs late—that's when she has trouble making her connection," Megan told him.

"Think I'll try to catch her and give her a ride home." Rusty smiled at Dan as he stood to leave. "We'll be back before it gets too late," Dan said.

As Rusty, Beth, and Megan went over the events of the day again just to be sure they hadn't overlooked anything, Dan turned the Corvette toward the Chicago School of Interior Design.

His store had been robbed, his daughter had chicken pox, and against his better judgement he had fallen in love. He was working on the first problem, and time would take care of the second. Tonight he and Jen were going to have a talk, a serious talk about the third.

CHAPTER EIGHTEEN

*D*an circled the block and found a parking place near the door. As he waited for Jen to appear, he caught a glimpse of a man he recognized as Bobby Moore. He couldn't have been more than twenty-five, Dan guessed, twenty-seven at the most. Since Moore was athletic and well built, Dan surmised he could, indeed, defend Jen if it were ever necessary.

Bobby was smiling at the young women coming out, and anyone watching would assume he was waiting for his girl or was interested in finding one. Dan opened the door to his car as he spotted Jen coming out.

"Excuse me, miss." A man stepped from the shadows. Jen glanced in his direction, and her hand flew to the scarf thrown loosely around her shoulders.

Bobby Moore stepped forward and grabbed Jen's arm just as the man tried to pull her toward the alley. Jen's books and purse scattered across the sidewalk, and the stranger darted away from the scene. Dan sprang from his car, and with a few long strides, he reached Jen's side and pulled her safely into his arms. Bobby turned toward Jen, saw that she recognized Dan, and immediately went in pursuit of the man.

"Jen! Are you all right?"

People around began picking up Jen's belongings and handing them to Dan. He quickly guided her to his car, and by the time he slid behind the wheel beside her, she was sobbing uncontrollably.

Dan instinctively reached for her, encircling her with his arms, and gently pulled her close. He began kissing her forehead.

"Jen, it's okay. I'm here. You're safe. I'm sorry, honey, I'm so sorry."

"There were two of them, Dan. I didn't know what to do. I couldn't even scream," Jen said through her tears.

"It's okay, Jen. It's okay." He held her and let her sob out her fear. "Jen, listen to me, Jennifer?"

"What?" she managed between sobs.

"One of those men was Bobby Moore. He's been watching out for you the last couple of days."

"What?" Jen straightened up and pulled away from Dan's grasp.

"Rusty and Megan are both convinced that someone has been following you for a while. We—well, I—asked Rusty to get someone to make sure you were safe. We hired Bobby."

"You mean someone has been following me?" Jen asked.

"I guess tonight proved that, all right."

"And no one told me?" Jen's fear turned to anger.

"Jennifer." Dan reached for her, hoping to pull her close again. "Come here, Jen."

"Get away from me." Jen's eyes flashed, and she began to shake all over.

"Jen."

"No one told me. I can't believe no one told me." She began to cry again. "Don't I have a right to know when I'm being followed? Isn't it *my* business? What is this? Megan gets into the thick of your investigation, and I don't even get told that someone is following me. What's the matter,

Dan, afraid I can't hold up? You afraid I might blow your whole little mystery?"

Dan had not seen this side of Jennifer before. "It's only my life, here," she went on. Jen found a Kleenex in her little purse and blew her nose. "But don't anyone tell her, after all, she might, she could . . . Well, you tell me, Dan Miller. Why wasn't I told, and why didn't I know I had a body-guard?"

"Jen, we didn't want to scare you."

"Scare me?" Jen was furious. "A strange man takes hold of my arm, and another stranger grabs the other—now why on earth do you think that ought to scare me?"

"I'm sorry,". Dan was beginning to get angry at her. "Look, Jennifer, I was only trying—"

"Trying to what? To protect me? To watch out for me? To make my decisions? To ..."

"Stop it, Jen. Just stop it. Bobby Moore was there just in time tonight, and even though you didn't know it, you needed him."

"Him? And what about you? How did you manage to be there, just at the right time?" Her voice was still tinged with anger.

"I was here because I wanted to be here. I came to offer you a lift home. I am here because . . . oh, forget it."

"No, no. I won't forget it," Jen said, still angry.

"Look, do you want a ride home or not?"

Jen looked into the night and into the faces of the few curious students still standing around to see what would happen next. "I would, thank you." She suddenly became quiet.

"Very well, then." Dan started the engine just as Bobby Moore appeared from the alley. Dan rolled down his win-dow as Moore approached the car.

"He got away, Mr. Miller. Not a trace." The young man

was winded. "Good evening, Miss Whipple. Sorry you got such a scare. I didn't see him until he grabbed you. Did he get anything? Your purse?"

"No, my purse is still here. He didn't get anything."

"Good." Bobby looked at Dan. "You'll see her safely home, then?"

"Yeah, if she'll let me." Dan looked at Jen. "She's pretty mad that she wasn't told about you."

"She didn't know?" Bobby seemed surprised.

"See, he agrees with me," Jen said.

"Don't get me into this," Bobby laughed. "I've got enough trouble without getting into a fight between you two."

"Need a lift somewhere?" Dan asked Bobby.

"No, I'm going to ask a few questions around here before I leave. Look, you guys get out of here." He motioned toward an oncoming police car. "Looks like somebody called the cops. I can handle them, unless you want to . . ."

"We'll talk tomorrow, first thing," Dan said as he put the car into gear, backed out, and pulled into traffic.

Jen rode silently beside Dan, trying to get her heart to stop beating so hard and fast. One of her ankles started to throb, and she bent over to rub it.

"You okay?" Dan asked.

"I think my ankle is swelling. I must have turned it."

Dan turned the car into an empty parking place under a streetlight. "Let me see."

"It's not too bad." Jen pulled off her boot and rolled down her anklet. Turning slightly in the bucket seat with her back against the door she put the injured foot up on the seat. Dan searched her foot and ankle with his fingers. She didn't protest, but she winced when he pressed on the inside of the swollen joint.

"I bet it's sprained," he said. "It'll need some ice."

"Great. Just what I need, a sprained ankle and a strange man following me for—God only knows what for." She looked into Dan's eyes. "Do we know *why* he's following me?"

"No, Jen. I wish we did. Maybe it would help us solve this whole ugly mess." Dan brushed her hair away from her face and wrapped one little curl around his finger. "I am sorry, Jen. I didn't want to upset you. You've had work, and school and well, I didn't think you needed the distraction right now. I'm sorry, I was wrong."

"Maybe not." Jen put her foot back on the floor and wrinkled her nose at the pain. "I shouldn't have taken it out on you. I was really glad to see you." She looked pensive, and Dan wanted to hold her close again. "It really scared me, Dan. Really scared me." She looked into his eyes, and he saw the tears in hers. He opened his arms and she leaned into him. There in Dan's car, she allowed herself to need him—something she had promised herself she would not do. Dan Miller didn't fit into her plans, nor she into his; but she fit into his arms. Frightened, she allowed herself to be comforted by his nearness.

Dan held her for a few silent moments, then lightly kissed the top of her head. "Jennifer?"

She tried to pull away but decided against it. "I came here tonight for a specific reason. I wanted to see you, to talk to you. I need to tell you something."

Jen again resisted his grasp, and he let her go. She didn't say anything, and he sat there groping for the words to begin.

"You don't have to tell me anything, Dan." Jen tried to make it easier. "You don't owe me any explanation. I already know about Marie."

Dan's head snapped toward her. "You do?"

"Yes, I do."

"It's been a long time, Jen. I didn't even know I had room in my life for anyone else, but then I met you."

Jen looked at him with wide eyes, and he thought he heard her slightly catch her breath.

"Does that surprise you," Dan asked.

"Yes, frankly it does." He saw her eyes glisten even in this dim light.

"Why?"

"Because, Dan Miller, I haven't room in my life for well . . . I'm leaving Chicago shortly. I'm finished here. I came to get an education, and it's almost over. Besides, even if I were staying, I don't see married men."

Dan felt as if she had slapped him. "Is that what you think? That I'm just another married man on the make?"

"Now who's getting angry?" Jen snapped back. "I'm not married, never have been. I have my dreams, and getting involved with a married man isn't part of them."

"I'm not married." Dan took her by the shoulders and turned her toward him. "Jen, I wouldn't do that to you. I wouldn't do it to Marie." Jen saw the anguish on his face. "I loved her, Jen. I probably still do, in some ways. But she's gone." Dan searched Jen's face intently. "She's dead."

Dan's pain seemed to stab directly into Jen's own heart. "She's what?" Jen said barely above a whisper.

"She's dead," Dan said flatly. He relaxed his hold on Jen and sank back into his seat. Covering his face with his hands, he wept. "I can't believe you would think that I'd . . ."

"Oh, Dan. I don't know what to say. It's just that when I was in your office . . ." Jen remembered Debbie's words: *That's Mrs. Marie Halloran Miller. Dan Miller's lucky wife.*

"My office?"

"I saw her picture, that's all." Jen realized that Debbie had misled her. "I assumed, that's all. I couldn't have been more wrong." *Why would Debbie lie?* she wondered.

"It's been four years, Jen, she died in an automobile accident." Dan slowly told Jen the whole story. Mrs. O'Halloran had never forgiven him for asking Marie to stop off at the library for him. "I needed a book to finish a paper due the next day. I didn't want to make the trip, and she said she wouldn't mind even though it took her a few miles out of her way. She was driving her mother's car. She might have been forced off the road; we don't know for sure. She hit a tree. The accident wasn't too bad, but she was thrown from the car and had a nasty bump on the head. She died of a fractured skull."

Jen reached for Dan's face to wipe away a tear, and he caught her hand and pressed his lips to it. "Wait," he said, "there's more."

"More?" Jen left her hand in his.

"There's Joy."

"Joy?"

"She was barely a year old when Marie was killed."

Jen couldn't believe what she was about to hear.

"She's my daughter. She's five. I'm not married, but I *am* a family man." Dan watched Jen pull away from him.

"I know what you've said about wanting a career and all, but—"

"You have a child?" Jen could barely form the words.

"Yes," Dan said simply, "and I want you to meet her."

"Oh, I don't know. I never thought that I'd . . . well, that I'd be very good with children. Someday maybe. But I don't know, Dan."

"Please, Jen. I'm not asking you for a commitment. I'm just asking you to meet Joy. I'm not asking for anything more after that. But I have a daughter I love very much. I can't go on—we can't—well, until you meet her. I should have told you about Marie before this; I should have told you about Joy."

"Look, Dan. I'm not what you'd call the motherly type. I'm not . . ." Jen felt her insides tighten and thought she might be sick. "You have never seen me with kids. My best friend, Cari, has just had her first baby and she wants me to be the godmother. Even that gives me the shakes. Please Dan, don't ask me to . . ."

Dan caught her face in his hands, and he saw the tears streaming down her cheeks. He pulled her toward him. "I'm only asking that you meet her, Jen. That's all." She began to weep softly as Dan Miller gently, but firmly pressed his lips against hers. When he released her, she wrapped her arms around his neck and burying her face in his neck, she wept softly.

Dan could barely make out her muffled words, "You have turned my life upside down, Dan Miller. I hate you for this."

He laughed and snuggled his face into her hair. "Yeah, I know. I hate you too."

CHAPTER NINETEEN

*W*here've you been?" Megan was upset when Dan helped Jen in the door.

"Well, we had a little trouble." Dan looked at Jen, who was more than willing to let him try to explain to the three angry people waiting for them at the apartment.

"A little?" Bobby Moore's voice came from the kitchen.

"How'd you get here so fast?"

"I've been here over an hour. I guess I took the more direct route," Bobby laughed.

"Jen's ankle is injured," Dan said, trying to change the subject.

"How bad is it?" Megan instantly softened toward Jen. "Let me see."

"I'll get an ice pack," Beth headed for the kitchen.

"We've got problems," Rusty said as soon as he could get Dan a little distance away from Megan and Jen.

"Oh?" Dan looked from Rusty to Bobby.

"Rochelle Lewis. I found her." Rusty paused. "She had an accident. Was left for dead is my guess."

Dan's eyes widened. "An accident?"

"She was hit by a car and left by the side of the road."

"She okay?"

"Well, let's just say she was ready to talk."

"What do you mean 'talk'?"

"Listen, Dan," Rusty began, "there is some indication

that Rochelle had stumbled onto some interesting things going on down in the shipping department. She found the belt she was accused of stealing from her department laying on the floor when she carried down some packages the guys had missed."

Dan looked at the two young men facing him and then looked up at Beth as she joined them.

"It seems that she spotted some other merchandise being stored down there, and when she asked Murphy about it, he just kept reading his magazine and wouldn't respond."

"What?" Dan couldn't believe what he was hearing.

"He ignored her, Dan, like she wasn't even there. She put the belt around her waist because she couldn't carry it with the packages she was bringing down for shipment. When she went back to the department, she was still wearing the belt. She was putting it back into stock when Halloran showed up and fired her." Rusty leaned his chair back on two legs.

"So when did she have this accident?" Beth asked.

"She called Mrs. Halloran later and tried to tell her about the other merchandise she saw in the stockroom. She thought the old lady would be grateful, would maybe believe her story and give her her job back."

"And?"

"Mrs. Halloran told her that she was lying. Then Rochelle told her exactly where the merchandise was, and Mrs. Halloran hung up on her."

"Did anyone ever call your office about this, Beth?" Dan asked.

"This is the first I've heard of it. I've ordered audits of the shipping department, and they have always come back clean."

"How are they done?" Rusty asked.

"The merchandise waiting for shipment is usually not

there for more than a day or two. I have simply written a memo, asking Yvonne to take an inventory of all merchandise being held there once in a while. A mistake, I'd say. I'm sorry, Dan. It's just that Murphy has been with the store for so many years, much longer than either you or I. I just didn't think that he could be suspected of anything."

Dan turned back to Rusty. "What else did Rochelle say?"

"She found another job, as a waitress working the late shift. A few days later she got a call from Mrs. Halloran with an offer to keep her mouth shut about what she saw in the stockroom. Funny thing, though, she wasn't planning to ever tell anyone about it anyway. But when she got the phone call, she got curious and decided to push Halloran to see how much she could get the offer up. Halloran got mad and slammed down the phone. Rochelle thought she'd heard the last of it—until the accident. Later she got an anonymous get-well card that said, *Be more careful next time*. She called Mrs. Halloran again and told her that she had been mistaken about the stockroom and that she was sorry she had tried to steal from the store."

"She what?"

"She gave in. She was scared, she was recovering from the accident. She wasn't able to work, and Mrs. Halloran sent her some money to help with medical expenses." Rusty stretched. "There is something very scary about all of this," he added.

"What's that?"

"Rochelle said there was someone watching her house, maybe even following her the few days before the accident. Her description of him fits the man we've seen tailing Jen."

Dan stood to his feet and began pacing back and forth in the small kitchen. "We've got to keep her away from danger, Rusty. I won't have anything happen to her."

"She's not going anywhere on that ankle," Beth said. "It probably needs to be x-rayed."

"She's sleeping," Megan said from the doorway. "She's exhausted. She studied most of the night last night—tonight was a big test for her. She's almost finished with her classes, but graduation is a few weeks away yet."

"I want to get her out of here," Dan said to the group sitting in the small kitchen.

Bobby Moore spoke up. "Where do you propose she go?"

"I don't know, let me think about it."

"You could take her to my mother's," Megan offered. "She loves to look after sick people. Even if you're not sick, she loves to look after you."

"Let's think about this," Beth said. "Maybe she doesn't want to go anywhere. She's going to be laid up a day or so on that foot anyway. If someone is here with her, won't she be all right?"

Rusty agreed that as long as she wasn't out walking the streets she would probably be safe.

They decided that Bobby would spend the night on the couch and that Beth would arrive first thing in the morning. Dan lifted Jen from the couch; she roused a bit and complained about her ankle. Megan and Beth helped her change into pajamas, and after Jen swallowed a few aspirin and elevated her foot, Dan came into her room to say good night.

"Jennifer," he said softly as he knelt beside her bed, "I won't let anything else happen to you. It's been so long since I even thought I could feel this way about someone, I can't—"

"Shh." Jen put her fingers up to Dan's lips. "Please don't say any more. Not until after I have met Joy."

"Yeah, you're right," Dan agreed. "I might as well tell you, Jen, she's pretty spoiled."

"Why do I get the feeling that my sprained ankle is minor compared to the trouble I can expect from one little five year old?" Jen laughed.

Beth approached the bedside. "Dan, maybe I could have the keys to the apartment. Then I can come in tomorrow morning after Bobby leaves without making Jen get up."

"Good idea, Beth, they're in my coat pocket." Jen pointed toward the coat draped over the chair in the corner.

"Which one, dear?" Beth said with a frown as she searched the pockets.

"I carry them in the right one." Jen propped herself up on one elbow.

Beth dug in both pockets and came up empty-handed.

"Maybe they're in your purse." Megan went for Jen's small purse, which she had left on the floor beside the couch.

"I don't like this," Rusty said to Bobby. "I better have a look around on the sidewalk outside the school."

"I'll look in my car," Dan offered.

"Look, Dan, you stay with the girls, let me look in your car," Rusty said.

Rusty appeared, empty-handed, fifteen minutes later. "They're not in your car, Dan. Bobby and I are going to take a trip downtown and see if they were dropped in the scuffle."

"Take the Corvette," Dan said to the two men. "I'll wait here."

Dan returned to his position beside Jen's bed. Megan stretched out on the other twin bed, and Beth curled up with a blanket on the couch to wait. It was an hour before Rusty and Bobby returned and let themselves in with Megan's key.

Dan had soothed Jen to sleep and adjusted the ice bag

on her ankle once or twice. He noticed that the swelling was starting to go down.

"We were tailed," Rusty announced calmly to Dan.

"Tailed? You sure?"

"Tailed. I'm sure." Rusty sat down and continued. "They seemed to follow too closely at times, then they would try to pass us. We thought they might be trying to force us over. That machine of yours was no match for them, though. It was pretty much a game of cat and mouse until we decided to lose them. That car really performs, I'll say that for it."

Bobby leaned against the side of the kitchen doorway. "This smacks of something bigger than Halloran. I wonder if she has ties to the mob."

"What'll we do?" Beth asked.

"We wait, that's what," Rusty said. "If they have keys, it's only a matter of time until they come to pay a visit. I think we'd better be here."

"We drove to your apartment," Bobby said, "parked the car in your garage, and then left by the side entrance. We took a cab back here and came in the side door."

"Let's all camp out here for tonight," Rusty said, "and make plans in the morning."

"I'll take the first watch," Bobby offered with a little laugh. "It's obvious we won't all sleep at the same time, there's no room."

Dan went back into the bedroom and curled up on the floor beside Jen's bed. He had lost one woman through his carelessness, but he was not about to lose this one.

Megan jumped to her feet when the phone rang early the next morning. She stumbled over the three people scattered across the living room.

"Hello?"

"May I speak to Jennifer Whipple, please?" the caller said.

"Well, she's still—I mean . . . Who's calling, please?"

"Dorthea Halloran."

Megan covered the phone receiver and turned to face three curious faces staring at her from behind. "Mrs. Halloran," she said. Uncovering the phone, she said, "I'll have to see if she's able to come to the phone. She had . . . well, let me see, okay, hold on."

"Thank you," Dorthea Halloran said. She took a long drag from her cigarette while she waited for Jen to come to the phone.

At Megan's summons, Jen shuffled into the living room and groggily took the receiver.

"Hello?"

"Jennifer, my dear, I just wanted to call and see how your schooling was coming along," Dorthea said.

"Fine, thank you." Jen was leaning on Dan; they each had an ear to the receiver.

"And how much longer will it be before you go back to California?" Mrs. Halloran asked.

"Well, I don't know. My plans are not that definite yet," Jen told her.

"I see." Dorthea blew a cloud of blue-gray smoke toward the ceiling, making a swishing sound into the phone. "Your bonus, dear, was it enough to help you get home?"

"More than enough, Mrs. Halloran. I really don't think I should accept it." Jen shifted her weight. Her ankle was beginning to throb.

"Nonsense, Jennifer. I want to see you get back home safe and sound. You know the city can be a dangerous place for a young girl all alone," the woman said sweetly.

"I know."

"You know?"

"I, well, last night . . ." Jen turned to face Rusty, who shook his head rapidly and held a finger to his lips, signaling Jen not to tell her anything.

"Yes, dear, go on," Mrs. Halloran said.

"I turned my ankle coming out of my class. I don't think I'll be able to come in to work today, I have to keep it propped up."

"I'm so sorry to hear that, Jennifer. I'm sure Mr. Jeffers will be too. He depends on you, you know. I'll call him for you. I'm sure you will be well enough by graduation, and then you'll, no doubt, want to take the first plane out. Let me call my travel agent, dear. I'd be happy to make all the arrangements, for you. Let's call it a graduation gift."

"Oh, no, Mrs. Halloran, I couldn't do that," Jen told her.

"Nonsense—besides, I want to say I knew you once when you become a famous interior designer. I'll call you later to get the exact dates and all. Don't you worry, I'll take care of everything."

"She wants you out of town," Rusty said to Jen after Dan told him about Dorthea's offer. "Why does she want you to leave so badly?"

"I guess she just wants me away from here."

Dan put his arm protectively around Jen. "Well, I don't."

"I haven't made up my mind yet." Jen tried to take a step away from Dan, but she found her foot was unable to take even the slightest weight.

"Let's try to find out why she's so determined that Jen leave Chicago," Rusty said. "What threat could one little redheaded Californian possibly be to one of the richest women in Chicago?"

"A big one, I'm afraid," Dan Miller said smiling at Jen. "Jen could be a threat to her whole world."

CHAPTER TWENTY

*B*y ten o'clock, Jen's apartment had quieted down considerably. Bobby and Rusty left to go out for breakfast and a "confab." "That's detective talk for a consultation," Bobby explained to the group.

"I never heard of such a word, and I've been in this business a long time," Beth said. "You guys better connect with me later, okay?"

The two agreed to call Beth at home later. Beth was going to stay with Jen during the day. She had to call in and give the store a reason for not being there. Dan decided to go by his small bachelor apartment and freshen up, then go on to work as usual.

"Where have you been?" Debbie asked when he got there. She looked frazzled and tired. "She's been trying to reach you all morning, and she says she has been calling your place all night."

"I wasn't answering my phone." Dan hurried inside his office to call Dorthea and check on Joy.

"Look, Dan," Dorthea began, more sour than usual this morning. "I have been trying to reach you for hours. You didn't answer your phone, and your service didn't know where to reach you. Is that being a responsible father?"

"Is there something wrong with Joy?" Dan asked, worried.

"She's miserable. She won't stop scratching, and the

doctor said if she doesn't leave the pox alone, she could have small scars. Thank God she doesn't have but a few spots on her face."

"God? You're thanking God?"

"Leave it alone, Dan, it was only an expression." He could hear the click of her long fingernails on the table over the phone. That meant she had something else on her mind, that she was irritated.

"What's so important you needed to talk to me about?"

"I suspect that Megan LaBianca has been shoplifting," Dorthea said.

"What? Who's Megan LaBianca?"

"She's that little Italian girl in fine jewelry. I want to move her to better blouses, down on the main floor. Just to keep an eye on her."

"I'm sure you have a basis for this suspicion?" Dan was interested in knowing how Dorthea could suspect Megan.

"I have my sources, Dan." She took a deep drag on her cigarette.

"What sources?"

"That's not the point here." Dorthea was not happy when Dan pressed for reasons for her actions. For four years now, he had stayed out of her way. Now, all of a sudden, he was beginning to try her patience.

"It's exactly the point, Dorthea. I don't like you shuffling my salesclerks around because you have some unfounded suspicion. You've moved girls around before, and I didn't say anything because even though I questioned your motives, I thought you might have good reason. However . . ."

Dorthea was indignant. "Just a moment, young man. What do you mean you questioned my motives?"

"I'll check out the LaBianca girl myself, Dorthea. I won't have her moved on a whim."

"You didn't answer my question, Dan Miller."

"I said I'd check on the girl myself," Dan repeated.

Dan hung up the phone and asked Debbie to get Yvonne on the phone.

Asking Yvonne about Megan, he found that she was willing—more than willing—to keep an eye on Megan. Yvonne was sent to work in the jewelry department for a few days.

"She makes me nervous," Megan said to Dan later that evening when he called to check on Jen.

"Just keep an eye on her," Dan said. "She thinks she's there to watch you, but I sent her there so you can keep an eye on her."

After talking briefly to Jen, Dan went to see Joy. He stopped on the way and bought her a small teddy bear that played "Jesus Loves Me" when he wound it up. He had persuaded the salesclerk to take a fountain pen and put little black spots all over the stuffed animal, but she had made him pay for it first.

Dan entered the house by the side door and went directly to Joy's room without seeing Dorthea. Entering, he found her playing quietly with her dollies and a tea set.

"Daddy!" she ran to him and threw her arms around him when he entered the room.

"Look at you!" Dan laughed. "How's my girl feeling?"

"I itch."

"I heard." Dan held her at arms length and then started counting the spots. ". . . twenty-five, twenty-six."

Touching every spot carefully, Dan counted the ones on her tummy, on her back, and even in her hair. Then he looked at her feet and found five spots nestled between her toes.

"My goodness, little girl, you're completely covered. I only know of one other person who has more spots than you."

"You do?"

"Look here, at little Bear." Dan produced the teddy bear from a shopping bag.

"What's the matter with him?" Joy wrinkled her nose at the sight of the bear.

"He's sick, just like you. He has chicken pox." Dan held out the bear to Joy. She carefully took him and started to count the spots.

"Daddy, he must have a thousand million spots. He has even more than me!"

Dan watched as Joy began to pet the small, prized bear. "Can he stay here with you?" Dan asked.

"Oh, Daddy, I think Bear is hungry."

"Shall we get him something to eat? Want me to call Elaine and have her fix him something?"

"No, Elaine doesn't know what to fix sick people." Joy looked entirely serious.

"She doesn't?"

"She thinks sick people only want soup and custard," Joy pouted.

"Don't they?"

"No, Daddy, they want hang-a-bers and french fries." She gave him a hopeful look.

"They do?"

"Please?" Joy looked so pitiful Dan couldn't help but laugh at her.

"Let's see, if you were to wrap up real warm, put on your fuzzy slippers and let me carry you, I could take you to the drive-in."

Without a word, Joy hurried to her closet and wrapped herself in a warm bathrobe and scurried under her bed looking for her slippers. Dan reached for a blanket, and with one scoop he lifted Joy, blanket, and bear all three. Reaching the kitchen, he confronted Elaine.

"I'm taking Joy for a ride," he said firmly.

"But Mrs. O'Halloran said she wasn't to leave her room," Elaine argued.

"Mrs. O'Halloran is her grandmother—I'm her father, and I'm taking her out. I'll be back soon."

"But what shall I tell Mrs. O'Halloran?"

"Just that." Dan crossed the kitchen and went out the same door he had entered earlier and put Joy in his car.

He took her to a drive-in, and together they shared "hang-a-bers" with all the trimmings. Joy only swallowed a bite or two of her sandwich, and she didn't like the french fries that much without catsup, which hurt her throat tonight. She sipped contentedly on the vanilla milk shake, offering to share once in a while with Dan and the bear.

On the way home, Joy leaned over to rest her head on the luxurious armrest between them. With his free hand, Dan played with her long, silky dark hair. She looked a lot like Marie. Too bad they had never really known each other. Dan looked at his daughter clutching her little spotted bear. Before two blocks separated them from the drive-in, Joy was fast asleep. Joy hardly ever asked any questions about Marie anymore. Her mother's absence, a tragic loss to him, was normal for her. *That,* Dan decided, *was more tragic than losing Marie in the first place.*

Before he arrived at the house, Dan decided that Jen and Joy needed to meet as soon as possible. Whatever was going on at the store, nothing was this important to him. Dorthea would pressure him, of course. And she would try to bribe Jen. But it wouldn't work. She could worship the store if she wanted to, but it wasn't enough for Dan.

"Even if I have to leave and let it go bankrupt." He looked at his sleeping daughter. "There are more important things than making sure you are rich when you grow up."

Before he left his sleeping Joy safe and sound back in her

room, he had formed a plan. Now he had to put it into play and to convince Jen to go along with it. *She's so stubborn,* he thought. *I'll have to work on that.*

Dan returned to his apartment and dialed Jen's number. He heard a faint click on the line and realized that his phone was probably tapped. He swore, which he hardly ever did, but Dorthea had gone too far this time. He hung up just as Jen answered.

Grabbing his coat on the way out the door, Dan hurried to a pay phone down the block. He had to hear Jen's voice once more to make sure she was all right and that she was staying off her foot.

Less than a month ago all he had to worry about was the store. Now he had met Jen, and somehow meeting her was making him more aware of Joy. Last month his life was busy; now he felt it was full. He had felt pinned in; now he was beginning to feel free. He had thought his life had ended, but now he sensed a new beginning.

CHAPTER TWENTY-ONE

*D*an, it's me." Dan recognized Rusty's voice on the phone and appreciated his caution. "Where can we meet? We need to talk."

"How about our usual place? I think it can be arranged."

"I don't think so. I'm more in the mood for hamburgers and french fries."

"Right," Dan knew he referred to the diner where they had gone before. "Fifteen minutes?"

Dan took his car and headed in the direction of his meeting with Rusty. As he drove, he thought about Jen and wondered how he could convince her to spend some time with Joy. Pulling into a parking space, Dan glanced around to be sure he wasn't followed. He entered the diner and saw Rusty sitting in the familiar red and gray vinyl booth.

"Hey, guy, how's it going?" Dan said almost cheerfully.

Rusty did not share his mood. "Sit down, Dan. I already ordered you a hamburger."

"Great," Dan said rubbing his hands together. "What's up?"

"You're not going to like what I'm going to tell you."

"What else is new?" Dan sighed.

"I can hardly believe it myself." Rusty smiled at the waitress as she put the plate in front of him. He grabbed the catsup bottle and shook it toward his plate. Dan handed him a knife, and he poked it inside the bottle to release the thick red ooze.

"What are you talking about, Russ?"

"It's just that I have had this hunch, you know? It's been a little weird and finally it's all beginning to make sense. Except for one or two pieces, I think the puzzle is almost complete. Unfortunately, those pieces are key pieces. Maybe you can help me out."

"I'll try. Let me hear what you've got."

"It's like this," Rusty said as he swallowed a hunk of his burger, "I've been doing a bit of snooping around, as you know, and the most interesting person I've talked to yet is Frances."

"Frances?"

"Yeah, she works in accessories. She's a bit of a snoop herself and has been wondering just how long it would be before the right person started asking, quote, 'the right questions.'"

"And?"

"And I learned some very interesting things," Rusty said.

"Such as?"

"Did you know that some merchandise that's ordered never arrives, yet there is no record of a short order ever being reported to a vendor, manufacturer, or supplier?"

"What?" Dan began to recall his conversation with the rep from Ship 'n Shore last week.

"Frances says that there was an order sent to their floor with the packing slip still attached. She pulled it out to put the order into stock and saw that the order had been checked in—you know, the paper was already initialed. But when she did a little checking of her own, some of the stock was missing. Yet every item was checked as being received in the quantities listed on the slip.

"Yvonne got really upset when Frances mentioned it and

said that somebody in receiving had really messed it up. She said she would check on it and file a report."

"So, if only a part of an order was received, why was the packing slip marked received in full?" Dan wondered.

"Or, if a whole order was received, where was the rest of it?"

"You think a whole shipment was received?"

"I *know* a whole shipment was received."

"Really?"

"Yes, really. Look, Dan, Frances went down to check on some trumped up problem with shipping and found Murphy napping. She sneaked around a bit and found an unmarked box in a bin marked *Christmas Returns*. She opened the flap, and what do you think she found?"

"Bingo," Dan said.

"Exactly," Rusty said. "She closed the flap, went around to where Murphy was snoozing, and woke him up to ask him a bogus question. Then she went on her merry way, but she didn't know what to do about her discovery."

"Is there more?" Dan asked.

"Later—I don't know if it was a few days or a week or two—she did the same thing again. This time Murphy wasn't at his desk, so she went looking for him, and walked right by the Christmas bin, intentionally of course. The box was gone."

"Gone? Is she sure?"

Rusty nodded. "She repeated this three times, Dan. Three times she saw merchandise that should have been on the floor but was ready for shipment instead. Three times it was stored in Christmas returns, three times she went back again and it was gone."

"Why didn't she get caught snooping around down there?"

"Oh, but she did," Rusty said. "That's when Halloran tried to fire her."

"What?" Dan almost choked on his Coke; he pounded his chest with his fist.

"Halloran called her in on some phony complaint, but Frances didn't budge. She's nobody's patsy, that's for sure. She told Halloran that she was mistaken and that if she had proof of misconduct she had better produce it."

Dan wondered what Dorthea must have looked like when someone actually dared to stand up to her. The thought of it brought a smile to his face.

"You think this is amusing?"

"I think Dorthea must have been ready to blow a gasket. I was just enjoying the thought of it." Dan wiped his mouth with his napkin. "What happened then?"

"Dorthea tried to transfer Frances to the designer's shop, but she refused. Said she didn't know the first thing about interior decorating and she wasn't in the mood to learn. She told Dorthea she was happy where she was and that she was going to stay. Even threatened to speak to the other clerks about it if necessary. I believe she mentioned talking to a union rep."

"We're not union," Dan said simply.

"No, and Dorthea wants to keep it that way." Rusty leaned back and took a long draw on his soda. "Then, she did something quite gutsy."

"Yeah?"

"She talked Peggy McKnight into looking up the invoices to see if the bills were paid in full or if the shortages were ever reported."

"Timid Peggy McKnight?"

"The very one."

"She's only an office clerk, kind of a mousey person. Seems afraid of everyone. She keeps the bookkeeping office in order and looks up—" Dan winked at Rusty. "She'd be perfect."

"She really took to this assignment. Maybe she felt she could really get back at people she thinks push her around."

"What did she find?"

"An invoice initialed for payment. Guess who's initials?"

"I already know. Mine," Dan said.

"You guessed it."

"But there is supposed to be an approved packing slip to back up every invoice."

"There was. Guess who's initials were on it?"

"Could be anybody's. We send down people to help when there is a big shipment."

"This wasn't anybody's; it was Yvonne's."

"Why am I not surprised?"

"There's just one thing, Dan. When I looked at the initials on the invoices—"

"You looked at the initials?"

"Doing a little night duty," Rusty said with an impish grin. "When I checked the initials, I compared them to other initials. It's a pretty good match, but still . . . Well, here, look for yourself." Rusty produced two documents from his pocket.

The first was an invoice and packing slip for the home furnishings department. The invoice initials were his; he remembered signing it because it was for kitchen gadgets and he thought some of the items were very funny. The packing slip had been initialed by Jen. The second, a blouse order from Ship 'n Shore, he couldn't recall at all. The invoice bore his initials, and the packing slip had been initialed by Yvonne.

"Rusty, this is signed with my pen. But it doesn't look exactly like my writing."

"How do you know it's your pen?"

"Imported ink." Dan pointed at his initials.

"Marie gave the pen to me for Christmas. The ink is maroon. I remember she said it was so much more refined than red. I keep it on my desk, in a pen holder with my name on the brass plate."

"Who has access to your desk?"

"Only Debbie," Dan answered.

"Debbie?"

"My secretary. Well, she's not just my secretary, she's Dorthea's too."

"That's interesting."

"She works down in my office area until Dorthea needs her for something."

"Then she goes up to Halloran's office?"

"Yeah, or on errands, taking her dry cleaning to and from the cleaners, delivering packages, etcetera."

"She sits right there at your office door, seeing everyone who comes in, taking every phone call before they come to you, watching everything you do, and knowing every place you go?"

"Just about."

"Does she know you're here with me?"

"No. I've been very careful to be vague these last few weeks."

"Good, then I have just one more thing to tell you for now."

Dan noticed Rusty's change of mood. His friend knitted his eyebrows together and began to twirl the wrapping from his straw between his fingers.

"I have reason—not *proof*, mind you, but *reason*—to believe that Jen could be in more danger than we thought."

"Rusty, don't say this unless you have very *good* reason."

"Dan, look, I didn't want to think that . . ." Rusty hesitated. Dan looked at his longtime friend across the table.

"Don't beat around the bush about this, Rusty. Just come right out and say it."

"I have been thinking about Rochelle. She got too close and was hit by a car. Frances has been threatened, as well."

"You didn't tell me about that."

"She wasn't able to prove anything, but she has had a couple of close calls and has suspected that someone was following her, too. She dismissed it as harassment, not a real threat."

"How does any of this make you think that Jen is in danger?"

"I've been thinking about Marie," Rusty said.

"Marie?" Dan's eyes widened, and he sat perfectly still.

"Marie." Rusty leaned toward his friend. "I have been wondering if—well, if her death might have been accidental, but not the accident."

Dan couldn't believe what he was hearing. His heart felt like it had leapt into the lower part of his throat and threatened to choke him.

"I know it causes you pain, Dan, to even think of such a thing. Really, I could be all wrong. It's just a thought. I've wondered about it for a long time. What if Marie was pulled from the car, instead of thrown? What if she was hit over the head . . . ?"

"You mean by a person?"

"Yes, Dan, I'm afraid I do."

"Then Jen could be—"

"That's my conclusion." Rusty reached for his wallet. "What's more, Elizabeth Simms agrees with me."

"Put your money away, Rusty, it's no good here. Unfortunately, your ideas are. Let's get out of here."

"Where to?"

"To get Jen out of town." Dan Miller threw a twenty-dollar

bill on the table and swung himself to a standing position. "Jen and Joy. It's time I protected them both."

As soon as they were seated in Dan's car, Rusty looked at Dan. "Where will you take them?"

"To the country, I guess. To farm country."

"Your folks?"

Dan nodded. "There's plenty of room for Jen and Joy. Mom and my sister will love having the both of them. Jen with her bad ankle, and Joy with her spots."

Rusty liked the way Dan decisively put his plan into action.

Dan continued.

"It's two-thirty now. I can have them there by ten. I'll get them on the road then call from a pay phone somewhere north of here."

"What do you want me to do?"

"You get Jen while I go get Joy. Have her pack and tell her it could be for a week or more."

"What about school? She won't want to miss school."

Dan pulled up beside Rusty's old Plymouth. "You handle that with her, Russ. Don't take no for an answer. I'll call Beth and have her meet you at Jen's. I want all three of you to meet me at the downtown Avis lot in an hour and fifteen minutes."

The two men then looked at a map, and Dan showed Rusty the route to the farm. As Rusty jumped out and grabbed the door handle on his old car, he said, "See you in an hour and fifteen at Avis." Dan nodded and pulled his car into traffic.

He was about to get some answers, he was certain of that. In addition, he was about to get Jen and Joy together, but first he had to get them to a safe place.

On his way to get Joy, he stopped at Avis and arranged to rent a Lincoln. While the clerk was processing the paperwork, he called Beth. She wasn't in her office, the secretary said, but somewhere on the floor. "No nothing urgent, I'll call her later." He hung up the phone and reached in his pocket, but before he put another dime in the pay phone he asked the clerk behind the desk to take the receiver and ask for fine jewelry when the store operator answered. "Good. Now ask for Megan. Thanks." The clerk walked away looking at him and shrugged as she returned to the counter to finish her paperwork on his rental car.

"Megan, it's me, Dan. I didn't want anyone to know I was calling. Listen, Megan, I need to get hold of Elizabeth. She's not in her office."

"She's over in accessories talking to McHenry," Megan told him.

"Can you get a message to her?"

"Sure. What's going on?"

"Rusty will tell you later. Right now, tell Beth I need her to meet Rusty at Jen's in fifteen minutes."

"Yes, ma'am, I'll put it behind the register until closing. If you haven't come in by then, we'll have to put it back in stock," Megan said.

"Someone listening, Megan?"

"Yes, ma'am, I know you. Yes, it will be right here next to the phone when you come in."

"Can you get away to get to Beth?"

"Don't worry, ma'am, I'm happy to do it for you."

"Thanks, Megan. You're the greatest," Dan told her.

"You're welcome, ma'am. Thank you for choosing Halloran's."

"I'll be back in an hour," Dan called over his shoulder on his way out of the rental agency. "Have her ready to go."

CHAPTER TWENTY-TWO

*A*ll I had to say was 'go see Grandma Miller.' She was thrilled to get out of the house," Dan said to Rusty as they met at the Avis lot. "I didn't say anything to the household staff except that I thought I might keep her overnight at my apartment."

"Where was Mrs. Halloran?" Beth wanted to know.

"Wasn't she at the store?" asked Rusty.

"No, I checked," Beth pulled her coat closer around her. "Goodness, I was hoping for spring to come along here pretty soon."

"This is her day to go to the hairdresser, spend the afternoon with her bridge club. She probably won't be home for dinner," Dan explained.

"That means she's out here somewhere on the streets," Rusty looked around. "She's got eyes everywhere, Dan. You better get going."

"Look, Russ, you drive my car back to my apartment. Park it in my regular place in the garage and then go upstairs and pack a few things for me. I want to be ready to go right back to the farm if things get unsettled here again."

Beth looked at Rusty then at Dan. "How about if I drive your old jalopy," she suggested to Rusty, "follow you there, and help you find the things Dan will need. I don't trust you to include all the essentials."

"Thanks. I will need help with that, I'm sure." Rusty laughed and poked gently at Beth's arm.

"Okay, I'll call you at your place tonight around ten-thirty or so," Dan told Rusty. "I can't call my apartment, the phone is tapped."

"Tapped? You sure?"

"There's clicking sounds on the line. I don't want to take a chance."

"Okay, Dan. Let's get these girls up to Grandma's." Rusty patted the Lincoln's fender.

Dan slid behind the wheel and looked at the pitifully spotted face of his little girl, then over to Jen as she fussed with the pillows she brought to prop up her foot as best she could.

"I'm hungry, Daddy," Joy said as they rolled around the corner of the first intersection.

"You are? That's wonderful! You haven't been hungry for a few days. In one hour I promise we'll get something to eat." Dan checked his watch. *Three-forty-five—we'll be there by ten if we don't stop too much.* He looked at his pouting daughter. *Or ten-thirty,* he thought.

"I'm hungry now," Joy said insistently.

"You'll just have to wait. See the clock there in the dash-board? When the big hand goes all the way around and the little hand passes the four, we'll stop and eat." Dan steered the car in and out of city traffic and headed for the freeway.

"That long? I can't wait that long. I want to eat sooner," Joy insisted.

"I'm sorry Joy, you'll just have to wait."

Jen jumped when Joy let out a loud wail and then suddenly screamed. "I want to eat! I want to eat!"

Dan tried to ignore the crying child and shot Jen a look of distress. She almost laughed out loud, but she was disgusted with Joy. This was not going to be an easy trip; this was not an easy child!

"Want some gum?" Jen opened her purse and took out a package of Juicy Fruit.

"I'm not allowed."

"Not allowed?"

"Grandmother says little ladies don't chew gum," the little girl explained.

"Oh, I see." Jen put the small package back and snapped her purse shut.

Joy grabbed for the purse and said, "But I want some gum."

"Okay," Jen opened the purse and handed her the package.

Unwrapping the gum took some time and kept Joy busy and quiet, to the relief of the two adults with her.

Finally, Joy put the gum in her mouth. Jen was anticipating what to do with her next. As soon as she began to squirm again, Jen showed her how to separate the foil from the paper of the gum wrapper. Then she got out a penny and pressed the foil on to it gently, showing Joy how to make an impression of the penny with her thumb against the foil. For several miles Jen entertained Joy with games she remembered from her childhood. She found pencil and paper in her purse and helped Joy write her name. She connected dots into squares and played tic-tac-toe. Finally Dan announced that the little hand had passed the four and it was time to eat.

"Yea!" Joy yelled in glee. "I want a hang-a-ber!"

"Okay, a hang-a-ber it is."

Getting out of the car, Joy turned around and spit her gum out on the leather upholstery. "Joy," Jen said, "little ladies don't spit out their gum. They wrap it carefully in the paper it came in."

"You do it," Joy said and slammed the car door. Jen

carefully picked up the gum and wrapped it in the paper. *Spanking,* she thought. *This child needs a good spanking.*

Jen carefully stood on her bad foot, and Dan came to help her.

"I want you to walk with me, Daddy." Joy ran around the car and Dan and Jen yelled at her at the same time.

"Joy!" They looked at each other in shock.

"You come here this instant!" Dan said gruffly. "Take my hand and don't let go." He reached out to support Jen with his arm around her waist. Jen loved being this close to him, but she wasn't sure she liked the idea of Joy being on the other side.

Within an hour they were once again traveling toward Dan's parent's. Crossing the state line, Jen noticed Joy leaning toward her, almost asleep. "Want to lay down, Joy?"

"I want my bed."

"I can make you a bed in the back seat if you'd like."

"You can?"

"If you want."

"Okay." Jen ducked as Joy scrambled over the seat and fell in the back laughing as she went. "Did you see me jump, Daddy?"

"I sure did," Dan said frowning at Jen.

Jen ignored him and turned in the seat to put one of her pillows under Joy's head and spread her own coat over her. Dan reached for the heater control, "You cold?"

"Not yet," Jen said. "There, how's that?" she asked Joy. She knelt over the seat to tuck Joy in. She brushed Joy's hair away from her face and the little girl pulled away from her touch. Jen just watched her for a moment, and soon the car's motor had lulled the child off to sleep.

Jen turned back around, and Dan encircled her in his free arm, pulling her closer to him. Jen felt the warmth of his body and realized that she was a little chilled without her coat. She let herself relax against him, and soon she too was asleep, her sore foot propped up on the seat beside her.

"Jen?" Dan whispered into her hair, "Can you wake up?" Jen felt his light kiss against her head. "We're here."

Jen straightened up and saw the large farmhouse immediately in front of the car. She quickly took in the size of the enormous porch and the wide shutters at every window. She could see a vapor light off in the distance next to a barn, and a light burned in an upstairs window.

"I hope they're still awake," Dan said straining his gaze toward the upstairs window.

"Didn't you call?"

"No, you were sleeping, Joy was asleep, and I was afraid that if we stopped she'd wake up." Dan glanced at the sleeping child. "As you probably noticed, she's adorable—when she's asleep."

A porch light came on, illuminating the entire front of the house and flooding the car as well. "Hal-loo!"

"It's me, Dad," Dan called from the car. "Got room for some tired travelers?"

"Well, mercy, if it isn't Dan. Come here, Mother," he called back into the house. "We've got company. Dan's here."

"Dan? Well, what a surprise." Mrs. Miller came wrapping a robe around her ample middle. "Who's this with you, my little Joy-Bell?" Bess Miller opened the door and swept the half-sleeping child into her strong arms. "And what's this? Spots?" Kissing her granddaughter's forehead, she walked quickly into the house. Bess took Joy upstairs and quickly tucked her into the small daybed she kept ready for visiting grandchildren.

Dan came around to Jen's side. Pulling her coat from the back seat, he wrapped it around her and helped her to her feet. When George Miller saw her limp, he too came to her side. "You hurt, girl?"

"I sprained my ankle," Jen said. Dan squeezed her waist ever so slightly. "I am sorry to be such a bother."

"Well, you know what we do with a horse when they pull up lame, don't you?"

"I've heard you shoot 'em," Jen said. Dan's father laughed. He helped her toward the huge kitchen and pulled out a chair from the table for her and brought another for her foot.

"Well, we don't always shoot 'em." George winked at Dan. "Not if they're pretty ones with curly red manes." Jen self-consciously reached with one hand to tame her hair.

"How's the foot?" Dan asked.

"Hurts. Feels better to hold it up, that's for sure."

Bess motioned toward the ceiling. "She's all snug for the night. We'll not hear a word from her until morning. Let me see what's the matter here." Jen shuddered as Bess reached for her ankle. "It's a mite swollen, my dear. How'd this happen?"

"I turned it the other night coming out of school. On the sidewalk."

"School? You brought us a schoolgirl, Danny?"

Dan gave his father a warning look. "Jen, I'd like to formally introduce my parents. George and Bess Miller, this is Jennifer Whipple. Jen is a second-year student at the Chicago School of Interior Design. She's supposed to graduate in about six weeks."

"Supposed to?" Bess scowled at Dan. "And what, pray tell, could keep her from graduating?"

"Well, it's a long story. But I assure you, it will not stop her from graduating." Dan pulled up a chair beside Jen, easily resting his arm across the back. Bess stood and pulled the belt of her chenille robe a little tighter.

"Then I'd better make some coffee. You two hungry? There's some ham and biscuits left from supper." Then without waiting for an answer, she turned to the cupboards and started laying out a little "snack," which looked like a banquet to Jen.

When Dan had finished his story and a good-sized helping of Bess's homemade biscuits and apple butter, he drained his coffee cup and leaned back in his chair.

"Put that chair down, Danny." Mrs. Miller scolded easily, "I can see that what I said all along is coming true."

"Now, Mother," George Miller warned his wife, "no sense harping on that now. Our boy's got troubles enough without an 'I told you so' from you."

"Just the same, she's up to no good. I've always known it and have always said so." Bess Miller laid a cloth wrung out in ice water across Jen's painful ankle.

"So, Jen and the baby need to stay here for a while." George Miller shifted in his chair.

"Well, Dad, they can't very well manage themselves with Jen's foot and Joy's chicken pox, can they?"

"Mama loves someone to look after, Jennifer. If you were to try do something on purpose to get on her good side, you couldn't have picked a better way to do it."

"Go on." Bess hit playfully at her husband.

"It's okay then?" Dan searched the faces of his parents.

"Of course it's okay." Bess turned to her son in seriousness, "But what about you? How long can you stay?"

"I'll catch a few hours sleep, but I need to leave in time to be back in Chicago by noon—to be back before Dorthea figures out that I'm gone. And certainly before she figures out what I've done with Joy. I'll have to tell her that I brought Joy here. But that can wait until later tomorrow."

"Let's get this little one to bed then." Bess stood and motioned toward Jen. "Take her upstairs to the front room. I put Joy on the daybed in the sewing room."

Dan stood and lifted Jen into his arms. "I can walk, Dan."

"Probably, but not tonight." He carried her easily up the stairs to the bedroom.

Dan's mother made it up the stairs ahead of them and opened the door of the spare room. She pulled back the homemade quilt and fussed with the window shades. "You might not like the sun streaming into your face bright and early tomorrow." In the bathroom immediately adjacent to the room, she puttered around, putting out clean towels.

George followed with Jen's suitcase and Dan's small bag of essentials. "Where are Joy's things?" Bess said in surprise.

"I didn't have time to bring anything for her. I only had an hour. I thought she might wear some of Tammy's clothes until I can get some things sent up."

"We'll manage. With grandkids and neighbor kids we've more than enough to fix her up. She won't look like little Miss O'Halloran, you can bet on that."

"She'll love it," Dan could only imagine her in clothing from Sears or J.C. Penny's. "Let her wear anything she wants, or you'll hear it for sure."

"We'll see about that, too." Mrs. Miller didn't look like she'd take too much grief from Joy without giving her granddaughter a run for her money. She looked at her husband and son. "You two, scoot, let me get this girl settled into bed. You can come and say good night as soon as she's proper."

Dan followed his father obediently out of the room, and Jen could hear their steps as they descended the stairway. "I really can manage, Mrs. Miller," Jen said. "I don't want to be a bother."

"Nonsense, just look at that ankle. You're no bother at all. And, young lady, by the looks of my son's face when he looks at you, you'd better call me Bess. I think we need to get to know each other." Bess helped Jen dress for bed, and before tucking her in, she leaned over her foot and examined it closer. "You have this thing x-rayed?"

"It's just sprained," Jen hedged.

"That's not what I asked," Mrs. Miller persisted.

"No, but I haven't been able to keep off it like I should. I'm sure it's just sprained."

"Well, tomorrow you'll do nothing but rest. I'll see to that. If it isn't better in a couple of days, we'll—"

"We'll what, Mom?" Dan had reappeared at the door.

"That ankle needs to be seen by a doctor, Dan."

"Please don't make a fuss," Jen begged. "Let's see how it is tomorrow. I've had a pretty long day, and I've been on it quite a bit." Jen felt tears begin to sting her eyes.

Bess reached out to Jen and pulled her into a warm hug. "Listen, sweetheart, I'm sorry. I go overboard sometimes. Don't mind me. I guess you've had quite a time of it lately. You probably need as much rest as that ankle." She stood up and looked directly at Dan. "The attention of a good man wouldn't hurt none either." She said a quick good night and left Dan and Jen alone.

Dan left the door open part way and knelt beside the bed. Jen looked so tired, and he was beginning to feel the activities of the day catch up to him as well. Jen took a deep breath and let it out slowly. Dan pushed a curl away from her cheek and then bent to kiss the place where it had been.

"I'll say good night, too," he said, though he didn't want to. He wanted to stay here with her. He wanted her to know she was safe here. He hoped she was.

"Don't leave without telling me, okay?" Jen's eyes pleaded with him.

"I won't, I couldn't. I wish I could stay. But . . ." Dan stood slowly. "I'll see you in the morning." He bent over and left a brief, light kiss on her lips before he turned and walked out the door, shutting it quietly behind him.

CHAPTER TWENTY-THREE

*B*efore it was light, Jen was roused by Dan's kiss on her forehead. She stretched and turned toward him, making him want to gather her in his arms and hold her. Instead he sat on the edge of the large bed and took one of her hands and pressed it to his lips.

"You leaving?" Jen realized he was already dressed and that she could smell coffee brewing downstairs.

"I'm on my way," Dan said. "I talked to Rusty last night after you went to bed. They have been working 'round the clock. Beth stayed at my apartment to make it appear as though I was home. The phone rang a few times, but she didn't answer it. I'm hoping this doesn't drag out too long, but I feel better about your being here."

"What about school? I only have a few weeks left."

"What will missing a week do, Jen?" Dan asked.

"Not much, really. Most of what I was supposed to finish is already done. I have a few sketches to do, some before-and-after stuff. If I can lay my hands on a layout pad I'll be okay."

"Dad would be glad to pick up whatever you need in town. He goes in a couple times a week. I'm sure there's an art supply store—check the phone book. It would be better if you called ahead and talked to them yourself so you can get exactly what you want. I'll leave some money with Mom."

"Dan?" Jen looked suddenly thoughtful, and he resisted the urge to kiss her. He didn't answer, but as he looked into her warm bluish eyes, she continued. "I want you to be careful. This whole thing seems so overwhelming and dangerous. Mrs. Halloran seems so rich and powerful. She scares me, Dan. She really does."

"She's not rich, remember? Joy is."

"Oh yeah, Joy." Jen's face furrowed with the thought of the five-year-old.

"What do you think of my daughter?"

"Don't ask me this morning, Dan, wait until you get back."

"That bad, huh?" Dan grinned playfully.

Pretty bad, Jen thought. She chose her words carefully. "I think she needs . . ."

"A strong hand, I know."

"I was thinking more of a paddle." Jen said it softly, wondering what his reaction would be.

"My mother agrees with you. She won't put up with anything from Joy—Dad either. She's like a different child whenever we leave here. Don't you put up with anything either. I mean it. If you can't handle her, let Mom know. She'll straighten her out."

"What about you?" Jen asked.

Dan seemed surprised. "Me?"

"Yeah. Why should your mother have to do it?"

"It's pretty complicated, Jen. Can we talk about it when I get back?"

"If I survive—you know, my ankle and all," Jen teased.

"Yeah, right." Dan smiled at the young woman he loved so much. "Listen, you. Don't you think you'll get away with anything either. Mom can keep you in line too."

"I have that same feeling." Jen liked Dan's parents; they

were so different from what she expected. Yet when she saw the three of them together, they fit comfortably.

"I have to go." Dan said turning a little toward her. "I wish I could stay and show you around. Maybe later."

"Do you know when you'll be back?"

"No. I won't be away any longer than necessary, I guarantee you that." Nothing in the city could compare with the importance of what he had right here.

Jen pushed herself to a sitting position and reached for her tousled hair. Dan leaned toward her, encircled her in his arms, and kissed her tenderly. She returned his kiss, wrapping her arms around his neck. Hesitantly, he pulled away. "Better go," he said softly and stood. He turned in the doorway and said simply, "See ya."

"I'll be right here when you get back."

"You better be, I'll tell Mom to make sure." He winked at her, then walked down the stairs and out the front door. Jen heard the car's engine begin to purr and the crush of the gravel beneath the tires as he left the yard.

"Oh, my gosh," Jen said aloud, "I've fallen in love. Oh, no! This doesn't fit into my plans at all!" She hit the pillow with her fist, buried her face in it, and began to cry, releasing pent-up emotions that suddenly refused to be contained any longer.

After a restless night, Rusty was up early, watching the clock for Dan's anticipated return. At nine o'clock he met Elizabeth Simms and Bobby Moore for breakfast. He couldn't help but laugh at the team he found himself working with.

Elizabeth was in her early fifties, unassuming and warm—warm, that is, unless she was dealing with a shoplifter or an unruly employee. Bobby Moore, just over twenty-five, he guessed, was a studious-looking guy who wore corduroy pants and a letter sweater. Because carrying a couple of books made him look like a college sophomore, Bobby was a perfect private investigator. The three of them had been working nonstop to put together the Dorthea Halloran story.

"I figure she's still out for the money." Bobby drank orange juice while he waited for his pancakes and sausage to arrive.

Beth sipped her cup of coffee, "And revenge. Don't forget revenge. That husband of hers was a real ladies' man. Frances' aunt even had a brief—well, shall we say 'relationship'—with Halloran himself."

Peggy McKnight had worked for two days turning up questionable invoices and shipping records. She had noticed them as they came through for filing and began to make mental notes of where to find things should she ever be asked—by the right people, of course.

"That girl's a wonder," Rusty said, "She's kept this all to herself until one day out of the blue, somebody asked her the right questions.

"Think of working for years, taking the kind of abuse dished out to her by those who considered her too dense to know what was going on. It must be pretty sweet to finally feel like it's paying off." Rusty reached for the salt.

"Don't you think you should taste that before you cover it with salt?" Beth asked.

"You sound like my mother," Rusty quipped.

"You need a mother," Beth said.

"You'd make a good one."

"How about calling the lawyer again? He said he'd be working late on getting the answers we need." Bobby was already hacking away at his pancakes and slathering them with butter and syrup.

"I told him we'd call by ten. It's almost that now." Rusty

said. "Dan said he'd be back by noon. He's supposed to check in with Megan at the store. I left a message with her for him to meet us as soon as possible at Mr. Piper's office."

"Do you think Mrs. Halloran suspects anything?" Rusty directed the question at Beth.

"I'm not sure. The theft sure hasn't slowed down any; if anything it's getting worse."

"How's that?" Bobby asked.

"A couple of manufacturers' reps were in to see Dan last week, and he turned them over to me. I talked to both of them for quite a while." Beth leaned back in the booth.

"Why didn't you say anything to us?" Rusty sopped up the runny egg yolk with a piece of his toast.

"I wasn't sure of the connection. But listen to this. Ship 'n Shore, a blouse company, has been sending us shipments that their rep insists are never displayed. He's been a little upset that his merchandise isn't being shown well at Halloran's. However, when we looked up the records, we found his shipments were on a markdown list—you know, put on sale—without ever being put on the floor."

"How's that work?"

"It's a bookkeeping thing. When you have merchandise so long and can't move it, you can either return it to the supplier, and pay a restocking fee, or you can discount it below cost and sell it to another supplier for whatever you can get for it. It comes out as a loss, and you absorb it in your regular profit margin."

"You mean there's a market for sale merchandise you can't even get rid of at the sale price?"

"You bet. It's not uncommon for a business to stock only overstock merchandise they have picked up for a song. They can get it so cheap they can sell it far below retail price and still make money." Beth swallowed the last of her coffee before holding the cup out for the waitress to refill.

"Is that what Dorthea Halloran's doing?"

"I'm not sure yet." Beth fished in her purse for her wallet. "We'll let you know as soon as we figure it out. Peggy has access to the records, but she can only work on them when Yvonne or Halloran are occupied somewhere else."

"We've got two hours before we can expect to hear from Dan," Rusty said. "Bobby, anybody at Halloran's recognize you yet?"

"Not yet, except for Meg of course."

"Good," Rusty began to lay out the morning's plans. "I want you to do a little snooping in Jeffers' department. See if you can pick up any strange things going on there, okay?" Bobby nodded.

"Beth, what about you? You think you can look around Minnie's desk without her knowing?"

"I can try. You really think she's involved?" Beth had wondered about the security office secretary and had been cautious around her.

"I can't tell yet. But someone is tipping people off to your whereabouts. Ever try leaving misdirections?"

"Worth a try. I'll need some help on this one."

"Peggy ever work the switchboard?"

"On occasion. It's right behind her office. Only a glass partition separates them."

"The next time she's on, have her page you. Go to a pay phone and call the store's number and then figure out some way to give Minnie some information that she wouldn't know any other way. Have Peggy watch her line and see who she calls."

"That won't be hard to do. What about you? How are you planning to spend the morning?"

"Napping," Rusty laughed. "No really, I need to move Dan's car, and I want to check out the shipping dock at the store. I want another word with Frances too. I guess I need to go shopping."

Rusty paid for breakfast, reminding Beth that he was on an expense account, and the three left to complete their assigned tasks before Dan Miller got back from his father's farm.

Heading for the city, Dan's heart became heavier the closer he got. He had always mistrusted his mother-in-law. He even disliked her. Looking back, he could see that she took advantage of his grief over losing Marie to manipulate him into leaving Joy with her and her household staff. He regretted surrendering his responsibility for his little daughter. She was Dorthea's granddaughter, however, and he had been in so much pain. Pain that meeting Jen was forcing him face once and for all.

He was beginning to see that part of the pain of losing Marie wasn't because of what he had with her but because of what was missing in their relationship. He grieved over what they didn't have as much as he did over losing what they did. He wouldn't make that mistake again. With Jen there was a whole new chance for happiness and fulfillment.

He remembered Jen's soft red hair spilling everywhere in unruly curls as she slept against his shoulder in the car. He knew that a life together could be wonderful. Now to convince Jen of that. He was almost glad she had an injury; it forced her to stay with his mother. He hoped he would be able to get back to her at least by the weekend.

But first, this unpleasant business. The city skyline loomed in front of him. He glanced at his watch—not quite noon. He was right on time, and Dorthea's control over his life and Joy's inheritance was coming to an end.

CHAPTER TWENTY-FOUR

*J*en managed to hobble to the bathroom and into the shower. The hot water felt good as it washed over her body. Her ankle throbbed when she stood, making her more than willing to stay in bed. From her room she could hear the activity of the house below.

"Where's my daddy?" Joy whined.

"He went back to the city, baby," George Miller said. "He left you here with us for a day or two. Isn't that going to be fun?"

"I want my daddy!" she shouted.

"He'll be back in a couple of days." Bess put pancakes on the plate in front of the child. "Look here who's smiling at you."

Joy examined the pancakes and found Bess had managed to cook smiling faces in them. She wrinkled her nose, "What is *that?*" She poked the pancakes with her fork. "I never saw this before."

"It's a happy face, honey," Bess explained.

"Yuck!"

"Better turn them faces over, Grandma, Joy doesn't want to be happy this morning." He reached for the plate, and Joy quickly grabbed it in defense.

"I didn't say that!" She looked at Bess. "Make him leave

my pancakes alone, Grandma." She picked up her fork and threatened George's hand with it.

"Grandpa," Bess warned, "don't tease her this early in the morning."

"How's our upstairs patient this morning?" George asked.

"I don't know yet. I'm taking her breakfast up now. Want to go with me, Joy?"

"No, I want to play with Grandpa. Do you have a TV? I want to watch TV."

Bess took a tray to Jen and left George to settle Joy's request for TV. She could hear the lively theme song to a Porky Pig cartoon as she approached Jen's door.

"Come in," Jen said in response to Bess's light knock.

"Good morning. Did you sleep okay?" Bess asked.

"I did, I really did, thank you. It is certainly quiet out here. I almost couldn't go to sleep because it is so quiet."

"It's quiet until Barney decides to chase a raccoon, then the whole county is awake," Bess laughed. "Here's some breakfast. I hope you're hungry."

Jen put her hand across her stomach. "You know, I believe I am." She hadn't realized it before.

"How's the foot?"

"As long as I keep it up, it doesn't feel too bad. I could begin to feel it, though, when I showered."

"Then it's bed rest for you today. I'll bring you some magazines and a radio to keep you company." Bess began to straighten Jen's covers even though she had hardly moved the night before.

Rest? Jen would gladly stay in bed and keep her foot elevated on a pillow, but with all that was going on, she could hardly rest.

"Dad's going into town. Is there anything he can get for you?" Bess offered.

"Yes, there is. I need a Biofang layout pad or some drafting paper. Let me write it down. Is there an art supply store?"

"Sure, Benny's Art Supply. He knows where it is."

Jen wrote her list. She would need a number four pencil or two, an art gum eraser, and the layout pad. She had brought a tote bag with her books and notes in it and grabbed her small T-square at the last minute. She could work on her assignment after all.

While Jen made her list, Bess produced a couple of *Ladies' Home Journals*, the newest issue of *Better Homes and Gardens*, and a small radio. "We get pretty good reception out here, one or two city stations and WCCO from Minneapolis," she said. She set it on the small painted table beside Jen's bed and took her list to George.

Jen propped herself up in a more comfortable position and turned the dial to a Chicago station.

"It will finally reach a springlike fifty degrees here in Chicago today, but don't forget your umbrella, we have a 60 percent chance of rain." Jen glanced at the bright white clouds outside her window. It wouldn't be raining here, wherever here was. Suddenly she felt a little lost and disoriented. She had no idea where she was. Somewhere in the middle of Iowa, driving distance from Ames, but in which direction? Upstairs in a house she assumed faced east, with strangers Dan Miller called family. And Joy, a completely spoiled five-year-old who could become a permanent fixture in her life—a thought she was totally unprepared for.

"Today, Chicago's mayor announced . . ." the radio announcer droned on.

Chicago. Not a place she had ever called home, and yet . . . she tried to force her thoughts to the magazine in her hand, but they refused to stay there. They were with the young executive who was driving a rented luxury car headed toward the city. It was not yet ten o'clock—by noon, he had said, he had to be back by noon.

Rusty paced back and forth while Bobby Moore watched him. Jen's small apartment had become their informal meeting place, sort of their unofficial headquarters. Megan had gone to work and promised to call them with the information Peggy McKnight was looking for just as soon as she heard anything. She was going to use a different pay phone each time she called.

"This really puts a funny slant on things, wouldn't you say?" Rusty stopped pacing just long enough to ask the question.

"Piper said it was true. He wasn't supposed to ever reveal the information, according to the will, unless Dorthea Halloran broke her agreement."

Jonathan Piper, a full partner at Jensen, Piper, and Reynolds had been handed the client's file when the elderly Mr. Jensen retired. He had handled the O'Halloran family's legal affairs for several years as had his father before him.

"Tell me again, how did he find this?"

"I went to see him, day before yesterday, to ask if there had ever been any lawsuits filed by a disgruntled employee against Halloran's. I had to wait until yesterday while he searched the files."

"Why would you even be interested?" Rusty wanted to cover all the bases, but this one he had overlooked. Bobby was a curious man, and this time it had paid off—he struck gold.

"I thought we might uncover a motive behind the missing merchandise. If there was a sour employee, maybe someone who kept their job but lost their case, or someone who settled out of court, I don't know. I was mainly just fishing.

"Piper called me and told me to meet him for coffee. He had some other business at the courthouse, so we met later. That's when he laid the papers on me."

"Dorthea met Mr. Halloran while working at the store." Rusty began to string all the facts together to see if there was a viable string to hold them all together. "Then she set about to trap him . . ."

"Now hold on. We don't know that she tried to trap him. We only know he was quite a bit older, ten years approximately, and she agreed before the marriage—I have a copy of the contract—to bear him at least four children, barring any physical complications or limitations, and she agreed to be examined by a doctor if requested."

"He wanted children, no doubt about it," Rusty said.

"And she agreed to give them to him." Bobby poured himself a cup of coffee and started picking a few dead leaves off of Jen's houseplants. He stuck his finger in the dry dirt around one of the ivy plants and reached for a glass of water. Rusty watched his friend check all the other plants before rotating them each a half turn. "For better light," Bobby said.

"Then what happened?" Rusty asked.

"Dorthea knew she couldn't have children when she signed the agreement," Bobby continued. "She brought him falsely certified medical information, and they got married."

"So, then," Rusty picked up the story at that point, "when he realized she wasn't going to have any children, he didn't divorce her because by that time she would have had a claim to Halloran's. Or at least a large settlement."

"Instead, he went about getting a child somewhere and bringing it home to Dorthea, for *adoption*."

Rusty let out a low whistle. "Boy, when you're rich, you don't have to break the rules, you can just rewrite them. Okay, if he adopted Marie, where'd he get her?" Rusty wondered aloud.

"That's what Piper is trying to find out. Adoption records are sealed—it's hard to crack them open. But hey, we're still operating on O'Halloran money. Let's see if it's still good." Bobby looked at his watch. "Dan should be getting here soon. I hope he keeps that rented car. His shouldn't be seen here."

Rusty peeked out the apartment window to see the man in the gray overcoat still at his post across the street. "He's still there; he doesn't have a clue that Jen's gone." He turned from the window. "He'll be good and wet before this day's over. It's starting to drizzle." Just then the phone rang, and Rusty picked it up.

"Hey, Mr. Piper. What have you got?" Rusty listened as Bobby watched with interest. "No kidding?"

Bobby heard steps approaching Jen's door, and he knew it was Dan when he heard the key in the lock. "Just a minute, Dan," he called. "The chain is on."

The two men exchanged greetings just as Rusty hung up the phone.

"What's up?" Dan looked at the two men he had hired to help him solve this case. "Anything happen while I was gone?"

"We're due in Piper's office in half an hour. Come on, Dan, we'll fill you in on the way." Rusty reached for his coat.

"Something new?" Bobby asked.

"Piper says it will blow our socks off."

"What's he got?" Dan was totally confused and acutely curious.

"Skeletons," Rusty smiled at Dan, "O'Halloran skeletons.

And they're about to come out of their closets. Let's get there in time to open the door."

Jen looked at the little electric alarm clock on the dresser; it was almost twelve-thirty. Dan would certainly be in Chicago by now. *I hope he is making progress,* she thought. She let her mind recall the tender kiss they shared early that morning and could feel her heart beat faster. *I want you to come back soon, Dan,* she said silently.

She heard loud voices below but couldn't make out what they were saying. Then she heard Mrs. Miller approach the stairway with a screaming Joy in tow—literally. By the time they reached the top of the stairway, Joy was wailing. Bess picked up the child and carried her to the little sewing room, shutting the door behind them. Eventually, Bess left her granddaughter on the cot, moaning and screaming for Dan.

Bess Miller stuck her head in Jen's room. "Sorry," she said as she shrugged her shoulders, "but somebody's got to take that child in hand before she is ruined completely." Jen turned the radio up a little louder, hoping to drown out the temper tantrum coming through the walls. As Bess shut the door, Jen slid between the covers and pulled the blankets over her head. *Oh, no!* she worried. *What have I gotten myself into?*

A moment ago, she was feeling love for Dan Miller. Now she was furious with him. *If he thinks I am . . .* Her thoughts trailed off.

But Dan wasn't thinking about Jen or Joy at the moment. Instead, Rusty and Jonathan Piper were bombarding him with incredible information he could hardly believe.

CHAPTER TWENTY-FIVE

*L*et me get this straight," Dan Miller stood in front of the lawyer's large desk surveying the papers spread before him. "Marie was Michael O'Halloran's daughter."

"Right."

"But Dorthea was not her mother."

"Right." Mr. Piper looked at his young client. "It seems that Mr. O'Halloran had adoption papers drawn up, but Dorthea refused to sign them. It's indicated by the documentation here. What she probably didn't know at that time is that Marie was Michael's."

"How do you figure that?"

"Because both names are included on the adoption petition. However, the petition is unsigned."

Dan turned away from the desk toward the window, then back again. "Okay. But how does that . . . ?"

"I began to ask myself how an unadopted child could stay in that home and inherit the entire estate. Mrs. O'Halloran would have been the legal heir, not Marie. I presume Mr. Jensen knew all this. However, I did not."

"So you went digging."

"I did. I didn't have to go far. According to the terms of the will, the contents of Mr. O'Halloran's safety deposit box were sent here to be stored in our vault. He didn't want Dorthea finding a way to open it. However, Marie was given the right to open it after she turned twenty-five." Piper picked his way through a stack of legal documents. "Here it is. Marie's birth certificate. Michael O'Halloran is the father, and the mother's name is Cleary. Then here is another document; wouldn't stand up in court, though. A contract for the woman to have the baby and surrender it for adoption." Piper handed Dan the contract.

Dan looked at the document, then passed it without a word to Rusty. "You mean he paid her ten thousand dollars to have his baby?"

"He bought himself a daughter," Piper said simply. "Here's the document that *would* stand up in court. She terminated her parental rights to the child. Took the money and left the country."

"Who knows, she may still be alive." Rusty said. "I wonder what she'd say if she knew all this."

"Dorthea was outwitted. Married him for his money and left to raise a daughter she was certain she'd never have."

"There's more," Piper said holding another document.

"More?" Dan could hardly believe there could be any more.

"A divorce petition. O'Halloran always kept a divorce petition ready to execute at any moment. He obviously threatened her that should she ever cross him, he would divorce her for marriage under false pretenses without batting an eye."

"And she would be out on her ear without a cent." Dan swept his hand across his forehead.

"You got it," Piper said. "Some marriage, huh?"

"Coercion, betrayal, adultery, blackmail . . . All money and no love." Dan thought of his parents and their struggles against the weather, pests that ate their crops, broken machinery, and the death of a baby. He remembered their financial struggles and their prayers of faith. But with all the hard times, he could never remember when they struggled against one another. With all their hardship, they had each other.

"I'd rather have love and no money, myself." His thoughts turned to the tousled redhead he had kissed earlier that morning.

"Well, we certainly have a motive for Dorthea's involvement," Rusty said. "I wonder what Beth has turned up. She was waiting for Megan's call. We might have to talk to Peggy McKnight."

"I need to get to the office, Debbie is probably wondering where I am by now." Dan shook hands with the lawyer. "Keep digging, okay? You never know what else we might find. I had better attend to business, or Joy won't have any business left to inherit." Dan ruefully wondered whether that wouldn't be better.

Jen finally was able to persuade Bess into letting her go downstairs to sit with her leg properly elevated. She didn't like being cooped up. It had been a long time since she had heard the pleasant noises a family made, and she didn't want to miss any of it.

Later in the afternoon, Doreen, Dan's sister, dropped by with a couple loaves of fresh-baked bread and some play clothes for Joy. She hadn't seen her niece in a few months and was happy to see her. Meeting Jen was also on her agenda.

"Let's see that ankle," Doreen said after a few moments of friendly chatter. "I'm an LPN, I could put Mom's fears to rest."

"It's much better this afternoon," Jen said, pulling up her slacks so Doreen could get a better look. "It still really hurts when I keep it down very long."

"You might have a nasty bruise in addition to the sprain. I can see the color coming to the surface. Ice will do the trick if you can stand having a frozen foot." As Doreen gave her advice, the phone rang.

"It's Dan." Bess Miller handed the phone to Jen. "He wants to talk to you."

"Hi," Jen said.

"Hi yourself. How's it going?"

"Your mother is spoiling me rotten. I haven't had this much attention since—"

"I know, she's loving it too."

"How's it going there?" Jen asked.

"It's been quite a day. I'm still at the store. I'm using the pay phone down by the shipping room. It drives Yvonne crazy." Dan checked around to see if anyone was standing near enough to hear him. "Listen, I've had some startling news. The details will have to wait until I come back out to the farm, but we've uncovered a reason why Dorthea would . . . well, would do what she's doing."

"You really think she's behind all this, don't you, Dan?"

"I know it. I also know why, and now all we have to do is figure out how she does it and how to catch her. Rusty and Bobby have some ideas, so I'll leave it to them. I'm not the detective, I have a store to run."

Jen loved the sound of his voice; she felt helpless to do anything about how she felt about him. She was also angry with him about Joy, but that would have to wait. That was something you didn't discuss on the phone. "When do you expect to come back?"

"As soon as possible, and not one minute longer." Dan paused as a customer walked by him. "I have to see Dorthea today and tell her I've taken Joy to Mom's. I'm not ready to tell her you're there, however. I don't know how I'll handle that quite yet."

"I wish this was all over."

"I do too. But then what?" Dan asked.

"What?" Jen responded.

"I'm still interested in having you redecorate my office."
Jen knew Dan was smiling even though she couldn't see
him.

"I'm still not convinced I shouldn't head for home right
after graduation." Jen smiled as well. "I have my expenses
all covered, you know."

"Oh?" Dan's tone was filled with mock surprise.

"Oh, yes. Have you forgotten? Dorthea gave me a nice fat
bonus check. She let me know it was to help me get home."

"You cash it yet?"

"No, it's there in my apartment."

"I wonder if she knew you were at my parents' if she'd
want to up her offer—or stop payment on the check." Dan
was silent again.

"Dan?"

"Yes."

"You're so quiet, I wondered if you were still there."

"I have to get back to work, but I hate to let you off the
phone. I miss not having you here. I can't even begin to
think of you going back to California," Dan told her.

After saying good-bye, Jen hung up the phone and stood
favoring her sore ankle. She turned around to face two
curious women.

"I'm sorry, I didn't mean to be rude."

"You weren't rude, dear." Bess patted the chair where Jen
had been sitting the entire afternoon. "Come get that foot
up. It'll be supper time soon. I'd better get on to the
kitchen. You girls have a nice talk and get acquainted."

"Jen," Doreen began, "how's the foot, really."

"It's just sore. Really, I've told you the truth. I'm a coward
when it comes to pain. If I thought it should be seen by a
doctor, I really would go."

"Okay. Then stay off it will you? You certainly don't have

to worry about inconveniencing Mom; she loves to take care of folks. Joy gives her quite a challenge, though." Doreen looked down at the floor and then back at Jen. "How long have you known Dan?"

"I've known who he is for a couple of years. But we've really just become acquainted in the last few weeks." Jen liked Dan's sister and wanted to confide in someone about her feelings for Dan and how those feelings confused her. She wanted to lean on someone a little older and blurt out how her dreams and goals were being threatened and how sad and afraid that made her. She also wanted someone to explain why those dreams seemed unimportant when she saw Dan or talked to him. She was in danger of losing not only her heart, but her whole self. Ever since junior high school she had seen herself in a career—certainly she would have to realize those goals before she could consider marriage and family. Yet here in the comfort and warmth of Dan's family, the dreams of a career seemed flat and without real purpose.

"Oh, oh, here comes Dad with Joy following right behind him." Doreen stood by the living room window. She could see George Miller coming from the barn with Joy. Barney followed as close to Joy as he could, and she petted him just enough to keep him nearby. As George approached the back door, Doreen turned to Jen.

"Get ready." She walked to the kitchen door. "She'll try to get Dad to let Barney in the house."

Doreen was right. Jen heard Joy's insistence escalate into a full-blown temper tantrum.

"Dad will only take so much," Doreen said. "She better calm down, or she'll end up with her bottom swatted."

"She needs it," Jen said quietly.

Doreen smiled at Jen. "I knew I liked you."

"She's selling it right out the back door," Beth told Dan over TV dinners and soda pop.

"You sure?" Dan looked back and forth between Rusty and Beth. Megan stood a little distance behind with Bobby Moore.

"Peggy McKnight has really taken this on as a project. She has turned up documents all but buried in the files," Beth said.

"I thought maybe she was getting the merchandise out somehow and disposing of it somewhere else. I thought she might even have opened shop in another city," Dan said.

"I thought so too, but as I examined the paperwork, I realized she is selling it right out of the store. At a fabulous discount, of course." Beth drained her orange soda.

"All marked down like sale merchandise, except it was never on the floor at full price. Then it's adjusted for in the inventory as unsalable, unreturnable merchandise and then sold—probably to a clearance house of some sort. You know, like an overstock dealer," Beth explained.

"I can't believe it," Megan said. "How could someone rob from their own business?"

"It's just like embezzling, Meg," Beth turned to look at the lovely young woman standing behind her.

"Not just like embezzling," Rusty corrected, "it is embezzling."

"I'd sure like a look-see in her office," Rusty said.

"She keeps it locked up tight." Dan knew that from the day she had the penthouse offices completed, she had kept the keys from him.

"What about Mike?" Bobby asked from his place in the corner of the small kitchen.

"Mike?" Rusty asked.

"He works in the housewares department. He's a locksmith among other things. He makes keys, changes locks—stuff like that," Megan offered.

"Can he be trusted?"

"I'm pretty sure. He's not much on words, but he doesn't have much use for Dorthea. They both came to work for Mr. O'Halloran about the same time." Dan had made friends with Mike shortly after coming on board following Mr. Halloran's death.

"Could he get us in?"

"Us?" Dan turned in the direction of the question. "You think we're letting you go with us, Megan?" he asked.

"Why not? I've gotten you a lot of information up to now. I bet I'd know what to look for. What do you guys know about filing systems?" Megan argued. "Dorthea is a woman, she'll keep the office like a woman. Come on, you guys need me."

"We've got Beth, thank you." Dan wasn't about to take Megan on such a mission. "You've got to get Jen's things together. She needs some clothes—well, here, I made a list." Dan produced a small piece of paper from his pocket of the things he thought Jen might need. She was supposed to graduate in a month and a half, but she still needed to rest her ankle. Someone needed to go to the school and find out how her absence would affect her. "I think you should do that, Megan. Tell them the doctor has ordered her to bed for a few weeks. See if they can let her finish her courses by independent study."

"Let them know that she turned her ankle right outside their doorway. You know, hint that she might have to see a lawyer if they resist," Rusty said as he stood and casually wrapped his arm around Megan's shoulders. She didn't move away from him.

"I'll be glad to take you," Bobby offered.

"She'll be all right alone, Bob," Rusty said. "We need you to go with us to the penthouse."

"How will we keep Dorthea away?" Beth asked the group.

"I have to go tell her I've taken Joy to my Mom's for a few

weeks. I'll drag out the confrontation as long as I can to give you plenty of time."

"We couldn't be ready before tomorrow night," Beth said. "We'll need time to talk to Mike, for Megan to go by Jen's school and to pack a few things. I want you to be able to leave town right afterward, Dan. It's important that we be able to move as quickly as possible."

"Why would I have to go so soon?" Dan asked.

"You might need to move Jen and Joy." Beth's face was dead serious. "We have no idea whether Dorthea's at the top in this, or if she's just a pawn in a larger picture. I don't want to be an alarmist, but we need to be ready, just in case. Better safe than sorry, you know."

Dan thought quickly. "We have an entire network of cousins scattered throughout the state of Iowa and even up into Minnesota. We've got lots of places to send them. I can always call my cousin Ken. He'd help us for sure."

"Okay then, Megan, you will go to work as usual," Rusty began, rehearsing the upcoming day's activities for each person. "Dan, you will do the same. Tonight, though, you need to call the house. Hopefully you will get one of the servants and tell them to leave a message for Dorthea that Joy is with you and you'll talk to Dorthea tomorrow night." Megan poured the group mugs of hot coffee while Rusty continued to outline his plan.

"Bobby, I want you to tag along behind Megan, just to be on the safe side. You-know-who is still posted outside. He may be waiting for her to leave to try to approach Jen. I'm pretty sure he thinks she is still here. Megan, you need to call in sick for Jen, talk to the personnel department just like you would under normal circumstances. Tell them she's asleep, from pain medication or something." Rusty blew on his coffee and paused.

"Beth, how would you feel about recruiting Frances and Peggy for a little filing duty tomorrow night?"

"If Debbie is out of the store and Yvonne is not there, I think it would be a good idea. They certainly know what we're looking for. They could be a big help."

"It looks like all this takes place during regular store hours. It's mostly paperwork, and the shipping was probably done within the normal routine." Dan helped himself to a sugar cookie.

"Beth, how about Minnie?" Bobby asked. Dan looked up from his cup at Bobby, then at Beth, waiting for her answer. "I saw her the other night coming out of a movie with Debbie," Bobby said.

"Is that right?" Beth began to smile.

"What's this?" Dan paused, suspending another cookie in midair.

"Ever since that day when we first questioned Jen, I have been suspecting that Yvonne arrived very conveniently to take over so Jeffers could come upstairs with us. I have been watching her, and I've wondered if she didn't have an inside line to my office."

"You mean she could be involved too?" Dan asked.

"Oh, yes, quite possibly." Beth surveyed the little band of investigators. "I am wondering how Jeffers fits in as well," she added.

"I've wondered about him myself." Megan grabbed a cookie from the package laying in front of Dan.

"And?" Dan asked.

"I think Halloran has something on him."

"Like what?"

"I've heard that he has a thing for gambling. I've also heard that Mrs. Halloran bailed him out of jail one night after he got into a fight over a poker game."

"Jeffers?" Dan couldn't imagine the timid man who

pored over his inventory figures and sales records doing anything without a sheaf of paperwork in his hands.

"I've also heard . . ." Megan poked her cookie in Dan's cup.

"What have you heard, Megan?" Beth was becoming a little impatient.

"Well, it's only gossip of course, but I've heard that Mr. Jeffers has a crush on Jen."

"Oh, really." The thought disgusted Dan.

"He always had her help him with his paperwork, filing, ordering, checking in stock. He found as many excuses as he could for keeping her in the stockroom with him— alone." Megan found the rumors entertaining. "He had sort of a signal he passed with the manager in ladies' shoes. Whenever he and Jen came out of the stockroom together, he would wink in that direction and the shoe department manager would give him a thumbs up."

"Did Jen know this?"

"Jen?" Megan wrapped her arms around her own waist as she laughed. "Jen has been totally oblivious to men the entire time she's been here. She has talked about nothing other than getting back to California the day after graduation. Other men in the store have tried to get her to go out with them, but she's always turned them down. It's because, the rumor mill says, she's involved with Mr. Jeffers."

"You know," Bobby spoke from his place a little distance away from the others, "if Jeffers is sweet on Jen, perhaps it's a weakness we could work on. If he knows she's in trouble, or in danger, maybe, just maybe he would be able to give us some dirt on Halloran."

"Megan?" Dan questioned her with his eyes.

"Well, maybe I could test the waters a bit. I can hint to Mr. Jeffers that she's been hurt. Maybe I'll tell him she was mugged. I can try to get a reaction out of him, anyway," Megan agreed.

Beth sighed. "We certainly have our work cut out for us. I guess I'd better call it a day." She stood to leave. "I wish you didn't have to stay here alone, Megan. I don't like the looks of that man down there. He may be waiting for the lights to go out to come snooping around."

"I wonder if he's found the basement entrance yet." Dan and Rusty had been using the delivery door to the apartment building to avoid being seen.

"He's a pretty lazy guy, if you ask me," Rusty offered. "I think he's just being paid to watch Jen and to let her know she's being watched. He probably thinks she is still here. You'd think Dorthea would spend a little more money and get herself a better snitch."

"Just the same, I wish Megan wasn't alone." Beth had come to admire and care for this brave young woman.

"I think I'll stay," Rusty said with a wink in Megan's direction. "You know, Jen's keys are still missing."

"I think that's a good idea." Bobby walked to the door and examined the locks. "Maybe I'd better camp out here too. You know, just in case there's trouble." Bobby picked up an afghan from off the back of a chair and spread it over himself as he stretched out on the sofa. "You take the first watch, okay, Russ?" Rusty looked at Dan. "Wake me at four," Bobby said.

Dan laughed and steered Beth toward the door. "I'll give you a lift home." Turning to Megan, he said, "We leave you in capable hands, my dear. Call the police if these two get out of hand."

Dan walked across the living room, noticing that here among Jen's things, he could feel her personality, see her touches. Her small apartment seemed so crowded with the five of them there yet so empty without her. He had to get back to her just as soon as he possibly could.

CHAPTER TWENTY-SIX

*A*t supper, Jen sat with Dan's parents and bowed her head while George said the blessing.

"Bless this food, our Father," he prayed. "We are so thankful for the bounty from which you provide for us. Thank you, Lord, for the strength to work the ground and the hands to prepare what only You can cause to grow for our benefit. We ask You for a special covering of protection over Dan, Father. Guide him to the right information, give him Your wisdom when facing decisions. We ask all this in the Name of Jesus, our Lord. Amen."

"Jen," Bess said as she offered her the large soup tureen, "help yourself to one of my special recipes."

Jen wiped away a tear with her gingham napkin. She took off the lid to the tureen and inhaled the aroma of stewed chicken and dumplings. "I'm starved," she said.

"I want peanut butter and jelly," announced Joy.

"Not tonight, dear." Bess dished some of the rich, hot dish on Joy's plate. "Tonight you have Grandma's good cooking."

"I don't like it," Joy pouted, lowering her face below the table's edge.

"Sit up, there," George said as he heaped his plate full. "Take a little bite. You'll see how good your Grandma cooks."

"I don't want it. I want peanut butter and jelly," Joy repeated.

"I guess you'll just go hungry, then." Bess picked up her dish and put in on the counter behind the large table.

"I want my daddy." Joy stuck out her lower lip and began to breathe loudly through her nose.

"In a day or two," Bess said in a nonchalant tone. "You'll need to eat, or you'll be hungry by morning."

"No, I won't."

"Joy," George's voice was sterner than before, "you need to sit up to the table like a good girl and eat your supper, or I will put you to bed right now."

"I hate you!" Joy screamed at George.

"Joy!" Jen was shocked to hear own voice. She had no right to get involved. She immediately looked away and began to eat her own dinner. This child's behavior was certainly something she would discuss with Dan. Or maybe not. Maybe she had best return to Chicago just as soon as it was possible, take her diploma from the Chicago School of Interior Design, and go directly to the airport. She could use Dorthea's money to get away from Dan—as far and as fast as she could.

The delicious food turned to paste in her mouth as her mind suddenly grasped the meaning behind Dorthea's generous check. *So that's it,* Jen realized, barely noticing as George picked up a screaming Joy and carried her up to her room. *Mrs. Halloran didn't give me a bonus. She paid me to get away from Dan.* Jen looked at Bess's curious expression across the table.

"What's the matter, Jen. You look like you just—"

"I just had an idea, Mrs. Miller. I'll work on it later." Jen swallowed hard. "I'll work on it later."

"My dear, please call me Bess." She smiled at Jen. "The only Mrs. Miller I ever knew was my mother-in-law. I decided then I wouldn't ever let any one of my children's friends call me Mrs. Miller." She laughed. "It makes me feel so old."

George rejoined them and said, "She's down for the night, Mother. No sneaking her food or going up to see her. She needs to learn that no matter what she does in *that* house, in *this* house we expect her to behave." He scooped up a generous forkful with delight. "You're a mighty fine cook, my love. Mighty fine."

Jen discovered confusing thoughts and emotions once again crowding in on her. She found herself wishing Dan would call, but she was glad he didn't. She needed time to think. *Why would Dorthea Halloran pay me to stay away from Dan?*

Later, up in her room, she lay in the darkness, listening to the quiet sounds of the farm. Crickets were not out at this time of year, but once in a while she could hear a dog bark in the distance and even a truck on a highway—probably somewhere nearby, she couldn't tell for sure.

Dan Miller, you have complicated my life. I don't know if I love you or hate you for it. The little clock on the nightstand said nine-thirty. She wished Dan would at least call and talk to his parents. She wanted to know what was happening and what he was doing.

"Glad to help out," Mike said to Rusty. "O'Halloran was a good man. We served together in the Pacific right after Pearl Harbor. Before we got home . . . well, I caught a shell. Took me a while to recover. Michael O'Halloran never forgot me. Gave me a job as soon as I could manage. That missus of his, though. She was quite another story." Mike followed Rusty to the stairway. "She partied the whole time he was away. Lots of things were rationed in those days, but that one, she never lacked for nothin'. There was Mr.

O'Halloran, out there with the rest of us, doin' without and riskin' his life, and she was back here livin' high and mighty." Mike set his toolbox on the floor and kneeled to get a better position to work on the lock. "Neglected that little tyke too. My sister told me. She worked in the big house, helped keep it runnin', throwin' parties, entertainin' high society." He poked around in the lock, changing his tools when necessary.

Rusty just listened. *This may be more important than what we find in the files,* he thought.

"My sister wrote to me and told me that most of the women she knew went to work in the factories, war support jobs, you know." Mike paused momentarily and looked at Rusty as if he were old enough to remember.

"She didn't qualify. Couldn't be around the powder or take the hard physical work." *Click, click,* the door opened, and Rusty patted Mike on the back.

"Good work, Mike."

"Yeah, it's been good work, for nigh unto twenty years now. Mr. O'Halloran, Major then, told me to write to my sister and tell her to go see Mrs. O'Halloran. I don't know what he told her, but Mrs. O'Halloran put her on. She felt good too, workin' for an officer and all. Made her feel like she was a part of the war."

"Thanks, Mike. I can't tell you how important this is."

"Don't have to."

"How's that?"

"Mrs. O'Halloran hasn't changed much in all these years. She's still after his money. Too bad. That little girl of his, she's the one who . . . well, it's no matter now. She's gone too. I just hope you find what you're lookin' for."

Rusty scanned the office. Beth, Peggy, and Frances would be here soon. Bobby was watching out for Megan. Dan was at the O'Halloran house. "Hey, Mike, can you open a few more doors?" Every door in Dorthea's royal office suite was locked.

"Sure can. And file cabinets are my specialty—want me to stick around?"

"How dare you, take a sick child out into the air like that!"

Dan watched Dorthea pace back and forth on the luxurious carpet of her expansive living room and blow cigarette smoke into the air over her head.

"She's my daughter. I took her to her grandmother's to recover."

"I'm her grandmother, too!"

"No—" Dan caught himself. It would not be wise to tip his hand just yet. "I know, but my mother is around more. She loves having her, and she loves having someone to watch out for."

"And I don't, I suppose."

"Well," Dan groped for carefully chosen words. "She's a handful on a good day. You've been busy."

"I have the staff to help me, your mother doesn't."

"Dorthea, let it alone. She's my daughter. She may spend most of her time here, but she is still my daughter. I did what I thought best for her."

"Why didn't you tell me?"

"I didn't want to fight with you about it."

"A fight?" She took a long drag on her cigarette. "Dan Miller, if I wanted to fight with you about Joy, it would have started a long time ago."

"I thought it had."

"I'm not getting into this with you, Dan." Dorthea stood and paced in her imported high-heeled shoes. "What did you take with her?"

"Not much, just her pajamas and robe. She had on a play outfit, and of course her coat."

"And what is she wearing?"

"I'm sure my sister found her some play clothes."

"You mean . . . ?" Dorthea could barely stand the thought of Joy wearing anything less than the most fashionable labels.

"I'm sure she's okay."

"She needs her own things. How long do you plan to leave her out there in the sticks?"

"It's not the sticks."

"How long?" Dorthea demanded.

"I don't know for sure. A week, maybe two."

"Elaine!" Dorthea screamed. "Get a suitcase, and help me pack some of Joy's things. At least she'll have her own clothes and a few of her own toys." Turning to Dan, she said, "When are you going out there again?"

"I planned to go for the weekend at least."

"I see." Dorthea decided to change her approach with Dan. "Well, at least you will spend time with your daughter. Goodness knows she sees precious little of you around here. Really, Dan, why do you insist on keeping that tiny little tacky apartment when you could live here with Joy and me?"

"It's not so tiny," Dan said, "and it's not tacky."

"I think it is . . ." Dorthea caught herself in mid-sentence.

"Oh? Have you seen it?"

"Well, no, not really. I drove by once. I wouldn't even get out of my car in that part of town, Dan. How can you even think of taking Joy there?"

"I won't discuss my choice of living quarters with you."

"I see. Elaine!" Dorthea never spoke the names of the household staff, she always screamed them. "I'd better go check up on that stupid girl. She doesn't know the first thing about what a little girl needs. She's never been a mother."

And neither have you, Dan wanted to say. "Wouldn't hurt to check, that's for sure," he managed.

Dan checked his watch as Dorthea disappeared up the stairway. He could hear her scolding poor Elaine. He checked the time. Nine-thirty. His parents went to bed early. He guessed Jen would already be upstairs. Had it only been yesterday morning that he had held her? It seemed like it had been much longer. It had been two long days and would probably be a longer night. But what time he didn't have to spend with Rusty, Dan planned to spend thinking about Jen.

CHAPTER TWENTY-SEVEN

*L*ook at this." Peggy McKnight quickly looked through the files and came up with some bills of sale, shipping receipts, and questionable invoices. "It's my guess some of this merchandise never made it past the shipping room before it was shipped out again."

"Look here." Frances was fingering a personal phone directory. "Lots of familiar names here. I guess we don't have to look far to find out which former employees you need to talk to," she concluded.

Rusty walked around the lavish office. *Excessive,* he thought as he thought of Dan's simple but tasteful working environment. *And not very practical.*

Surveying the shelves, he spotted sculpture and paintings he knew werc probably bought as merchandise but never put on the floor. She never intended them to go on the floor; but ordering them for the store was a way to buy them wholesale. As long as they remained in the building they could be inventoried as merchandise.

Not a single family picture or memento was displayed in this suite. Not even a picture of Michael O'Halloran, the man who had put this all just outside her reach.

It was obvious, to Rusty at least, why Dorthea didn't have a picture of Marie sitting somewhere. Beth must have read his thoughts. "She *says* it's too painful for her to have Marie's picture out," she explained.

"No kidding," Rusty remarked. "Dan must have heard that line a thousand times."

Beth checked the time. "Well team, it's nine-thirty," she said. "Guess we'd better clear out. Good, Frances, you've made a list. Peggy?"

"I've got vendors' names and invoice numbers. They will have copies. Mr. Miller could get them without too much trouble."

"Rusty?" Beth noticed Rusty standing with Dorthea's personal checkbook.

"Look here," Rusty said. "I believe some of these names match the list you have, Peggy." The two compared the list with the register. "And look at the size of these deposits. Wow!"

"Wait a minute." Frances was looking over Peggy's shoulder. "Look who's listed here." She pointed at Yvonne's name. "Sales commission." For twenty minutes they examined Dorthea's check register and took notes.

"What do we do now?" Frances asked.

"We get out of here and meet Dan. We're already twenty minutes later than we planned." After checking to make sure that all the documents were refiled and the office appeared undisturbed, Rusty led the way out the door to the stairway. Mike locked it behind him. The group made their way down the stairwell all six flights to the second floor.

"Wait a minute," Rusty stood perfectly still and listened. He could hear an elevator moving in another part of the building. "Someone's going up—let's see where to." He led the way to the elevator area and checked the dial above the door. "That's what I thought, the penthouse."

Mike stood back and then said, "You better leave the back

way." He motioned, and the group followed him back to the stairway. They went down two more floors to the basement and through his department. He showed them the basement entrance, which had outside stairs leading up to the alley. "It's a fire escape," Mike said, "I changed the locks on it a long time ago. I haven't told anyone or given anyone a key. I don't even know how many people realize it's here."

"Mike, you're a genius," Beth said. Mike pulled out the enormous key ring he kept on the end of a heavy chain attached to his belt loop.

"Here," he took off a key and gave it to Beth. "I have an extra. You can come in this door anytime without being noticed. I've done it for years. I like to come to the store sometimes—it's nice when all the people are gone. It's so quiet."

Beth gave the old man a quick hug. "Mike, you've been the best."

"Anythin' else you need, don't forget, I'm your man." Mike smiled and let the group out the back door. He left with them and locked the door behind him.

After a few quick instructions, the group dispersed to meet again at Jen's apartment. One by one, they went in the apartment building's underground entrance, much like the one the group used leaving the department store.

"It's like something from an old movie," Frances whispered to Peggy on their way up to Jen's apartment.

"I was thinking more like hiding from the KGB." The two giggled, enjoying themselves completely.

"I haven't had this much excitement since Christmastime when I was a little girl!" Frances reached to knock on the apartment door just as it swung open.

"Get in here," Rusty said looking quickly in the hallway. "You two are giggling like a couple of schoolgirls."

Peggy immediately sobered, but Frances couldn't help

but laugh out loud at Rusty. Bobby and Megan were there waiting with him, and so was Beth. Dan was due back any minute as well. He had to drive his Corvette back to his regular parking spot at his apartment and drive the rented Lincoln to Jen's place.

After everyone was introduced to Bobby, Megan put on a fresh pot of coffee and heated some milk for hot chocolate. "Hi," Dan greeted the group as he came in. "How'd it go?"

"Great," Beth said. "She has kept files on everyone, and everything they did."

"That's because she didn't trust anyone and had to have answers if she was ever asked," Rusty said.

Beth and Rusty filled Dan in on their discoveries.

"Why weren't those records ever included in an audit?" Dan asked.

"Because, as far as the store is concerned, they don't exist," Beth said. "The checkbook is a personal account. The files are personal too."

"We'll have to have a good reason for searching them, openly," Rusty commented. "Maybe we don't have it yet, but we'll find it." Beth nodded.

"Where's Mike?" Dan looked around the room. "Didn't he come with you?"

"Said he was tired," Frances said. "I think he went home."

"Well, without his help, we couldn't have done it," Rusty noted.

"Now what do we do?" Dan asked.

"Can you all go back to work tomorrow as if nothing happened?" Rusty was in charge of the investigation, and he decided to give orders to his unlikely team. "It's important that we don't give away our information to anyone outside this room."

"Oh, yeah, there is one more thing, Dan." Rusty turned

to his friend and employer. "Just as we were leaving, we heard the elevator. We checked—it went to the penthouse."

"Those elevators are locked at night. Did you see who it was?"

"I assumed it was Mrs. Halloran."

"I doubt it. She was having a midnight cocktail party for a few friends who had gone to the opera. She didn't go because she knew I was coming."

"At her house?"

"Um-hmm. She wasn't even dressed for it when I left. I assure you, she's at home."

"Can you call and check?"

"Yeah, I can ask Elaine." Dan excused himself to make the call.

"Who all has keys to the elevator?"

"Yvonne, I suppose," Beth said. "I don't—the penthouse is considered private, almost like a royal residence. No one goes up there except the queen."

"I'm glad we left," Frances said. "I've had enough excitement for one day."

Rusty looked at Frances and decided she was about Jen's height. A little heavier, maybe, but certainly not so much that someone would notice in passing.

"Frances, could you spend the night here?" A plan was taking shape in Rusty's mind.

"I guess so, but why?"

"I have a plan. Do you think you could stand a little excitement tomorrow?"

"What's going on in your head now?" Beth looked at the young investigator.

"I just think Jen could use some fresh air." Rusty turned Frances around. "With some of Jen's clothes and some crutches, we might be able to entice Dick Tracy out there to leave his post."

"And go where?" Beth asked.

"Anywhere," Rusty answered. "It really doesn't matter, as long as he reports back to his boss that Jen's still in town."

"Maybe she could go buy an airline ticket," Megan joined in. "You know, like she's planning to go to California."

Dan felt his heart drop with the thought of Jen leaving. He checked his watch—ten-thirty; she was probably asleep by now. "Dorthea's getting ready for her party," he said. "Elaine says she's been in all evening. Said she was mad after I left, though, and then she got a couple of phone calls."

"Then it was someone else in the store," Beth said.

"I think we can probably guess it was Yvonne." Rusty glanced at Peggy and then at Frances. "How about it, Frances, are you willing to let us use you as a decoy?"

"Sure, I don't have to be on the floor until one tomorrow. I work until nine." Frances looked around at the small apartment. "Where will I sleep?"

"In here, with me." Megan led the way to the bedroom. "It will be nice to have some girl company for a change." She glanced over her shoulder at Bobby and smiled.

Rusty overlooked the nonverbal exchange between Bobby and Megan. "Let's get some sleep, shall we?" he said. Bobby sat down on the sofa, staking out his territory. Rusty continued, "I'm going back to my own bed tonight. Dan, how about dropping me? I can leave my car here in case Bobby needs it."

"Sure," Dan picked up his jacket. He wanted this all to be over. It was almost spring and the magic of the changing seasons shouldn't go unnoticed. He wanted to share it with Jen.

Jen hobbled over to the chair by the window and lifted the shade. Unable to sleep, she stared out into the clear starry sky. *Why did I have to meet Dan now?* Tears filled her eyes and escaped down her cheeks. *This isn't at all what I had in mind for my life.* She made her way over to the bag that held her books. *I know I stuck it in here somewhere.* She rummaged around and finally pulled out her small Bible. Without turning on a light, she hopped back to the bed. Pulling the covers over her, she clutched her Bible to her stomach. Like a small child with a teddy bear, she found comfort just holding it close. *Oh, dear God, please tell me what to do,* she prayed. Finally she drifted off to sleep.

Bess lay awake in the next room. Joy had been asleep when she checked on her before she joined George in her own bed. She heard the sounds of Jen moving around. "I'm going to have a talk with that young woman," she said quietly into the darkness.

"Hmmm?" George mumbled.

"Shh. Go on to sleep," she whispered. "It's nothing, nothing I can't handle with the Lord's help."

CHAPTER TWENTY-EIGHT

*A*fter breakfast, Doreen came with her two youngest children and announced that she planned to take Joy home with her for the day. Joy waved cheerfully to her grandmother as she left with her cousins. Jen said good-bye, but Joy ignored her.

"She doesn't even know how to be polite," Dan's mother shook her head as she began to clear the table. "I'm changing all the beds today and doing a couple loads of towels. When I'm ready to fold, maybe you could give me a hand. Would you mind?" she asked Jen.

Jen was happy to help out. "I'm not much good with this ankle, but I can sure fold clothes. I'd be more than glad to help."

"I thought you would," Bess said. "An energetic young woman like you won't be happy just sitting for long."

"I don't like it at all. I wish I could go out and look around the farm."

Bess nodded. "Next month it will really start to look green again. End of April is real pretty, unless we get lots of rain. Then it's real muddy. But May and June, well, we'll just have to get Dan to bring you back out when the weather is warmer."

"I'll be heading home to California soon. With finals and graduation, I probably won't be able to make it back." Jen hated making such a decisive announcement, but she had to keep her eyes on her goals. She read the verses from Proverbs just last night: *Let thine eyes look right on, and let thine eyelids look straight before thee. Ponder the path of thy feet, and let all thy ways be established. Turn not to the right hand nor to the left: remove thy foot from evil.*

God had spoken to her, she was sure of it. He would give her the strength to do what she knew she had to do.

Settling down in the living room with piles of clean clothes beside her chair, Jen started folding while Bess Miller pulled out the pieces that needed mending.

"Are you so sure you'll be heading back to California right away?" Bess asked.

"I have always known," Jen said simply. "Since I was a freshman in high school, I have known I was going to be an interior designer. I started working as soon as I was fifteen, saved my money, and worked my way toward college. I finished my first two years in basic business and art at a junior college back home. Then I applied for a scholarship to the school I'm attending now."

"You seem to have it all planned."

"It's been my dream, Mrs. Mill—I mean, Bess." Jen folded a large fluffy towel with every corner matched perfectly. She had developed habits of perfection at Halloran's where towels were concerned.

Dan's mother stopped what she was doing and looked at Jen. "May I ask you a very personal question?"

"Of course." Jen laid a tea towel in her lap and turned her attention toward Bess.

"Jen, do you know the Lord?"

"Yes, I do. I accepted him as a very young child. My parents are Christians, and I have attended church all my life. It's all I do know, Bess. Right now, I'm somewhat confused, but . . . well, I have asked the Lord to help me get through this situation. I just want to get home safely."

"I see." Bess reached for her sewing basket and threaded a needle with heavy thread to replace a button on one of George's work shirts.

The two women were silent for a few moments; then Bess spoke. "Have you asked the Lord if you're supposed to return to California?" she asked.

Jen jerked her head up toward Bess then slowly turned her face away, trying to hide the sudden tears she felt spilling on to her face.

Bess crossed the room and put her arm around Jen's shoulders as she rested on the arm of the overstuffed chair where Jen sat surrounded by clean laundry. "I'm sorry, my dear, it's just that I see such hope in Dan's eyes. It's been a long time since he even looked alive, let alone happy. And Joy—well, I couldn't help but wonder if you might be the answer to my prayers for Dan."

"No, I'm not." Jen absentmindedly wiped her tears on a clean hand towel. "I'm sure I'm not. Maybe God used me to wake him up, but I have my goals and Dan's life doesn't fit into them at all."

"Does God?" Even Bess was amazed at her boldness to invade Jen's personal business in this matter. She hardly knew the girl.

"What do you mean?"

"Is there room in your plans for God's will?"

"This is God's will."

"Are you sure?" Bess moved a little closer and took Jen's face in her hands. "It seems like you have all the answers, but do you have the *right* answers?"

"I think I do."

"But does God think so?"

"I don't . . . I mean I . . ." Jen stammered.

"You don't know what God thinks about your plans, do you, Jen?" Bess pulled a clean flowered hanky from her apron pocket and handed it to the young woman she already loved.

"I guess I just always thought that—"

"Thought? Jennifer, you don't have to guess, or think about what God's will is. You can *know* His will for your life."

"It's just that I want so much to have a career. My mother never had anything."

"Oh, I see. Tell me about your mother." Bess rose and resumed her mending project.

"She's a wonderful mother. She's worked hard all her life, keeping her house just so and her family was always— well, we are all, really *all*, she has." Jen frowned and kept folding towels, laying them in neatly organized stacks around her chair. "She loves us, my Dad and me, but she seems so limited. She's a wonderful cook, a good house- keeper, and involved in church. But she's also intelligent, well-read. Yet her world is so small."

"My, my," Bess said, "sounds terrible to me." Jen noticed a slight grin playing with Bess's mouth.

"No, it's not terrible, it's just not enough. There's a part of her that's wonderful, happy, and even outgoing. But there's also a part of her that's unhappy, searching. Kind of an unspoken disappointment," Jen said.

"She's not fulfilled?"

Jen nodded. "That's it. She seems unfulfilled."

"And so you have to go to college, get your career going, and live a life your mother would find fulfilling?"

"No, that's not it at all. I want a life that *I* find fulfilling. I don't want to be just busy, I want to have meaning and purpose."

"You think you'll find those things by having a career?" Bess asked.

"You don't?"

"Of course I do. I am proof."

"But you're just a—" Jen stopped in mid-sentence, embarrassed and unable to say the word out loud.

"Housewife? A farm wife at that," Bess said for her.

"I didn't mean to—" Jen began.

"It's okay. I had this conversation myself with George many years ago. Before we were married, in fact."

"With George?"

"Of course. George and I talk about everything that's important to either of us." Bess saw a painfully pensive expression cross Jen's beautiful young face. "Did your mother ever tell anyone about her unhappiness?"

"Not that I know of."

"Your father. You think he knows?"

"I doubt it. He works all day, comes home, eats dinner, and watches TV. He goes to bed, and it starts all over again the next day. On Saturday he mows the lawn, trims the hedge, washes the car, and hoses down the driveway. On Sunday it's church and sports on TV—unless we have company or go to someone else's house for dinner."

"How is he with other men?"

"Outgoing, friendly. He really gets into a football game when he watches it with his friends."

"I see. Then he and your mother don't talk much to each other," Bess concluded.

"No, I don't think they do." Jen finished the pile of clothes given her to fold. "I'm done here, any more?" she asked.

"In a minute. I'll get the last load out of the dryer." Bess wasn't about to let this conversation end just yet. "Tell me, Jen, does your father love your mother?"

"Of course he does."

"Does she love him?"

"Certainly."

"How do you know?"

"Well, they never fight. They . . . well, they just do."

"Does George love me?" Bess asked.

"I am sure he does."

Bess smiled. "You've been here two days, yet you know George loves me. How can you tell?"

"He seems happy, he's affectionate, he even complimented your dinner the other night."

"Your father ever do that?"

"No. Mom always said you could tell how well he liked her cooking by how much he ate."

"Jen, there's a lot of years between George and me, years of building a relationship that you can't even conceive of, only being here a short time and all. But George and I—well, let me put it this way. I understand your need and desire for a career. I had a career in mind when I met Dan's dad too. I wanted it in the worst way. Fortunately for me, he wanted the same thing. So, we became partners."

"Partners?"

"Yes, we run this farm as partners—business partners. I have my share of responsibilities, and he has his. We discuss the future of our farm just like any partners would discuss the future of a business. We work side by side, but more importantly, we talk. We're not just business partners or marriage partners, we're friends. We not only love each other, we *like* each other."

"Is this your career?"

"Oh, yes. I always dreamed that one day I would live on a farm, that I would marry a farmer." Bess smiled at Jen's shocked expression. "I think it's interesting that you had to come all the way to the middle of Iowa to meet a real career woman. You know, Jen, you've met lots of working women, but how many real career women have you met?"

"Not many," Jen had to admit. "Most of the women I

know are working, waiting for the right man to come along and take care of them so that they can quit."

"I didn't want to quit," Bess offered. "In fact, I didn't even really begin my career until I found the right partner. This farm is too much for one person."

"Are you fulfilled?" Jen asked timidly.

"Oh, yes. But, Jen, it's not the work, it's not the farm, it's not even George that makes me feel fulfilled. It's knowing that I am living in the security of God's will for my life." Bess stood to answer the buzz of the dryer from the back porch. "If you were to become a successful interior designer, a single career woman, do you know for sure you would be in the center of God's will?"

Before Jen could answer, Bess held up her hand. "Don't answer me, ask Him." She pointed to the ceiling, then turned and left the room.

Jen's thoughts turned homeward just as George Miller came in the back door. She heard Bess laugh and scold him, "Keep your hands to yourself, George Miller, can't you see I'm busy?"

"Oh, my Bess, how can a man keep his mind on his work when he knows he's got a beautiful woman like you back in the house?"

Jen blushed and tried to remember if she had ever heard her father tease her mother that way. She couldn't even remember him using her mother's name. He just came in the house, and if he spoke at all it was to announce that he was hungry, tired, or broke. In fact, as far as Jen could recall, almost every sentence her father spoke to her mother began with the word *I*.

"Jen, dear," Bess called from the kitchen, "Dan's on the phone." Jen had been so deep in her own thoughts she hadn't even heard the phone ring.

His voice caused Jen to take a deep breath. "Hi, how's it going out there?"

"We're doing fine," Jen answered.

"How's your ankle?"

"The bruise is showing up more, but the swelling seems to be going down."

"And Joy?" Dan asked.

"She's okay. She went with Doreen for the day."

"Did she talk Dad into letting Barney in the house yet?"

"No. He really knows how to handle her."

"It's not over yet. She'll get that dog in, wait and see."

"How are you?" Jen asked.

"Well, I had an encounter with Dorthea about Joy last night. I went to the house and got some of Joy's things. She's not too happy about Joy being with my mom. But I think that spotted children do not fit her image of perfection."

"How are you?" Jen repeated.

"Finally got some sleep. Megan and Bobby went to your school last night. They talked to a Mr. Magnusen, I think."

"The dean of students," Jen confirmed.

"Yeah, he said you could complete whatever assignments you have left by independent study. You're so close to completion, Jen. He said you're a straight *A* student. I didn't know about that. I'm impressed."

"Dan?" Jen persisted. "In addition to finally getting some sleep, how are you?"

"Rusty and Beth took Frances and Peggy to Dorthea's office last night. They found some interesting files and names and are checking them out. They called our lawyer, Mr. Piper. He wants to meet with us early this afternoon."

"You're not answering my question, Dan. I want to know how *you* are." It was frustrating to have him skirt the subject.

"You really want to know?"

"I wouldn't have asked if I didn't want to know."

"I miss you."

Jen closed her eyes and felt her stomach tighten. Dan heard her take a deep breath and let it out slowly.

"Sorry you asked," he said, "aren't you?"

"No, I'm not." Jen leaned her forehead against the wall by the phone. "When are you coming back?"

"The store is open late tonight. I need to be here." Dan mentally calculated the work that needed his attention spread out on his desk up in his office.

"Where are you?"

"I'm in the customer service department. Peggy is on the switchboard so I know no one is listening in."

"How's Megan?"

"She's doing fine." Dan smiled. "She's enjoying the attention of *two* private eyes at the moment."

"Rusty and Bobby?"

"I have to laugh at them. They're so good at their jobs, but when it comes to Megan, they're like two school kids stumbling all over themselves and each other to get her attention."

Jen laughed at the thought of Megan and her two suitors.

"You didn't say when we could expect you?"

"I plan to leave around noon tomorrow. Beth is taking the rest of today off and will cover tomorrow. I meet with Piper and Rusty in a couple of hours. If everything goes okay, I'll call you later." Dan wanted to keep her on the line, even if he had nothing else to tell her. He was content to listen to her breathe.

"You found lots of information?"

"We found some interesting things. I can't go into it now, but maybe later tonight—after I talk to the lawyer." He paused. "Jen?"

"Yes."

"I'm sorry all this has happened to you," Dan said. "I

wished we had met sooner. I am sorry you got hurt. I want to—" He paused again. "Well, I'd better go. I need to talk to you, but I don't want to . . ."

"I'll see you this weekend," Jen said.

"Tomorrow night. Will you wait up for me?"

"I will," she promised.

"We need to talk, Jen," Dan told her.

"I know. I just don't know what to say, Dan. I've been thinking . . ."

"Oh, no! That's just what I don't want you to do."

"You don't?"

"No. You'll talk yourself into going back to California!"

"Dan, I've never been talked out of it."

"I'm going to try. You might as well know, I'm going to try," Dan warned.

"Is that a threat?"

"I was hoping you'd hear it as a promise." Dan knew it was only the first of many promises he wanted to make to her. "I'll see you tomorrow night," he said. Dan hung up the phone, and Jen slowly placed the receiver in its cradle on the wall. She turned just in time to walk into Bess's warm embrace. Jen first felt tears swell in her eyes, then sobs from deep in her chest. She released both into Bess's soft shoulder.

"What am I going to do?" she sobbed, her voice muffled into Bess.

"Pray, that's what you're going to do. This time don't tell God what to do. Don't ask Him for strength, ask Him for wisdom. Let Him speak to you, Jen. I'm sure He's got something quite wonderful to say." Bess pulled back and wiped the tears from this precious young woman's face with the back of her hand. "You've got twenty-four hours."

"That's not very much time." Jen sniffed then blew her nose into the hanky Bess had provided earlier.

"If God created light and separated it from darkness in one day, don't you think it's enough time for Him to speak to you?" Bess helped Jen get to a nearby chair. "How long did it take to talk to Moses from a burning bush? How long did it take to calm the sea during the storm? You only need a word, Jen, just a word. But you need it from God—not from me, not from Dan."

"Thank you, Bess." Jen put her arms around Dan's mother. "He certainly knew I needed you, today."

Later, after supper dishes were done and Jen was up in her room, Bess excused herself from George and Joy. "Where're you going?" George asked his wife.

"To have a little talk with God. I want to give Him some advice." She winked at her beloved husband.

"Oh, boy." George said to Joy. "God better watch out tonight—Grandma's coming."

CHAPTER TWENTY-NINE

*A*s soon as Dan finished his conversation with Jen, he got another phone call.

"It's Rusty," Peggy said from her spot on the switchboard.

"Dan, I've got some news," Rusty said. "The girls left the apartment, and Dick Tracy followed them. Bobby tagged along behind, and when the girls went into an art supply store, Dick Tracy ducked into a phone booth—and it's our lucky day. Bobby was standing right next to the booth, watching the whole thing. The guy was so intent on watching the girls, he didn't even see Bobby."

"Where is he now?"

"Still following the girls as far as I know. But Bobby watched him dial the phone. He called Dorthea Halloran's number."

"Did he talk to her?"

"Bobby couldn't say for sure, but he thinks so."

"It's not a surprise. I thought for sure she was behind it, but why? That's what I can't figure out yet. Why does she want Jen followed?"

"I think it's to harass her. Dorthea wants her out of town."

"I guess so." Dan looked up to see Peggy frantically motioning him to cut his conversation short. Yvonne entered the office and caught a glimpse of Dan talking on the phone. He smiled and waved at her. "Thanks, Russ," he said and hung up.

"Good morning, Mr. Miller. I wondered if you had taken off for a while. I haven't seen you around the store for a couple of days."

"I've been busy with business outside the store," Dan explained. "You know, sales reps and the like."

"I see. Well, I was just asking."

"Thanks, it's nice to be missed." Dan wondered what she was up to. "How are you?"

"Fine. Didn't sleep too well last night. I'm a little tired this morning."

"Try going out for a while; that always works for me." Dan pushed his way out of the chair and stood directly in front of her. "Did you stay in, Yvonne?"

"Yes, I did. I should have thought of going for a walk or something. But I just stayed in and watched Jack Parr, then a Boris Karloff movie on the late, late show."

"Do you need some time off?"

"No, I'm fine. I have some paperwork to attend to. Mrs. Halloran will be in later, and I should have it done by then."

"Well, don't expect her in too early. She was up late too," Dan said.

"Oh?"

"Yeah, she threw a midnight cocktail party for a few of her society friends." Dan thought he saw a flash of anger cross Yvonne's face, but it quickly disappeared.

"Well, then, there's no hurry. Guess I'll get a cup of coffee before I begin."

"Excuse me, there's my page." Dan glanced at Peggy with her back to him talking on the phone behind the window. Yvonne turned and left the office and went toward the escalator. "Dan, here," he said into the phone.

"Sorry," Peggy said, "but Mr. Jeffers is on the phone. He says it's urgent."

"Put him on." Dan waited for Peggy to make the connection. "Jeffers, what can I do for you?"

Peggy watched while Dan listened to Jeffers. Dan motioned for Peggy to listen in on the conversation. "Listen, Mr. Miller, I'm worried about Mike. You know him? He works down in housewares."

"What seems to be the problem?"

"He didn't come in this morning," Jeffers said.

"Oh?"

"I called his house. His wife said he didn't come home last night."

"He didn't?" Dan and Peggy exchanged expressions of surprise.

"She's worried too. She called the police, but they won't even take a report until he's been missing forty-eight hours."

"I'll check on it, Jeffers. Thanks for calling."

"Let me know what you find out, okay?" Jeffers asked.

"Sure thing," Dan said. He hung up the phone just as the regular switchboard operator came back from her lunch break.

Dan walked with Peggy toward the back of the store. "Call Mike's wife. I don't even know his last name," he said. "Then call me in a half hour at Piper's office. Better use a pay phone."

The elevator doors opened, and Dan stepped inside. "One, please."

Just as the doors closed, Dan heard Peggy say, "Cleary, Mike's name is Cleary." But he was almost out the front door of the store before he realized where he had heard it before. Without bothering to get his car, Dan hailed a cab.

Dan headed directly for Piper's office.

"Mr. Miller, Mr. Piper's waiting for you—" Dan swept

right past the secretary posted outside the lawyer's office. "Go right on in," she finished with a shrug.

"I've just had quite a shock." Dan paced back and forth trying to put this latest piece into the puzzle. "Let me see Marie's birth certificate again."

"What's this all about, Dan?"

"I'm not sure." Dan grabbed the document from Piper's hand. "There, look there." He pointed at the birth mother's name. *Emily M. Cleary.*

"What about it?"

"Mike, the old man who works in the store, his name is Cleary."

"Is there a connection here?"

"What's this?" Rusty joined them in Jonathan Piper's office.

Dan told him about his most recent discovery. "I don't get it, Dan. What's it got to do with anything?"

"Only this." Dan turned to include them both in his next comment. "Mike Cleary is missing."

Rusty sat down slowly and rubbed his hand through his curly brown-black hair. "I knew something was on his mind last night. He went on and on about his friendship with Mr. O'Halloran. He doesn't have any use for Mrs. O'Halloran at all. Says his sister worked for her during the war when Mr. O'Halloran was in the military."

"His sister?"

"Yeah, she kept an eye on Marie while Mrs. O'Halloran partied during the war."

"Oh, my God." Dan sank into the nearest chair. "I can't believe it—you mean Emily M. Cleary?"

"Marie's mother." Mr. Piper released a low whistle.

"Wait a minute, you two. Let me get my bearings. You say Mike was with you last night, Rusty?"

"Yeah, he let us into Dorthea's office. He also let us out

the back basement door when we heard someone come in after we were out of the office."

"Someone came in?"

"I thought it must be Dorthea."

"She was at home, though; I checked with Elaine."

"Okay," Jonathan Piper said, "let's see what we have here." He took his place behind the big desk and grabbed a large yellow pad to make notes. "You left the office at what time?"

"Ten—or a few minutes before," Rusty said. "We were supposed to be out by nine-thirty, but I discovered Dorthea's checkbook in one of the bottom drawers. We looked it over and took some notes." Rusty produced some folded pieces of paper from his jacket pocket. "Look Dan, I compared this to her phone directory and several names show up both places."

"Then what did you do?" Jonathan asked.

"We left. Mike went out with us and when we reached the landing between the second and third floor, we heard the elevator start up. You can't help but recognize that whine and grind as the elevator."

"Then?" Jonathan wrote as Rusty talked.

"Mike showed us a way out through a stairway in the basement through his stockroom. It's sort of a fire escape from the basement—it goes up instead of down."

"They're pretty well all sealed up, now. But several years ago, they were required. Now we just have to have two inside stairways in separate locations."

"They're unused then?" Jonathan asked.

"I thought so," Dan said.

"Mike opened the one by his department. He used to come down and spend time there when it was quiet. He's a strange man, kind of sad in a way," Rusty said.

Jonathan wanted to know what Rusty knew about Mike

and his relationship to Mr. O'Halloran. Rusty told him all he could recall from his conversation with Mike the night before.

"He didn't have anything good to say about Mrs. O'Halloran, that's for sure."

"Then when you left the store, did everyone go back to the apartment with you?"

"Everyone but Mike. I thought he went home."

"Did he leave the store with you?"

"He walked us to the end of the alley. We all went separately. He stayed with me until the women were headed back to the apartment. I said good night, and he went back down the alley."

"Back to the store?"

"I assumed he was going home."

"You didn't see him go back into the store?"

"No. I walked down the street to my car and left."

"Let's leave Mike alone for a minute and look over what you found in Dorthca's office." Jonathan turned the page on the yellow pad and began a new one. "I wish you had not broken into the office."

"We didn't, we had a key—or rather Mike did. At least he had one that he could make work." Rusty smiled at the young lawyer.

"Great, Rusty. There's not much difference between breaking and entering and unlawful entry. You'd better hope we don't have to defend you on either." He reached for his phone. "Yes?" He paused, then handed the phone to Dan. "It's a Peggy McKnight."

"I told her to call me here." Dan took the phone and put it to his ear while Rusty and Jonathan waited. "What? Oh, no!" Dan said. "Don't panic. I'll be right there."

"What's up?" Rusty was already standing.

"Mike's dead. A customer found him in the stairway a half hour ago."

"I'd better go with you. You may need an attorney close by. You know anybody in the police department?"

They gave instructions to Jonathan's secretary to call Jacob Smith and Elizabeth Simms. "This is Beth's afternoon off. She's not going to like this at all," Rusty said.

The three men crowded in to Rusty's old Plymouth. Halfway to the store, Rusty wailed, "Oh, no! There'll be police all over that place!"

"Yeah?" Dan didn't understand Rusty's concern.

"Our fingerprints are all over that office."

"You sure?"

"Positive."

"I'm counting the legal fees already. I'm going to get rich off you guys," Jonathan Piper quipped from the back seat. "You better hope Jacob Smith is a policeman you can trust to keep the evidence out of the papers until we can put our heads together. A leak to a reporter right now could do real damage."

Rusty pulled up in front of the store, which was already teaming with reporters and police. A yellow ribbon had been strung and the store was being evacuated as the police took the names and addresses of everyone shopping there at the time of the discovery. Employees were being questioned in the shoe department, where the police had gathered them all together.

Dan Miller walked quickly to the store's escalator. "Upstairs, Mr. Miller, fourth floor," an officer said when Dan identified himself.

As he approached the stairway area, he was glad to see Jacob Smith among the plainclothes officers on the scene.

"Looks like an accident—can't be sure yet," he told Dan.

"Coroner will have to determine the time of death. I'd say it's been a few hours, ten or twelve maybe."

"How do you know?"

Jacob grimaced. "He's cold as ice and stiff as a board."

Dan felt his stomach turn. He thought he might throw up. Mike's body was covered with a sheet, and police were marking it's location and position with chalk. "They examined the stairway for evidence and checked for fingerprints." Jake was perfunctory and unemotional about the whole thing. "Won't do any good, though. It's a public building. Who know's how many people pass through here in a day's time?" He shrugged and reached for a small pad.

"When's the last time you saw Mike, Dan?"

"We'd better go somewhere where we can talk in private, Jake." Rusty commented from the side.

"Yeah? You know something?"

"Let's go to my office," Dan said. Debbie was with the other employees, so he knew they wouldn't be overheard.

A couple of hours later, Dan sat back on the large leather sofa. He was suddenly tired. He closed his eyes out of sheer exhaustion and opened them only when Jake said, "We'd better get Peggy and Frances up here. I'll have to take a statement."

"I hate to involve them in this." Dan regretted ever asking their help.

"They're already involved. If they corroborate this tale of suspense and intrigue, we'll be looking to talk to them some more. It could be we're looking at more than an accident here."

Dan leaned back again while he waited for an officer to accompany the two women to his office. He noticed Marie's picture on the shelf.

"That's funny," he said to Rusty. "I put this picture away

a few weeks ago. I know I didn't get it out. I put it right there, in the bottom drawer." Dan pointed to his desk.

Dan stood and reached for it, but Rusty restrained his hand. "Don't touch it, Dan. Let's see if Jake's guys can tell us who put it back." He raised his eyebrows, and Jake shrugged his shoulders.

"You never know, it might be important. Let's get Sam up here to dust it," Jacob said.

"Thanks, Jake," Rusty said.

"Yeah, well, never mind. Let's get this case solved before we open another one."

"I think they're the same one, Jake," Rusty said.

"You might be right, but I'm hoping it was an accident."

"Where's Beth?" Dan asked.

"I sent her with one of my men to break the news to Mrs. Cleary. Mike has other family too, although I understand some of them live out of the country." Jake stood as a policeman escorted Frances and Peggy into the office.

"Don't be afraid, ladies." Jake held out a chair to Frances. "Here, sit down, won't you?"

"It's okay, Peggy." Dan stood and put his arm around the frightened woman. "Jake knows about our little escapade last night."

"I'm overlooking it at the moment. After all, you were working late for Mr. Miller here, and even the penthouse office is part of his building. He has a right to have his employees search company records," Jacob explained.

Peggy relaxed against the comfort of Dan's brotherly closeness. Frances answered all the questions she could as accurately as she remembered. Peggy confirmed all Frances said and then added, "It's hard to think you might have been with someone—well, you know, were the last ones . . ."

"To see him alive," Jake finished her sentence for her. "But we're not sure you were."

Dan looked at the women, sorry he had asked them to be involved at all in this case. Surely there must have been another way to get the information they needed.

"What do you mean?"

"You have all stated that you heard the elevator as you were leaving. How do we know the person taking the elevator didn't see Mike after you did?"

"Oh, my gosh." Peggy put her hand to her mouth.

"We've got a real mess, here, folks. A real mess, indeed."

"Captain? You're wanted at the scene. The coroner wants to talk to you before he removes the body."

"Ladies, wait here. Dan, you and Rusty come with me."

"It's no accident, Jake," the coroner said. "Look at this." He lifted the covering from Mike's body and Dan had to work hard to keep from vomiting. Rolling the body slightly, the coroner revealed a little pool of blood beneath Mike's back.

"He's been stabbed, Jake." The coroner rolled him back and tucked the covering around Mike's arm. "It's a small but deep wound. Probably didn't kill him, though; I can't say for sure, but my hunch is the fall did. He probably lost his balance after being stabbed."

"Either way . . ." Jake rubbed his chin.

"Either way, looks like you've got a homicide on your hands here, Jake. Good luck."

"This is turning into a real night's work, Dan." Jake led the way back into Dan's office. Rusty followed closely behind. "I'll need to take a look around that office myself. Do you mind?"

"Of course not." Dan had nothing to hide.

"Wait a minute." Jonathan Piper stepped forward. "I want you to get a search warrant."

"Is that really necessary, Jon?" Dan asked.

"It is. If they enter the room without Dorthea's permission that's one thing—the building is really under your authority. But if they open any files that do not belong to the store—well, just to be on the safe side." Jonathan walked to the opposite side of the room. "Let's make sure everything you find is admissible in court. That okay with you, Jake?"

"Some smart lawyer you got yourself here, Dan. He may be able to solve two cases at once." Jake reached for the phone.

"It has to go through the switchboard, sir." Peggy started for the door, "I can get you through." She left, an officer escorting her, and put Jake's call through to the necessary official to get a court order.

Dan checked his watch—seven-thirty. Jen expected him to call around nine. *Guess I won't be getting back as soon as I had hoped.* His heart was heavy, for Mike, for his wife, and for himself too. He felt guilty for thinking about Jen at a time like this. But then she was always close to his thoughts, to his heart.

"Let's go have a look upstairs," Jake said, slapping Dan's knee, "shall we?"

CHAPTER THIRTY

*J*en took Mrs. Miller's advice and went to her room early. She needed time alone, and Joy's annoying presence only clouded the issue. Jen had never made plans to have children. She didn't plan *not* to either, but such a spoiled child . . . Jen felt guilty for wishing she had never heard of Joy.

Laying across the bed, she once again turned to Proverbs, the fourth chapter.

Let thine eyes look right on. Jen had read the words many times before. Years ago she had underlined the verse with a red pencil and memorized it. She turned to it for encouragement whenever she found herself short of money or so tired from both working and going to school that she wanted to quit.

Let thine eyelids look straight before thee. Determination was something Jen had plenty of. She made it a habit not to let distractions deter her from her goals. *Ponder the path of thy feet.* Jen took that to mean plan, budget, and be careful not to get sidetracked.

Let all thy ways be established. Turn not to the right hand nor to the left; remove thy foot from evil. Jen wished Dan would call so that she could hear his voice. *It's a word from God you need, Jen.* Dan's mother had said.

"I do, dear heavenly Father, I really do." Jen put her face in the pillow and let the tears once again flow freely.

"Dear, Father, show me Your will for my life," Jen prayed aloud when the crying subsided. "I want what you want for me." She got up and knelt by the bedside.

"I can't do this by myself, Lord. I think I love Dan. I don't see how I can fit him and my plans together. I am sorry that I have to bother You with this mess I seem to have gotten myself into. Please help me understand what You want me to do—to be what You want me to be. Bess says I need a word from You, God. Isn't the Bible enough? Isn't it Your Word? Look here, I've already underlined this passage. Do You have anything else You want to say to me? Please God, hear my prayer and give me a word."

Drawn back to the passage again, Jen picked up her Bible and sat back on the floor, looking at the underlined words. She sat quiet and still and read them over and over again. Suddenly she realized she was seeing the same words but a different message.

Open your eyes, Jen, she heard within her heart, *look at what I have put right in front of your face.* She knew the Lord was speaking to her. *Think about what you'll gain, but also think about what you'll lose, if you continue down the path you have chosen for yourself. When you have done that, you will know what to do. You will know My will, and I will give you the strength you need to make the right choice. Don't be distracted by what you always thought you wanted. Let me show you desires that you have had in your heart that you don't even know about yet. Don't be so stubborn and shut Me out. I have chosen you, and I have brought you here to this place. Look to Me, not to your hopes, dreams, and ambitions.*

Jen clutched the Bible to her breast and began to rock slowly back and forth, crying softly.

"Dear God, I'm so sorry. I used You to help me get what I wanted without regard to what You wanted. I used Your Word to motivate me toward my own selfish goals." She looked at the words again and read them with new understanding.

"Is Dan what You have put right in front of my face? Have You brought him into my life, just before it was too late?" She sobbed as she laid her Bible aside and gathered her knees up under her chin, wrapping her legs with her arms. "But what about Joy? Oh, dear God, what about Joy?"

Jen didn't hear the door open slowly; she wasn't aware of the child creeping toward her.

"Don't cry, Jen," Joy whispered softly. "It's no fun to cry."

Jen lifted her face to see the tears streaming down the little girl's cheeks. She opened her arms to this little one, so spoiled and yet so uncared for. Joy flew into the waiting arms and snuggled as closely as she could to Jen.

Together they cried and held each other. Jen began rocking Joy and soon they were both soothed by just being together.

When they were quiet, Jen smoothed back Joy's long, straight hair. Jen felt a sudden chill from sitting on the floor. "Want to sleep with me?"

"Can I?" Joy scrambled into Jen's bed. "I never slept with anyone ever before."

Jen thought of her sleep over parties with Cari and how they snuggled under the covers and giggled together until Grandma Ginny scolded them and Grandpa Will came and hit them playfully with pillows.

"I wished I could have curly hair like yours," Joy said.

Jen laughed. "I wish mine was straight and dark like yours," she told Joy.

Under the covers Joy snuggled close to Jen and soon slept. Jen closed her eyes once more to lift a prayer to God. A prayer for help—not to do what she wanted but to do what He wanted.

Across the room, her Bible lay open where she left it on

the floor. On the facing page was another underlined verse Jen had memorized as a child: *Trust in the LORD with all thine heart; and lean not unto thine own understanding. In all thy ways acknowledge Him, and He shall direct thy paths.*

Noticing the light still burning under Jen's door, Bess tiptoed into the room. She picked up the Bible from the floor and placed in on the nightstand. She looked at the two sleeping girls in the big bed and smiled.

God is still on duty, she thought as she pulled the covers up a little and turned off the bedside lamp, *and, hallelujah, He's taking my advice.*

Dan watched as the police went over Dorthea's office. He looked at his watch. Eleven o'clock. Too late to call now. He hoped everything was going all right—that Jen and Joy were getting acquainted. His hope was almost, but not quite, a prayer. But for Dan Miller, it was closer to being a prayer than anything had been in quite a while.

Early the next morning, Jen and Joy descended the stairs slowly and carefully because of Jen's injured ankle. They tried to sneak down ahead of the Millers and planned to make breakfast. Opening the door to the kitchen, they found Bess sitting in the semidarkness with her Bible open on the table in front of her.

"Well, well," Bess said, "who have we here?" Her eyes twinkled with delight as the two quietly entered. "What are you two up to?"

"I'm sorry. We didn't think anyone was up. We were going to come down and make you breakfast," Jen said.

"Well, go right ahead, I'll just sit here and watch. It's been a long time since I had anyone make *me* breakfast. Let's see, I'll have—"

"French toast!" Joy and Jen shouted. They had made menu decisions before climbing out of bed.

"Okay, french toast it is," Bess agreed.

"Point me to the pantry!" Jen said standing at attention.

Getting out the bowl for mixing the eggs and milk, the whisk, and griddle was easy. Walking back and forth to the refrigerator proved to be a bit harder for Jen. She reached for the door to the refrigerator and stooped to find the eggs when Joy sneaked in front of her, knocking her off balance and forcing her to use her sore ankle to keep from falling.

"Oh!" Jen cried.

"Joy, be careful!" Bess warned from her place at the table.

"I want to carry the eggs!" Joy elbowed Jen in the stomach.

"Joy!" Bess warned again. "Let Jen carry the eggs. You have to be careful!"

"I want to carry the eggs!" Joy demanded loudly.

"No, sweetheart," Jen said sweetly, "I'd better do that. Why don't you get the silverware and set the table?"

"No. I want to carry the eggs." Joy yanked at the carton of eggs stored on the bottom shelf.

"Joy!" Jen reached to steady the carton. Joy, thinking Jen was about to take them from her hand, yanked them in the opposite direction and eggs flew everywhere.

"Joy! Now look at the mess you've made." Bess quickly crossed the large kitchen to stand at Jen's side, steadying her with one hand and grabbing Joy's arm with the other. "Look, at this mess!" she said again.

"I didn't do it, Jen did!" Joy began wailing and flailing at Jen.

"Stop it, Joy, this instant!" Bess commanded.

"Jen made me do it!"

"Joy!" Jen virtually yelled at the screaming child. "You get hold of yourself and calm down!"

"No, you made me get in trouble, I don't like you anymore! I hate you! I hate you!"

Joy sobbed uncontrollably, burying her face in Bess's robe. "Oh, no you don't, miss." Bess held her back at arm's distance. "You don't get yourself in trouble and then come running to me." Bess looked at Jen. "You've not only broken the eggs, you've hurt Jen's feelings. You need to tell Jen you're sorry!"

"No, I won't. She made me do it. She did it!"

Jen hobbled over to the sink, took the roll of paper towels from their yellow plastic holder and started for the mess on the floor.

"Jen, let me do that," Bess said.

Jen surrendered the paper towels and glared at Joy who looked slightly triumphant. "Get down there and help your grandmother!" Jen commanded. "You did this, and you need to be responsible for cleaning it up."

"You can't make me," Joy taunted.

"Oh, yes I can!" Jen reached for Joy's arm and grabbed her before she could run out of the room. With her other hand she reacted with a swift swat to Joy's bottom. Then Jen stood in shock as Joy stiffened and screamed at the top of her lungs.

"What on earth is going on down here?" George opened the kitchen door and paused briefly to assess the situation. Without hesitation, he crossed the kitchen, picked Joy up and carried her from the room.

Jen's eyes filled with tears, and her heart pounded with anger and embarrassment. She turned away from Bess, who was still mopping up the slimy mess on the floor. Jen's ankle throbbed from the sudden shock of bearing her weight. Unable to hold her emotions, she leaned against the refrigerator and sobbed.

Bess finished cleaning up the mess on the floor and

turned to the mess inside Jen. She put her arms around the young woman and gently helped her to a chair at the table. Jen put her head down on her arms and continued sobbing.

Finally, when the initial emotional outburst had subsided, Bess spoke softly.

"Jen, Jen, it's not your fault. She's been so spoiled by Dorthea O'Halloran and ignored by Dan. I guess it's not really her fault either. It's going to be a challenge, and Dan's going to have to face his responsibility toward her one of these days. I wish I had been able care for her when Marie died, but I wasn't in very good health at the time." Jen looked at the gentle, healthy-looking woman sitting beside her. "Oh, I'm fine now. It was a bad time for all of us. By the time I was on my feet again, Dorthea had pretty much taken advantage of the situation and was in total control."

Bess wiped a tear from her own eye. "Looking back, we see that we should have been more firm with Dan. But he was already in so much pain, we didn't want to cause more. Too bad Dorthea didn't have the same attitude. We could have spared that child so much."

Jen reached out her arms and pulled Bess into a warm hug. "I have never seen such a spoiled child up this close before. It's awful. How can anyone like her, let alone love her?"

"I love her because it's the right thing to do." Bess returned Jen's hug then pulled away and faced her. "Love is given, Jen, by a decision of your will. Joy will never deserve anyone's love as long as she's like this. But it is love that will change her. We love her because she needs it, not because she deserves it."

Bess threw a glance up toward the ceiling. "I can almost bet that George is up in Joy's room right now, calming her down and talking to her about her options."

"Options?" Jen wiped her nose on a napkin.

"Choices. She can either come down and apologize to us for what she has done, or she can stay up there without breakfast, all alone. He will give her the choice, then she will have to live with not only the consequences of her actions but with the consequences of her choices following those actions."

"Why do you even bother?" Jen asked. "Dan will be back soon and take her right back to that house, and Dorthea will undo in a few minutes what it took days to begin."

"We bother because it's the right thing to do." Bess stood and reached for the coffee pot. "I could use a cup of coffee, how about you?"

"Bess," Jen began, "I was wrong to swat her, wasn't I?"

"Maybe not. You can't ever tell immediately. And you certainly can't tell by Joy's reaction to your discipline. It will take time, my dear. How much time are you willing to give it?"

That was just it. Jen didn't know how much time she would be willing to give to Dan, much less his daughter. "I don't know."

"Then best leave the discipline to those of us who are committed to her. You just focus on being her friend for now. Can you do that much?"

"I can try," Jen said.

"Good, she needs friends. Too many people pull away from her already. If she just knows you want to be her friend, Grandpa and I can manage correcting her."

Dan, Jen thought, *I wonder how you would've wanted me to handle this. I wonder if you even expect me to.*

Dan, meanwhile, wasn't even thinking about Jen or Joy or wondering how they were getting along. He had other things pressing on his mind. Mike had been killed in the store, stabbed, and probably pushed down the stairway, where he lay until a customer found him.

"It's a small deep wound," the coroner had said. "Bigger than an ice pick, but smaller than a knife. I have ruled out a dagger. The flesh is torn, so the object was not as sharp as the blade of a knife, probably had ragged edges."

"There wasn't as much blood as you'd expect," Jake said. His voice shocked Dan back to the present. Sitting across the desk from Dan he leaned toward him. "You all right? I've been talking over here, and I don't think you've been listening."

"I'm sorry. I can't believe any of this is really happening," Dan said.

"It's happening, Dan," Rusty said from his slouched position on the couch.

"I'm taking Peggy and Frances back up to the penthouse for a look-see before Dorthea is allowed up there. I want to find out if anything has changed since they left last night." Jake stood and headed toward the door. "Want to come along?"

"Yeah, I guess so." Dan walked numbly toward the door and Rusty followed.

Up in the penthouse, Frances and Peggy McKnight walked around, careful not to touch anything. "Everything looks the same to me," said Frances.

"Me too," added Peggy. Turning to leave Dorthea's desk, Peggy paused. "Wait a minute. Fran, wasn't there a letter opener laying there by the blotter?"

"Yes there was. It was a matching one. It had the same pattern on the handle that is on the corners of the desk blotter. It also matches the phone directory."

"What phone directory?"

"It's in the drawer." Frances pointed to the left hand desk drawer. "In there."

Jake shook out his hanky and, covering the drawer handle with it, he pulled the drawer open. "In where?"

"I left it right where I found it, in there."

"It's not here now."

Jake reached for the phone, "Get me a search warrant," he barked into the phone. "The O'Halloran residence." Hanging up the phone, he turned to Peggy. "Can you remember anything else about the letter opener?"

"It was one of those real sharp kind. We have some down in stationary. It has a serrated edge on the blade and if you're not careful, you can cut yourself . . ." Peggy's voice trailed off.

Dan crossed the room to stand beside her. The thought of the letter opener penetrating Mike's back was too much for both of them. He put his arm around her, and she turned her face to his chest.

"Captain." An officer entered the room and placed a report in Jake's hands.

Jake examined the paper. "That's odd. No prints except one set," he said. He looked at Dan and raised one eyebrow. "Seems someone wiped the place clean but left one clear set behind. How do you suppose that happened?"

Dan wrinkled his forehead and reached to smooth back his hair. "One set? But, there were five people up here last night: Rusty, Beth, Frances, Peggy, and Mike."

"Maybe six," Jake said. "You have some names from that directory?" He addressed the two women.

"I gave the list to Rusty."

"We've got our work cut out for us, Dan. I'm afraid the papers have already gotten a hold of this. Sorry. It couldn't be helped. You might want to make a statement to the press."

"What about Dorthea? Let her make the statement." Dan didn't want to talk to anyone except Jen at the moment.

"I'm afraid Dorthea isn't talking to anyone but us at the moment."

"What?"

"We've picked her up for questioning. She's at headquarters right now. They're taking an initial statement from her and then they'll wait for me." Jake headed for the elevator door. "I trust none of you are going out of town for a few days."

"Jake, I took my daughter and Jennifer Whipple to my folks' farm in Iowa. I need to go get them. When can I tell them I can come?"

"Not any time soon, Dan. I'm sorry."

The phone on Dorthea's desk rang. Frances answered it and handed it to Dan. "It's Bess Miller," she said.

CHAPTER THIRTY-ONE

*A*fter Bess filled Jen in on what was going on back at Halloran's, she helped her up to her room and left her alone to lie down. Jen felt sad. Mike had always been friendly to her as he was to most of the other employees at Halloran's. She couldn't believe he was dead. *Who could have done such a thing?* she wondered. *And why?*

Knowing Dan wasn't coming back until this latest twist was cleared up threw an unexpected pall over her already dark mood. Her foot throbbed, and it didn't seem to be getting any better. Joy was in her room sulking. Bess was downstairs mopping the kitchen floor after the disaster with the eggs, and George left the house to busy himself in the barn.

Later, Bess came up with a sandwich and cup of soup for Jen. "I remembered you didn't have any breakfast." Bess was quiet and seemed somewhat distant to Jen.

"Thank you." Jen didn't feel like eating, but she was grateful for the kindness. "What about Joy?"

"I'm going to check on her in a minute. She's a stubborn one, that's for sure."

Bess sat on the side of the bed near Jen's foot. "Let me see how this is coming along." She bent over it and tenderly touched the purple bruise. "Jen, I think we've waited long enough. This has to be looked at. I'm calling the doctor."

"I guess you're right. It's just that I don't—" She couldn't finish the sentence.

"It's all right, dear. Dan will take care of the expense. He told me so before he left. He feels responsible, so just let him take care of everything." Bess patted Jen's leg and went to the phone. Returning in a few moments, "The doctor will see you now if you can come. He's had a cancellation."

George came in the house to watch after Joy, and Doreen came over to accompany Jen and Bess to the doctor's office.

"Nothing to worry about," Bess announced to George upon their return. "The X ray shows a deep bruise but nothing else. He thinks the bone might be bruised." Jen walked in on crutches, displaying a cast from the knee down. Her toes stuck out and were caked with excess plaster. "He said she needs to protect it. This morning's disaster convinced her of that too." Bess walked to the stove and put on the tea kettle. "How's Joy?"

"Asking for Jen."

"I'll go up to her, then," Jen said. "That is, if you think it's all right."

"I don't think so," George said.

Bess looked at him, then at Jen. "And why not?" she asked.

"It's time she came to Jen. She's the one who's at fault here, let her do the making up." George looked at Jen with a serious expression, "Let her do the repair work. And don't make it too easy for her. Let her understand that she hurt you. Let her feel your pain. She only thinks of herself—it's time she learned to think of others."

"But she's only a little girl," Jen jumped to her defense.

"She will still be a little girl—even if we make her behave

like a responsible person. It's time she learned, Jen, from people who love her."

"But, I . . ." Jen stopped in mid sentence. She didn't even *like* Joy, much less *love* her. "I think I'll just go to my room for a while. I'm tired." The day had exhausted her with more than just Joy. She needed time to think—to think about Dan, about Mike. And she still had graduation to think about.

Sadness gripped Dan Miller's heart like a vice. His head pounded with the pain of intense confusion, and he felt responsible for Mike's death. He stretched himself out on the sofa in his office.

"She took it pretty hard," Beth said, referring to Mike's wife.

"Something doesn't make sense here." Rusty paced the length of Dan's office. Beth stood in front of the windows and stared in the direction of the lake, which was obscured with fog and a light rain.

"Spring."

"Huh?" Rusty turned toward Beth.

"Spring. It's finally here. Last month this would have been snow. Now it's drizzle." She wrapped her arms around her ribs and leaned slightly forward, then gave way to her tears. Crossing the length of Dan's office with long swift strides, Rusty wrapped his arms around the older woman and pulled her toward him.

Dan stared at the ceiling. *I did the right thing,* he said to himself. *Jen is safe at the farm.*

"We're going to the apartment—I want to be with Megan," Rusty said to Dan.

"Bobby's over there," Dan said.

"Frances is too," Beth said as she picked up her raincoat from the credenza by the door.

"Coming?" Rusty turned to look at Dan.

"Maybe later." Dan didn't move. He looked at Marie's picture across the room from where he lay. *This is a real mess, Marie. First you then* . . . Dan didn't finish his thought before he stood up and walked to the picture. *I know I put this away. Who would get it out again?*

Sam, one of Jake's men, had come and checked the picture for fingerprints. The report from the lab would be a few days in coming. Dan would know whose fingerprints were on the picture soon enough. He had more important things to think about right now. *Jen,* Dan looked at Marie's picture once more before moving to the window.

"Mr. Miller?" Debbie entered his office without knocking.

"Yes," Dan resented the intrusion.

"Captain Smith is on the phone. He's asking for you." Dan reached for the phone, and Debbie checked Marie's picture. She could see slight smudges of the powder used by the police lab clinging to the glass. No one saw as she closed her eyes tightly against the realization that she would probably be questioned about the picture. Why had she let herself be talked into getting involved? Covering her mouth with her hand, she left the office as Dan talked with the police investigator.

"We have the murder weapon, Dan." Smith's voice was matter-of-fact. "I think you'd better come down here."

"I'll be right there."

"I'm afraid," Debbie said into the phone as soon as the office suite door closed behind Dan. She paused waiting for a response. "I don't care . . . I just want . . ."

Debbie fidgeted with the papers on her desk. "I don't think we should. It might be dangerous. Whoever thought they'd do this to anyone? I didn't even know Mike knew anything." Debbie caught a glimpse of Yvonne approaching the office through the window leading out onto the fourth floor of the store. "I have to go." Quickly she hung up and turned to the typewriter, inserting a piece of paper.

"Debbie, how're you doing?" Yvonne glanced around to see if anyone was watching. "How's he?" she asked, nodding toward Dan's door.

"He's okay. He's lying down." Debbie lied. "He's pretty washed out."

"This isn't easy for any of us." Yvonne bit the side of her fingernail. "We need to keep our mouths shut. Remember, if even one of us . . . well, I don't have to tell you what could happen. Mike's accident speaks loudly enough, don't you agree?"

"I'm afraid, Yvonne. Aren't you?"

"Of what?" She reached for the doorknob. "We've got nothing to be afraid of—if we keep our heads and our silence."

Debbie watched Yvonne walk through the fourth floor departments, speaking to a few store clerks. As she stepped on the escalator, Debbie picked up the phone and dialed a three-digit number. "It's me again. She was just here. I think she threatened me."

"No," Debbie said into the phone, "not directly. She just reminded me that Mike was . . . Okay, after work, then. Yeah, I know where that is. Okay, see you then."

"We found the murder weapon at Dorthea O'Halloran's home," Jake said, "along with the missing phone directory. She swears she was home all night. Had a party until one-thirty or two and went right to bed. The maid said she thought Mrs. O'Halloran was in all night, but that she did hear a door close about three-thirty. She assumed it was a boyfriend leaving."

"What does Dorthea say?" Dan asked.

"Said she didn't have anyone in last night." Jake sat

sideways on the desk. "The maid didn't clean up after the party. She was told to go to bed. Maybe Dorthea wanted to have company but didn't, maybe she left and came in at three-thirty. Maybe not. Maybe, maybe. I hate this—all maybes and nothing solid."

"You mean, maybe she's telling the truth?"

"She might not be." Jake followed the line of his jaw with his knuckle. "Not the whole truth anyway." He stood from his position on the desk and stuck both hands in his pockets. "Anyone else have a key to her house?"

"Me. But I was at the apartment with Beth and Rusty."

"Yeah, I know. Anyone else?"

"Not that I know of."

"Is there a spare key kept anywhere?"

"No. Wait. She keeps an extra set at the office. In her little safe, would be my guess."

Jake made a note on the desk. "I'll have someone check it out. You know how to get in the safe?" Dan reached for his wallet and produced a small slip of paper with a combination on it. "Thanks, this will help," Jake said,

"Where's Dorthea now?"

"We're holding her for questioning. I can't hold her much longer without a lawyer. Maybe you ought to talk to her and find out who she wants. I suggest you get a good one. She's in a lot of trouble."

"Jake?" A large balding police officer stuck his head in the door. "I think you'd better come and talk to these people."

"What's up?" Jake asked.

"Won't say. They'll only talk to you."

"Be right there. Dan, go home. Get some rest and let us handle this now. She's going to be here for the night. Call your lawyer and get him down here, but you go on home."

Dan opened the door to his small apartment. *Home,* he

thought, *this isn't home.* He let his thoughts turn toward the farm and Jen. Suddenly he ached to hold her, to let her nearness give him strength; her softness, comfort. Overwhelmed, he went to the kitchen, reached into a high cupboard, and brought out a bottle of wine. He looked at the label, not even knowing if it was good wine or not. It was a gift from Yvonne, and he had almost forgotten it was there. Unwrapping the foil top and examining the cork he knew it was useless. He didn't even have a corkscrew. He tossed the bottle in the wastepaper basket and reached instead for the aspirin bottle. Gulping two down with half a glass of water, he turned and walked out of the kitchen.

Alone in the darkness of his small bedroom, he slipped between the sheets. He lay alone, his clothes tossed carelessly across the chair in the corner. His thoughts of Jen competed with pictures of Marie flashing through his mind. He wondered how Dorthea was and if Piper found her a criminal lawyer. Eventually the weariness of the past few days overtook him, and he slept. He didn't even notice that tears streamed silently down his face.

Jen carefully washed the plaster from her toes and checked the heavy dampness encasing her leg. The doctor had said that tomorrow her cast would be completely set and that she would welcome the protection it would provide for her injury. Using the crutches she made her way to the bed, and with only a little difficulty, she crawled into the warm comfort it offered. *Tomorrow,* she promised herself, *I'm going back to Chicago. I have a life after all, a life of my own. I have my own plans and goals,* she reiterated, though they seemed less important than they used to. *I only have a few weeks until graduation. If nothing else, I owe myself that much. After coming this far and working so hard,* she thought, *I will finish at least.*

CHAPTER THIRTY-TWO

*J*en settled back in the seat of the Greyhound bus once it was underway. She closed her eyes against the memory of Bess's last words.

"Don't go, Jen. You told Dan you'd be here when he got back. He won't be long. This whole thing is probably just a few days from being solved. He thinks you are safe here, and he isn't sure about what could happen to you there."

She looked out across the rolling land, which was soon to feel the farmer's plow and welcome the spring planting. She glanced at her watch—nine-thirty. She would be in Chicago by four. Her mind drifted first toward California, her parents, and Cari and the new baby. She felt suddenly homesick and displaced. She longed to see palm tree lined Center Street and go down Brookside Avenue between the orange groves. She remembered the mustiness of Smiley Library and the way the sunsets stretched pink and purple streaks all the way across the sky.

She thought about how sad she was when she visited Grandpa Will's grave at Monticito Cemetery out on Barton Road. She smiled at the thought of Cari and having a milk shake at Winn's with the kids from church.

I want to go home. Tears found their way to her cheeks and plopped on the gray and white angora sweater Megan loved so much. *I need to go home.*

"You all right, dear?" The woman across the aisle noticed her tears and handed her a purse-sized package of Kleenex.

"Yes, my foot hurts." It wasn't really a lie, but it wasn't the whole truth either.

"How'd you break it?"

"It's not broken. It's just a deep bruise and sprain. My doctor thought I should have a cast so that I could finish school."

"Oh, my," the woman said. "You probably should stay off it."

"Yeah, that's what he said. But I'm only a few weeks from graduation, and I've worked for four years toward this. I can't take a break just now."

"I have a bottle of aspirin, would you like a couple?" she asked, and without waiting for an answer, she began digging in her large purse. "I know they're in here somewhere. Oh, good, here they are."

"Thank you," Jen said taking them from the woman. She held them in her hand for a while; then the woman produced a bottle of orange soda.

"It's probably warm by now," she said. Snapping off the top with a small opener she handed the soda to Jen. "It will sure be better than swallowing those pills without it."

Jen took the soda and swallowed the aspirin. "You're very kind, thank you," she said. The orange pop was refreshing, and in a few minutes she drank the whole thing.

"Do you mind if I have the bottle back?" The woman reached across the narrow bus aisle. "It's two cents' refund."

Jen smiled and handed the bottle back to its owner. She turned slightly in the seat, grateful that the one next to her was unoccupied. Stretching her leg, she managed to elevate her injured ankle. Settling herself, she leaned the seat back as far as it would go and covered up with her coat. Soon the motion of the bus and the warmth of her jacket lulled her to sleep.

"Miss, oh, miss." The woman across the aisle was standing over her. "We're in Chicago. Is that where you're getting off? Let me help you with your things. My son and daughter-in-law are meeting me here. Can we take you home?"

Jen roused herself and quickly gathered her few things around her. She had put her suitcase in the baggage area and didn't have much on board with her. "Thank you." She looked at the woman's kind smile. "I just need to get a cab. My apartment isn't too far from here."

"We wouldn't mind dropping you," the woman said as they made their way out the bus door. Jen carefully lowered herself using the handrails, then reached for the crutches.

"Thank you," Jen resisted. "But if you'd just help me catch a cab. I couldn't inconvenience you. You've been so kind already."

Just then Jen heard her name. "There she is!" Megan grabbed hold of Bobby's arm and steered him toward her friend.

"Meg!"

"Look at that cast!" Megan exclaimed.

"Megan, how'd you know I was coming?"

"Dan's mother called and talked to Beth." Megan grabbed Jen's purse and the smaller bag while Bobby took her suitcase.

"Nobody could find Mr. Miller, I guess," Bobby commented. "Otherwise, I'm sure he would have been here instead of us."

It hadn't been easy, but Dan had convinced Jake Smith that Jen was important to the case, and Jake agreed to let him go back to the farm to get her. Driving the distance through the countryside and watching the clouds play with the horizon, he knew that soon the land would be alive with tractors scratching deep grooves in the earth.

Leaving just before nine, he planned to get to the farm before three. He and Jen would have some time to talk before dinner. Two days, Jake made him promise to be back in two days, three at the most. He knew Joy needed some time with him as well, and he intended to get her settled for an indefinite stay with his parents before he and Jen drove back to the city.

Jen was just as glad that Dan hadn't met her. She didn't want to face him just now. She had to clear her mind—her focus had to be on finishing school.

Megan chatted on and on about the things that had happened in the few days that Jen had been away. The man stationed outside the apartment had disappeared since Mike's death. Bobby had been with Megan almost continually, "My own bodyguard!" Megan smiled toward Bobby, who winked back at her.

"Rusty?"

"He's been working with the police as much as possible. He and Jake Smith, that's the officer in charge of the case, have been friends for a long time." Megan helped Jen up to the apartment and opened the door. "Bobby's good with plants. It's a good thing, too. They would have all been dead by now."

"Have you heard from—" Jen changed her mind about asking the question. "It's good to be back. I want to hang up my things and lay down a while." Jen opened the door to the bedroom and surveyed the mess.

"I haven't been alone, Jen." Megan tried to hurry and pick up clothes strewn around the room.

"I see."

"Frances and Peggy McKnight have been staying with

me. It's been a little crowded. Our apartment is barely big enough for two, let alone four!" Megan laughed.

"Four?"

"Rusty insisted that Bobby stay, too. Your keys have never turned up."

Jen felt strangely crowded and frustrated with the chaos in her life. With eyes brimming with tears, she turned away from Megan.

"Jen, look, Frances and Peggy can go home now that you're back. We're stuck with Bobby, I think. But he's quiet, and I'm sure we can manage . . ." Her voice trailed off as she reached for Jen's shoulders.

Jen spun around and faced her friend. "I'm tired, Megan. Tired of this whole thing. I'm sorry I ever heard of Halloran's, sorry that I ever came to Chicago. I should have stayed in California and gone to a school in L.A. I'm sorry I ever heard of Dan Miller. I should have never gone to the farm or met Joy!" Megan, stunned by her friend's sudden outburst, stepped back a few feet before sitting abruptly on the side of the bed.

"Look at this mess!" Jen's arm swept through the air, and Megan quickly looked around the room. "Not *this* mess, Meg! The big mess that my life is in!"

"Is your life in a mess?"

"Of course it is," Jen cried. "I don't know what I want anymore. I thought I wanted to finish school, go home, and spend a couple of weeks on the beach with Cari and the baby. I wanted to get a job in a design studio or with an interior designer for a couple of years before branching out on my own."

"Isn't that what you still want?"

"Yes, it is—I mean, I think it is." Jen pulled a length of toilet paper from the roll in the bathroom and hobbled back toward Megan blowing her nose. "Then this whole thing happened."

"This whole thing?"

"You know, at work. Getting mixed up with Dan Miller, this whole cloak and dagger routine. I've missed almost a week of school, and I haven't been able to concentrate on studying for my finals!" Jen thumped her cast on the floor as she walked around the foot of the bed and sat opposite Megan. "Look at this mess!"

"You said that already."

"I think," said Bobby from the doorway, "that you've fallen in—"

"Don't say it!" Jen yelled. "I don't want anyone to say it, you hear me?"

Bobby turned and silently made his way out to the kitchen. Megan heard him open the refrigerator door and pop the cap on a Pepsi bottle. "Jen," she began, "why not take the time you need now to get ready for school. Isn't there a class tonight?"

Checking her watch, Jen noticed that she had about an hour before class time. "I could make it," she said. "I'm not sure how I would get there."

"Bobby can take you. He's been driving Rusty's Plymouth. Let me ask him, and you get yourself ready. Need help?" Jen held up her hand and motioned her friend away. "Didn't think so," Megan said.

"I'm going to do this," Jen said stubbornly to her reflection in the mirror over the bathroom sink. "I came this far, and I'm going to finish—Dan Miller or no Dan Miller."

As he drove up to the house, Dan was surprised by his mother's greeting.

"She's not here, Dan. She took the bus back to the city this morning."

"She what?"

"She wanted to get back to her classes," Mrs. Miller's face begged Dan for understanding.

"I came to get her."

"I tried to get her to wait a little longer. It just sounded so indefinite. She's a strong girl, Dan. She's got this thing about—"

"I know, finishing school. And," Dan added, "having a career."

"It's her dream, son. You can't blame her for having a dream."

Dan turned away from his mother to study the familiar landscape. "I had a dream once," he said softly. "I thought I had another. Maybe I was wrong."

Bess's heart ached for her only son. "No, honey, you aren't wrong." She longed to hold him and take away his pain. "But you have to make room for her dreams too."

"Daddy!" Joy burst out the door, and Dan's thoughts were temporarily suspended while he opened his arms to the one girl he knew loved him.

"Hi, Joy-Baby, how's my girl?" Dan said as he scooped Joy up into his arms and started toward the house.

Bess touched his arm, and he turned to look down into his mother's face. "Give her space, Dan. Give her time."

"Even if it means I risk losing her?"

"Is she yours to lose?" Bess looked deep into her son's blue eyes. "I think this whole situation needs prayerful attention. Do you think you could consider doing that?"

"Maybe so, Mom. What else can I do?"

"It's not so much what you *can* do, but what you *should* do. You'll only know that after you pray."

"Yeah, I guess you're right. After I pray." He hugged Joy tighter and kissed her cheeks. "After we eat, right Joy?"

"I haven't missed much." Jen told Megan after class. "I had worked so far ahead that I'm not even behind. I just have a few projects to finish and a couple of books to review. I think I'll be all right."

From her room, she could hear Bobby and Megan laughing at Jack Parr on *The Tonight Show*. Limping her way to the bathroom, Jen closed the door, and without turning on the light, she sank to the floor in the darkness. "Dear God," she began, "I need to talk to you about Dan Miller, my future, and me . . ."

Two hundred and fifty miles west, Dan lay in the darkness of his boyhood bedroom, and into the stillness he whispered, "Dear heavenly Father, I need to talk to you about Jennifer Whipple, Joy, and the possibility of our future, together, as a family . . ."

CHAPTER THIRTY-THREE

*D*an turned the car toward the highway as Joy stood beside his father on the porch waving good-bye. He had promised Joy he would return for her just as soon as Grandma O'Halloran was home from her "trip." Joy clung to her grandfather's neck and waved bravely as long as she could see Dan's Corvette.

The two days spent at home with his family had provided Dan with time to think and to renew his commitment to Christ with his parent's gentle encouragement. They had prayed together as a family for the first time since he had met Marie O'Halloran. Dan hadn't realized how much he had shut God out of his life—nor did he have any idea how quickly God was willing to welcome him back.

His prayers about Jen and the future had not really given him any answers or clear direction or strategy to follow, but they had brought a strange peace. He would not crowd her. He loved her, he was certain of that. He was also fairly certain she loved him.

"Just give her time." Bess's advice rung in his ears. "If God is in this, it doesn't matter if she goes back to California or to Timbuktu. God's hand is not shortened by miles or circumstances. Only people can stop God from working. If you will just give this to him, Dan," his mother had said, "He will work it all out. And it will be right." He loved his Mom, and he knew her words were true. "Right for you, right for Jen, and right for Joy," Bess had added.

Give her space, Dan thought ruefully. *What I really want to do is to go directly to her apartment, take her in my arms, and tell her how much I love her.* He shoved thoughts of the situation at the store and Mike's death aside. *I want to tell her that we can work it all out—her future, a career if that's what she wants, and Joy. It will all work out. God will help us—I know He will.*

But the situation at the store wouldn't be shoved aside for very long. Reality was waiting for him the moment he set his suitcase down inside his bedroom.

"Hello," he said, answering the insistent phone.

"Dan, I'm glad you're back," Jake Smith said. "Can you come to headquarters? We have a lot to talk about."

"Two days," Dan said, "I've been gone two days. Can so much have happened in that short time?"

"It can when you have a confession."

"A confession?"

"Can you be here in ten minutes, twenty?"

"Half an hour." Dan hung up the phone and began to dial Jen's number. After only five digits, he hung up. *I'll call her later.* Now he was needed at the police station.

"What's up?" Dan said to Rusty, who was waiting at the front desk.

"You won't believe it!" Rusty walked him up the back stairs to the small office where they had met Jake before.

"How well do you know Yvonne?" Jake asked once they were seated around the small table.

"Just from work. She tends to be a private person. She has worked at the store for several years. Before I came, anyway," Dan said.

Rusty stood pacing as Dan and Jake talked.

"Can you think of any reason she could possibly have

to—well, is there anything she might have on . . ." Jake looked toward Rusty for help.

"What Jake means is, do you know of anything that could link Yvonne and Dorthea together?"

"You mean outside work?"

"Outside, or inside, for that matter," Jake said.

"I don't know . . ." Dan said.

"Listen, Dan, Mr. Jeffers—you know, from home furnishings."

"That's Jen's department. Yes, I know him."

"Jeffers and Debbie—your secretary, I believe—"

"Yes, Debbie is my secretary."

"They came and talked to me day before yesterday. They say that Mrs. O'Halloran and Yvonne have some connection. They have all been a part of a—"

"They all? Who's all?"

"Debbie, Jeffers, Yvonne, and what's-her-name—you know, the little blond who works the desk in the security office."

"You mean Minnie?"

Jake shuffled some papers and found some scribbled notes. "Yeah, Minnie."

"I don't understand," Dan said, rubbing his forehead.

"They've all been working for Dorthea O'Halloran."

"I know that."

Rusty spun a chair around and straddled it facing Dan. "No, not for the store, but *in* the store."

"Look, guys, I'm totally confused."

Jake stacked his papers together, picked them up, and tapped the edges on the table to make them neat. "Look, Dan, I'll be as clear as I know how to be. Jeffers and Debbie came to see me. They told me they have been working for Dorthea for quite a while. They have been helping her get merchandise out of the store, passing it from one department to another, finally shipping it out—right from Halloran's shipping room. They don't know where it's been going. They're paid to keep their eyes open, their mouths shut, and to look the other way whenever they're told to."

"Do they know who killed Mike?" Dan looked from one of the two men to the other.

"No, they say they don't. However, they do say that Yvonne has been showing quite a bit of temper lately—impatient, you might say."

"So what's this all leading to?"

"We decided to check up on Yvonne. We did a little checking into her background, her family history, and we discovered quite a bit of surprising information about her."

"Oh?"

"Dan, she was Mike's daughter." Rusty waited for the shock of the news to sink in. "Yvonne Markim is Yvonne *Cleary* Markim."

"Wait a minute." Dan groped for a thought that he couldn't quite put words to.

"There's more," Rusty said.

"Cleary," Dan said. "The same name as on Marie's birth certificate."

"Emily M. Cleary—Mike's sister."

"No wonder Mr. O'Halloran felt responsible for her when she couldn't find a job during the war." Dan paused and thought about the young woman hired to work in a house where her own baby was living as the O'Halloran's daughter. "He was a cruel man."

"He?" Jake asked.

"Mr. O'Halloran."

"Not really, Dan. Just ruined by money, that's all. Raised to buy whatever he wanted all his life. Even people."

"Even a baby." Dan was disgusted and glad Marie never knew. "Okay, so . . . ?"

"So," Jake continued, "Yvonne must have been working for Dorthea O'Halloran until she could get close enough to turn the tables."

"You mean you think she's the one behind all this?"

"I think she was blackmailing Dorthea," Jake said.

"I think," Rusty smiled at Dan, "that you've probably heard enough for one night."

"Not on your life," Dan said. "Let's hear it all."

"All we know," Jake said, "is that Debbie, Minnie, and Jeffers were helping them get merchandise out of the store. Yvonne was in charge, and as far as we can figure, Mike wasn't involved. He may have known something, but he wasn't involved with the whole plan." Jake stood and stretched. "I can't help but think that Yvonne came to work for Dorthea but eventually found a way to make Dorthea work for her."

"It's possible, Dan," Rusty said. "After all, Emily Cleary was Marie's mother. Don't you suppose her family knew she was carrying a baby?"

"O'Halloran didn't count on that, did he?" Dan remarked.

"I don't know. After all, he did give Mike a job and pay him well for all these years. And he did arrange for Emily to work for Dorthea while he was away during the war."

"There's something else." Jake sorted through his stack of paperwork. "Here it is." He pulled one sheet from the sheaf of papers and handed it to Dan.

"What's this?"

"It's a report from the lab. Dorthea's fingerprints were the only set found in the penthouse office."

"That means she was there after we were."

"Yeah, but it also means someone else was there in between."

"How's that?"

"Someone was in the office, wiped the place clean and then left it before Dorthea came in. After all, why would Dorthea leave her own prints after wiping away everyone else's?"

Dan remembered the picture in his office. "Whose prints were on that picture of Marie?"

"Yours, of course. And one other set. It's strange, but it doesn't match any of the others in your office. But it does match one set, just one. We found it on the button marked *door close* inside the elevator. Guess whoever used it couldn't wait for the door to close automatically when the first floor button was pushed."

"Any idea whose it is?"

"We're questioning her right now." Jake nodded toward another office.

"Why did Jeffers and Debbie come forward?"

"Scared, I guess. Theft is one thing, but murder is another. Jeffers also has a thing for Jen. He was afraid for her safety."

"He knew she was being followed?"

"By Ken Markim."

"Ken Markim?"

"Yvonne's husband. Jeffers knew who it was."

"Now what?" Dan asked.

"Just putting the pieces into place. Once we do that, we'll wrap it up. Dorthea's still in jail. We've been holding her without bail for murder, but we will probably release her tomorrow. Once we get Yvonne, we'll know for sure whether she really had anything to do with it or not."

"How will you get Yvonne?" Dan wondered out loud.

"I know this is stressful for you, Mrs. Markim. You had such trust in Mrs. O'Halloran." Jim Sweeny was very sympa-

JEN'S PRIDE AND JOY

thetic. "We knew you'd be able to help us with our case against her for murdering your father."

"I still can't believe it." Yvonne dabbed at her eyes with a handkerchief. She rubbed her temples with perfectly manicured hands.

"Could I get you something?"

"I just have a headache, that's all. It's nothing. It's just such a shock, that's all."

"Here, Mrs. Markim, have a drink of water." Jim handed her a clear glass filled with cool water. "Would you like some aspirin or something?"

"No, thank you, water is fine." Jim watched her down the water and set the glass on the desk. "Thank you," she said softly. He reached for the glass, and carefully handling it by the rim he handed it to a man waiting outside the office.

"No, ma'am," he said casually, "thank you."

CHAPTER THIRTY-FOUR

*G*ive Jen time and space," Bess repeated when Dan called to check on Joy. Dan repeated those words of advice to himself more than once during the past two weeks as he worked to replace Jeffers and Debbie.

Elizabeth had asked for Megan to be transferred to the security office to fill in while she looked for a suitable replacement for Minnie. The store was buzzing with gossip, and Dan found himself fielding questions and squelching rumors many hours out of each day. He was tired, he missed Jen, and he wanted to make a change in his life. He liked the security of the family life out at the farm but could not quite see himself settling down there, or even in Ames. Saddled with the store and Dorthea's problems he felt trapped and overextended.

It had been fifteen days since he last saw Jen. He was trying to be patient, but he had phoned a couple of times, only to be told that she was at school, studying, or just not available. He had asked that she call him back, but she had never done so.

Finally, he could stand it no longer. He left the store and glanced at his watch. He knew she would be leaving class and heading for the bus at the corner. He turned the Corvette toward the Chicago School of Interior Design. He eased the small car into a truck-loading zone near the front entrance and waited for Jen to appear.

He waited until she was well out the door before he got out of his car and approached her. "Hi," he said simply.

"Hi." She stopped and faced him.

"Want a ride home?" he asked.

"Okay."

Dan opened the car door for her and resisted brushing her hair with his hand. He noticed her cast was missing and that her ankle was wrapped in an ace bandage. He slid in beside her and started the engine.

"How's your ankle?"

"Better. Still sore."

"How's school?"

"Okay. It's almost finished. I turned in the last of my projects tonight. I don't have to come back until finals."

"When's that?"

"Three weeks from now."

Dan nodded. "What'll you do in the meantime?"

"I was hoping to go back to work," she said.

"Can you?" Dan asked, glancing toward her ankle.

"I think so. I might not be able to stand all day."

Dan had an idea. "Could you work in my office?"

"Dan, I don't think—"

"Good, if you think about it you won't. So don't think." Easing the car into traffic, Dan glanced at Jen. "Hungry?"

"No." She paused. "Well, maybe a little."

"Good," he said, "I know just the place."

Jen excused herself to call Megan as soon as they reached the restaurant. Dan said something to the hostess at the little Italian place on the shore of Lake Michigan. She smiled at him as he pressed a twenty-dollar bill into her hand. She glanced over her shoulder at Jen. "She's a lucky girl," she whispered to Dan.

Jen felt awkward and wished Dan would say something instead of just looking at her while she ate. "You're quiet," he said.

"Me?" Jen said. Her meaning was not lost on Dan.

"Well, I'm just so glad to see you, I don't know where to begin."

"You could tell me how things are at the store. I called to ask Mr. Jeffers if I could come back to work, and I got Janie Fariday. She said Mr. Jeffers was off for a while."

Dan leaned forward in his chair. "I have a few details to fill you in on."

An hour later, Dan checked his watch. Ten-thirty. He had gotten so involved telling Jen what had happened at the store, he hadn't even begun to approach what he really wanted to say to her.

"Yvonne? Mike's daughter? It's hard to believe." She played with her napkin, folding it several ways, then unfolding it and starting over. "I'm sorry to hear about Mr. Jeffers. He's always been nice to me."

"Yeah, well, that isn't hard to do," Dan said.

"Dan?" Jen ignored his comment. "Why would Debbie and Minnie get involved?"

"Money." Dan hated the word. "Some people will do anything for it."

"And Mrs. O'Halloran?"

"She really doesn't have any money of her own, Jen. She lives off Joy's money. As long as Joy will let her—or really, as long as I let her, she will live in Joy's house and will be paid as Joy's caretaker. And then, she has her position at the store. Or rather, she did have until all this came out."

"Where is she now?"

"Being held as a material witness, I think." Dan was not sure how or why Jake was able to keep Dorthea O'Halloran in custody.

Dan noticed how tired Jen was getting and decided to take her home. She didn't hate him, he was sure of that now. She didn't give away her feelings exactly, but he hoped she was glad to see him again.

"Jen?" Dan turned to her in the car after parking in front of her building.

"Um-hmm?" She leaned her head on the car window away from him.

"I've been wondering how you and Joy . . . well, how'd it go?"

"Didn't you talk to your mother?"

"She said you were getting along as well as could be expected."

Jen smiled. "She's a generous woman. I like her." She didn't know exactly how to tell Dan what she really thought. "Joy is a challenge, Dan. You know that. I don't think I did very well. In fact, I didn't do well at all." Jen stared out the car's windshield. Dan studied her profile and wanted to kiss her. "I, well—" Jen paused. "I'm not ready to pursue . . ." she couldn't finish her sentence.

"Jen, I love you," Dan said.

"Dan, don't."

"Jennifer, I love you," he repeated.

Jen dropped her eyes to her lap and studied her hands. Dan reached for her hands and covered them with his own. Jen turned away and looked out the car window.

"Jen, please look at me. I want to tell you about Marie."

Jen turned around, curious and confused. "Marie?"

"Marie was over at her parent's house. She had a terrible fight with Dorthea and was on her way home. She didn't have her car, and I didn't want to come and get her. I was studying." Dan said with a disgusted tone. "All I thought about was finishing my degree. Back then, Marie waited and waited for my attention and never complained." Dan ran his fingers through his hair while keeping his other hand safely on Jen's. "She often quarreled with Dorthea. So I didn't think it was any different. But that night, she begged me to come and get her. But no, I had to finish a paper. She took her mother's car. She called me again just before she left. She was much calmer—I assumed they had patched things up. I asked her to stop off at the library and pick up a book I needed. She was furious with me for asking. I was furious with her for refusing. She slammed down the phone, and I never saw her alive again."

Jen looked at Dan and saw the pain and regret in his eyes. "I didn't know why, but I have known for some time that you felt guilty about her death."

"Guilty? Of course I feel guilty. I'm responsible."

"For what, Dan? For being selfish, maybe, but not for her death."

"If I had only—"

"Oh, right." Jen felt anger swell within her.

"Jen, you don't understand."

"No, Dan, I don't. I met your parents, and I know they taught you about forgiveness. You made a mistake, okay. But your mistake was not what killed Marie. I know you don't believe that—you'd rather believe Dorthea who has kept you under her thumb and has almost ruined your daughter because you'd rather believe you killed Marie than realize that you made a mistake that can be forgiven. People make the same mistake you made everyday and no one dies—they simply make up and go on with their lives. You can't make up, but you can certainly go on—can't you?" Jen was shocked at her own outburst.

"Jen, don't. You weren't there."

"No, I wasn't there. I am here, I am now. I live in the present, Dan. You live in the past. Joy is getting bigger everyday, and you hardly notice. Dorthea has been stealing from her own granddaughter for years, right before your very eyes. How long are you going to feel guilty about that? How long are you going to be willing to live under her thumb rather than start a new life for yourself and for Joy? She's ruining her, Dan, and you won't even put a stop to it."

Dan had never seen Jen this angry. She was saying what his mother had been saying for four years.

"You know God can help you, Dan." He turned to her and realized her eyes were filled with tears. "Why have you turned your back on Him? I see the strong faith of your family. Why did you turn your back on all they taught you?"

"Marie," Dan said quietly. "She became more important to me than anything else. I didn't want anything else but her. She wasn't a Christian, and I knew it, but I wanted her more than anything—even more than God."

"Pride," Jen said flatly. "You listened to your pride."

"Pride?"

"You thought you knew more than God about your life and what you needed. You didn't even ask Him before you married Marie, did you?"

"No, I didn't. I knew that—"

"That you were stubbornly going about your own way, living your own life, doing just fine without interference from Him."

Jen began to cry. She buried her face in her hands, and Dan sat quietly as she sobbed. "Jen?" he said after a few minutes. "Jen, I didn't do that with you."

She sat up and wiped her tears on her sleeve. Dan reached into his pocket and handed her his hanky. "Didn't do what?" she asked.

"Not talk to God." Dan turned and searched her eyes for encouragement. "I prayed about you and me. Jen, I love you, I really do." He traced her jawline with his fingers. "I prayed for us, Jen."

"You what?"

"I prayed for us."

"You did?"

"I even asked my parents to pray with me. I don't want to make the same mistakes again." Dan slid his hand around the back of Jen's neck. "I have shut God out in the past, Jen. But I can't do that anymore—I don't want to do that anymore."

Jen's voice caught in her throat. "Dan, I don't know what to say. I've been screaming at you for shutting God out and I—I didn't know."

"I love you, Jen." Dan pulled her face close to his. "I love you," he whispered just before he kissed her. Before Dan could let go, Jen's tears reached his face. She buried her face in his neck and let him hold her while she sobbed.

"I love you too." Dan could barely understand the words. "I don't know what to do about it." She straightened up and tucked a long curl behind one ear. "I just don't know."

"Do you have to know what to do about it?"

"Yes. I have always known what to do. I knew where to go to school after high school, and I knew to come here and finish. I got my job at the store and worked my head off getting to where I knew I wanted to go next."

"Did you pray about it?"

"Stop it, Dan." Jen didn't like being questioned about her decisions.

"I mean it, Jen. I didn't pray about Marie, I admit that. Did you pray about what you were supposed to do after you finish here, or did you just assume you knew and didn't have to pray?"

"Are you saying . . . ?" Jen tossed her head to one side sending her long hair behind her shoulder.

"Pride." Jen's forehead wrinkled in response to the ugly word as Dan continued, "I have faced my failure, faced my pride—I've even repented."

"Pride?" she asked quietly.

"Awful, isn't it?"

"I don't think you of all people have any room to talk to me about pride."

"Jen's pride." Dan began to tease her.

"If you want to talk about pride, let's talk about you."

Dan went on, ignoring her. "And, of course there's Joy." Dan laughed, pulling Jen close again, and kissed the top of her head. "Jen, would you consider going back to the farm?" Dan felt her stiffen in his arms. She couldn't believe what he was saying. Hadn't he heard a word she had said?

"You can't be serious, Dan. I've got work to do."

"What work to do?" She pulled away. "You told me you don't have any work left at school."

"I need to work. I've got expenses to meet." Jen's eyes flashed with independence.

"I have the authority to keep you on the payroll, you know." Jen pulled away, and Dan could tell she was angry. "Don't do this, Jen," he said gently.

"Do what?" she snapped.

"Let your pride get in the way. You only have three weeks before graduation, before you go off to California." Dan's eyes pleaded with Jen. "Please, give it another try."

"Is that what you think this is? My pride?" Jen felt tears sting her eyes once again.

"What do you call it then?"

"Look, Dan Miller. I had a life before I met you. I am three weeks away from graduation. You want me to spend those three weeks with a child that is spoiled, almost beyond—"

"What, Jen? Beyond hope?"

Jen let his remark pass. "I just met the child. You have been her father for five years. Don't ask me to do in three weeks what you should have been doing all along." She opened the door and stepped to the curb. Dan followed quickly not wanting to leave her alone on the city street so late at night.

"Jen, that's not fair!"

"No, Dan, it's not. Not to Joy, not to me—and not to you. You go spend the three weeks with your daughter. You're her parent, not me. I don't even think I want to be a parent, much less to a child that's been ruined by neglect and taken advantage of by all the adults who should have loved her."

"Wait, Jennifer," Dan followed her into the apartment building. They fell silent as they entered the elevator, not wanting to awaken the other tenants.

"Look, Dan." Jen turned toward him as they entered her apartment. "Before I met you I had a life, my own life. Then you came along and upset my whole plan. I didn't plan to meet you, I didn't plan to meet Joy. I didn't plan to get mugged by some hoodlum working for Dorthea O'Halloran, and I didn't plan to fall in love with you."

Dan grabbed her and tried to pull her into his arms. "Get away from me!" She wrenched herself free and put too much weight on her sore ankle. "Ow!" Dan reached to steady her, and she leaned into him.

"You said you loved me." Dan smiled at the angry young redhead, still holding on to her arm.

"I did not. I said I don't plan to—"

"No, you didn't, you said you *didn't* plan to fall in love, but you have, haven't you?" Dan's face was beaming with the realization that Jen loved him.

"You talk about pride! You Dan Miller, have the biggest ego of any man I have ever met."

"I don't care what you think about me," Dan laughed. "I only care that you love me."

"Get out!" Jen shoved him toward the door, and he caught her and wrapped her in his arms so tightly she couldn't get away. "I'm going to scream," she said—just before he kissed her good night.

CHAPTER THIRTY-FIVE

*T*here you are!" Rusty burst into Dan's office.

"Boy, with no secretary at the front desk, you never know what can get in the door." Rusty's clothes were wrinkled, and he sported a day's growth on his face. "You look awful," Dan said. "You been up all night?"

"Yeah, I've been up all night, all right." Rusty plopped down on Dan's large leather sofa.

"Doing what?"

"Listening to a canary sing, that's what."

"What're you talking about, Russ?"

"Yvonne. Another woman ruined by money."

"And jealousy," Dan added. "Don't forget that insidious monster."

"Can a person really be so jealous and greedy that she'd actually kill their own father?" Rusty wondered aloud. "I'm pretty convinced she didn't plan it, Dan."

"Or temper. Mike probably took her by surprise. I bet she gets second degree, not first."

"How sad. O'Halloran's obsession for a child has ruined so many lives. It's too bad he never really got to know Joy. What will happen to Yvonne now?" Dan asked.

"She's not going to go to prison all alone, I can tell you that," Rusty said. "She's taking everyone with her she possibly can. Including, no one less than Dorthea O'Halloran herself."

"Dorthea will have to spend some time in some sort of facility, I was pretty sure of that."

"Not some facility, Dan. And not some time—she's probably looking at a life sentence. That's my guess, anyway."

"For what?"

"Murder."

"No way. I thought you and Jake figured that all out. She was framed by Yvonne. Her fingerprints? You forget all that?"

"Not Mike's murder. We've pretty well wrapped that up. Jake's got a strong case, done a little wheeling and dealing with Jeffers and Diane. He'll probably get a lot out of Minnie, too. Did you know her real name is Minrette?"

"Not Mike's murder?" Dan's eyebrows knitted together. "You mean there's been another one?"

Rusty looked at his puzzled friend. "You're not going to like this, and you may not believe it, but Yvonne says Dorthea killed Marie."

Dan felt the blood drain from his face, and Rusty watched him turn pale. "Sit down, Dan." He helped him find a chair.

"Are you guys crazy?"

"Jake pulled the files. He read the autopsy report." Rusty watched the pain of the night four years ago return and settle on Dan. "He said the report showed a blow to the back of Marie's head that was inconsistent with the accident."

Dan scratched his head and leaned forward resting his elbows on his knees. "I vaguely remember somebody mentioning that at the time."

"Yeah, but never since, I bet."

"No, I don't think so."

"Know why?" Rusty took his seat on the sofa again. "Money, that's why. Yvonne knew who, when, and how much. It all checks out. She's been blackmailing Dorthea for years."

Dan felt almost as numb as the night he was told that Marie was dead. "I can't believe it."

"It gets worse, Dan. Guess who kept the lid on the report. Someone in the coroner's office by the name of Markim."

"Yvonne's husband?"

"One and the same. Except they weren't married then. He came to her trying to sell the information Dorthea paid him to keep quiet about. But Yvonne didn't have any money. Instead, they formed a partnership and well, you know the rest."

"I don't know if I do or not." Dan was trying to take in this latest information and fit it in to make a clearer picture. "I still don't know why Dorthea would do such a thing."

"It's simple. Marie found out Dorthea wasn't her mother. She suspected it for some time because of some of the comments some of the household servants made. Dorthea got rid of most of them and intimidated the rest into silence. Mr. O'Halloran finally told Marie himself. He knew he had a bad heart and that Dorthea would try to take everything she could from the estate. He was trying to stop Dorthea from having *any* of his estate."

"Fighting over money, putting Marie in the middle." Dan waited and then asked, "Did Mike Cleary know about all this?"

"Only that Marie was his niece. He didn't know Dorthea had arranged to . . ."

"Then Yvonne was Marie's cousin." Dan stood and paced in front of his desk. "If it could be proved, she would be Marie's next of kin, except for Joy." Dan stopped and faced Rusty. "That's why Dorthea was so desperate to keep control of Joy."

"Why didn't Yvonne simply report this to the police at the time of Marie's death?"

"Because Emily Cleary had surrendered Marie for adoption. Yvonne had no legal rights, only damaging information. And she used it to her own financial advantage."

"Selling stolen merchandise, stealing from a child's inheritance. There must be a special place in hell for people like this." Dan's anger flashed and then subsided when he thought of how first Marie and then Joy had been victims simply because they had been born into wealth. He needed to do something to protect Joy from further harm and to make sure she was never taken advantage of again. He had to remove her from Halloran's—maybe even sell the store. Several national chains had shown interest from time to time. Perhaps a complete change was what she needed.

"Let me have a car, and charge it to the Halloran account." Jen fairly barked the instructions to the clerk behind the counter.

"Any preference as to style and color, miss?"

"It's for Mr. Miller, just give me whatever he usually gets."

"Is he coming to get it himself?"

"No, I'm taking it to pick up his daughter."

"Then you want to drive a Lincoln?"

Jen remembered the size of the huge car and decided something smaller would be more suitable. She had not driven in two years; since she had been in Chicago, she traveled by city bus.

"I have a Mustang, it's quite a bit smaller. Would that be all right?"

"Fine, I'm sure it will be fine. Does it have an automatic transmission?" Jen knew she'd need all her concentration just to find her way out of the city, let alone try to manage shifting gears as well.

Two hours later, she pulled off the highway to get something to eat and calm herself after driving through the city traffic. She bought a map and asked directions. She hoped she would remember the way to the farm once she got close. She had Doreen's phone number and could call, if necessary. She checked her watch and decided that Megan wouldn't be home for another hour or so. Bobby had taken to seeing her home more and more, even though he had other duties to help find the necessary evidence to fortify the case against Yvonne. Rusty didn't seem to notice Bobby's attention and Megan's responsiveness; Jen knew he was in for a surprise when the case was over and their lives returned to normal again.

Normal? Jen shook her head as she pulled the small car onto the highway headed for the Millers' farm. *I thought I had a normal life, a normal future all planned.* She hoped she wasn't about to ruin everything she had worked for all her life.

"Jen there?" Megan recognized Dan's familiar voice.

"No, Dan, she's not. She left a note saying she was going away for a few days. She's packed some of her clothes, and I noticed that her stuff is missing out of the bathroom."

"Is all her stuff gone? Megan, did she go back to California?"

"I don't think so. She's been packing, but she's not finished with that yet. I think she went somewhere to be alone. You know, she seems like she's mad about something. I thought about going back to my mother's. But then I'd have to be away from . . ." Megan stopped herself before she admitted how much she wanted to be near Bobby.

"Where could she have gone?" Dan wondered.

"She'll be back, Dan. She's okay. I know it." Megan didn't sound convincing. "Don't worry, she'll be back," she repeated.

Jen pulled over to the side of the road and pored over the map. She was lost, and she was furious. She retraced her route on the map, found where she had missed a turn, and turned the car around to head back. Stopping for gas, she counted her money and decided against eating or staying in a motel for the night. She would continue driving. Her five-hour drive had already taken eight. She had to be close. Before leaving the gas station she considered calling ahead, then decided against it. She needed to do this alone, without anyone's help.

"No, I haven't heard from her." Bess's tone was filled with worry as she talked to her son, but her words were reassuring. "She'll get in touch with you, Dan. Let's pray."

Dan listened to his mother's prayer and hoped that God was listening as well. After hanging up, he paced the small rooms of his apartment waiting for Jen to call or for Rusty or Bobby to find her.

She didn't buy a bus ticket, and she didn't take the train. She hadn't taken a plane, Rusty checked on that while Bobby had checked the other two. She had simply disappeared. Dan didn't know if he was more worried or angry. He had no choice but to wait. Certainly he would hear something soon.

Finally Jen found the remote road that led to the farm. A quick check with the man at the all-night gas station near the interstate, and she was on her way again. Pulling into the driveway, she saw Barney trotting to meet her oncoming car. Soon the porch lights lit the front of the familiar farmhouse, and Jen felt the relief of reaching her destination sweep over her.

"Jen? Is that you?" George Miller shaded his eyes from the porch light and tried to peer into the darkness.

"Yes, it's me." Jen tried to keep her voice light, even though her heart threatened to pound its way out of her chest.

"We've been so worried, dear." Bess quickly approached the car. "Dan called, and he's frantic. You come in and call him."

"I don't want to talk to him."

"Jennifer, don't you be so stubborn. He's worried sick, and he won't sleep a wink until he knows you are safe. Whatever possessed you to come all this way by yourself, anyway?"

"I came to get Joy."

"What?" Bess shooed Jen in the front door and led the way to the kitchen. "I never heard of such a thing."

"Sit down, mother." The smile in George's eyes belied his serious tone. "Let the girl catch her breath—after all, she's had quite a drive. How long did it take you, child?"

"I left this afternoon." Jen avoided the question.

"Let's see, it's past ten-thirty. You must have hit rush hour traffic if you left close to five." George wasn't about to let Jen off the hook that easily. "What time did you leave?"

Jen was embarrassed to tell them that she had been on the road over nine hours.

"How'd that little car do on gas?"

"Okay, I guess." Jen didn't want to talk about her trip. She was on a mission. "I came to get Joy. I thought that since I had a couple of weeks before graduation, I could let her stay with me, or I could go stay with her and she'd be in her own house for a little while." Jen accepted the cup of hot tea offered by Bess and continued. "Dorthea's in a lot of trouble, I guess you know that."

"We do," George said, silencing Bess with a look.

"She might not be with Joy for a long time. She's going to prison."

"We know."

"I've been wondering about Joy. Shouldn't she have the chance to pack her things if she's coming out here to live with you?"

"Is that the plan?" Bess asked quietly.

"I'm assuming that it is." Jen looked at them both. "Where else would she go?"

"Well, we thought—"

"We haven't heard Dan's plans for Joy yet," George interrupted his wife. "Maybe you're right. Maybe you could take her back with you and help her get packed. She might need that time to make her adjustment to a new situation. You know—preparation." George winked at his wife.

"But first, my dear, you must get a good night's sleep." Bess took up where George left off. "Doreen will want to see you before you leave. And, of course the children will want to see Joy. Do you have to leave tomorrow? Couldn't you wait a day or two?" Bess noticed George's slight nod of approval.

"I really want to get back," Jen said.

"What's the hurry? You said yourself, you have a couple of weeks."

"We can talk about this tomorrow," George decided. "Mother, take our girl here to her room. And check that ankle before you leave her. I'll get her bags and park that car out of the way. If the neighbors see that, they'll accuse me of going into my second childhood."

Jen gave George the keys, and he promptly put the

Mustang in the garage stall next to his tractor, then closed and locked the door. "You'll not go anywhere until we're ready to have you go." He patted the padlock and whistled as he crossed the yard in the faint light of the vapor lamp high on a pole above the barn.

Quietly crossing the kitchen to the living room, George was glad Bess had talked him into getting a phone extension. She was right when she said it might come in handy from time to time. And this was one of those times.

Upstairs Jen settled in the comfortable bed, grateful for the ice pack Bess put on her ankle. Bess Miller went to her room and fell to her knees. At Doreen's, Joy slept in the top bunk above her cousin. And, in Chicago Dan put his Corvette in gear and screeched the tires as he headed for the farm.

CHAPTER THIRTY-SIX

*D*arkness had not yet yielded to dawn when Jen was awakened by voices and footsteps outside her door.

"Let her sleep," Bess pleaded.

"Let him be," George said.

Jen's eyes were momentarily blinded by the lights as Dan entered her room. "Get up, Jennifer."

"No." Dan was not who she wanted to see or deal with at the moment. "What time is it?"

"What difference does it make?" Dan pulled back the covers and grabbed her hand. She fought back.

"Leave me alone."

"I will not."

Jen grabbed the covers just as Dan snapped them from her hand. She reached for a pillow and smashed it hard across his face. He tossed it back at her and with his other hand reached and took possession of another pillow. Raising it above his head, he slammed it toward her just as she rolled out of the bed and onto the floor, wrapping her arms around his feet and sending him sprawling backward.

She ducked as he swung the pillow wildly and caught him off balance as he struggled to get up. Once on the floor he grabbed her good ankle and she tried to scramble away from him and out the door. He pulled her back into the room, and she began to laugh.

"You think this is funny?" He ducked as she swung a pillow around her head, aiming for his face.

"I think you are funny!" She managed to escape his grasp and leaped up on to the bed. She grabbed the covers and rolled them into a ball and tossed them in the corner and stuffed the pillows behind the bed. She stood in the center of the bed and placed both hands squarely on her hips.

Dan crawled to a chair and pulled himself up into it. She stood glaring at him from her position of victory, and Dan slumped, defeated, in the chair. "I give up," he said.

"What, so soon?"

"You've had a good night's sleep, I've been driving all night."

"Pardon me, Dan Miller. I've had half a night's sleep."

Dan caught a glimpse of his dad standing in the hall out of Jen's sight with two large pillows in his hands. Quietly he crept toward Dan and handed him the pillows. Dan tossed one at Jen and then began to pummel her with the other. She fell on the bed and Dan continued his attack. She squealed with delight, and Dan's laughter filled the upstairs room. Eventually she lay exhausted on the bed, and Dan took her hand and pulled her up to face him.

"You scared me to death!" Dan's voice was suddenly husky, and she met his eyes with her own. "Please, don't ever do that to me again."

"I just wanted to . . . well, I'm not sure what I wanted to do for sure. I thought I wanted to come and get Joy. I don't know."

"Jen, I thought something had happened to you. I thought I'd never see you again."

Jen reached for her robe and covered her flannel pajamas. Her hair was wild from the pillow fight, and Dan thought she had never been more beautiful.

He pulled her close and as he kissed her, he decided he had better leave her room. "Go back to bed," he said. "We'll talk later after we both get some rest." He walked toward the door and then turned to face her. "You had better be here when I wake up."

"I will," Jen said, and she knew that her plans, her dreams, were all about to change.

"Promise?"

"I promise," Jen said as she held up her three center fingers. "Girl Scout's honor."

"That's your left hand, Jen," Dan laughed.

"I know it."

"We've some serious talking to do, Jennifer Whipple."

"About what, Dan Miller?"

"California. I've never seen it. I've been thinking about going. Thought I might like to take my daughter. Want to go?"

"Can we go to Disneyland?"

"On one condition," Dan said with a smile.

"What's that?"

"Will you marry me first?"

"No," she teased, "but maybe after."

Down the hall, Bess Miller lay next to her husband, perfectly still. Every word of Dan and Jen's conversation could be heard throughout the entire upstairs of the silent farmhouse.

Hearing Jen's response, Bess sighed and closed her eyes tight.

I don't know about you, Lord, but these two have worn me out. Now maybe we can all get some rest.